THE ENDLESS WEEK

Originally published in French as *La semaine perpétuelle*

First edition, 2025

Art on cover © Pierrette Bloch, *Untitled*, 1973, black ink on paper, 30.5 x 37 cm
Photo: Adam Rzepka
Courtesy Galerie Karsten Greve Paris, Köln, St. Moritz, © ADAGP, Paris

The publisher wishes to thank Hannah Kofman and Amy Peltz.

Library of Congress Cataloging-in-Publication Data
Names: Vazquez, Laura, 1986- author. | Niemi, Alex, translator.
Title: The endless week / Laura Vazquez ; translated by Alex Niemi.
Other titles: Semaine perpetuelle. English
Description: Saint Louis : Dorothy, a publishing project, 2025
Identifiers: LCCN 2024058346 (print) | LCCN 2024058347 (ebook) | ISBN 9781948980272 (paperback) | ISBN 9781948980289 (ebook)
Subjects: LCGFT: Novels.
Classification: LCC PQ2722.A97 S4613 2025 (print) | LCC PQ2722.A97 (ebook) | DDC 843/.92—dc23/eng/20241212
LC record available at https://lccn.loc.gov/2024058346
LC ebook record available at https://lccn.loc.gov/2024058347

ISBN: 978-1-948980-27-2

Design and composition by Danielle Dutton
Printed on permanent, durable, acid-free recycled paper
in the United States of America

Dorothy, a publishing project books are distributed to the trade by
New York Review Books

Dorothy, a publishing project | St. Louis, MO
DOROTHYPROJECT.COM

THE ENDLESS WEEK
LAURA VAZQUEZ

Translated by Alex Niemi

Dorothy, a publishing project

For Patato

For now we see only a reflection as in a mirror;
then we shall see face to face.
Now I know in part;
then I shall know fully, even as I am fully known.
—1 Corinthians 13:12

FREE ME FROM MY STRESS THROUGH BITCHES

1

A head doesn't just fall off, it can't fall off. It's connected to a thin string that goes all the way down to a person's feet, and if the head falls, so does everything else. You should avoid breaking your head, but you can break your limbs. When you break a limb, you remember the limb is there. When a tooth gets infected, it vibrates inside, almost as if it's speaking. When you pinch your hand, it suddenly appears. If a person puts an eye out, it becomes the main thing about them. In truth, the body is soft. People are soft. Their hands are soft, more tender than wood, softer than plastic or shells, they are softer than fruit, more tender than the majority of things on Earth. You can pierce through them with a needle, with a nail, it would be easy, you wouldn't even have to push that hard. There's nothing easier than piercing through someone's hand with a pike or a piece of wood. If you lose your hands they might as well rot, there will still be arms left behind. Not your head. A head doesn't just fall off.

Some robots wear heads like ornaments. You can change their heads, unscrew them, you can change their appearance, but their minds stay the same. Salim was imagining robots, several cities full of robots run by robots. A family of robots in a normal house, the sound of their feet on the stairs, their talking, eating. A regular family. Then he stopped imagining. He was looking at himself in his phone screen, his face was changing. The reflection was speaking, the reflection was proud and sad. Salim said: What do you want? The reflection stayed silent.

The father had little black wrinkles on his lips, he said: What do I want? I want the house to be clean, but you all leave so many marks behind I can't even count them. If I count one fingerprint, I look more closely, and it's really ten, and if I count ten, I look even more closely, and it's really 100, and if I count 100, I spend the whole day counting. It's like you and your sister have 1,200 fingers, do you really have 1,200 fingers between the two of you? You and your sister? How many fingers do you have, one million? Do you and your sister have eight billion fingers? That's the real question. That's the real question, Salim.

This father's lips produced short, abrupt sounds against his gums. He wrung out a sponge and dunked it in water, wrung it out and dunked it again. He pointed a fork at the ceiling and said: You need to understand that you can't just do whatever you want. One day, the police are going to ring the doorbell and they're going to take you away. They'll put both your hands behind your back, and then what? What will you do then, Salim? Standing there with both your hands behind your back? Think about it, you have to think.

The father's hair was like dead grass on his skull. Just one match, and the whole thing would go up in flames, there would be nothing but ash. Salim imagined his father on fire, then he imagined his father in ashes, then he imagined his father alive with shining hair. He took a photo of his father. He added a filter to his father, and the father had long, soft, blond hair. He said: Are you listening to me? Salim formed the word: Yes. And the word: Dad. He repeated the word: Dad. He felt as if his voice were something outside of himself, as if his voice came from the walls or the surfaces around him, as if his own voice didn't come out of his throat but the air surrounding things, as if his voice didn't exist. He said: Da-a-a-a-ad, but he didn't hear his own voice, he heard the outlines, he heard the edges.

When a voice finishes a word, it disappears.

The voice was coming out, it was alive. It said: Dad, dad, dad,

dad, and the word was a movement in his mouth. He said: Da-a-a-a-a-ad, and the voice was a thing in the world. Maybe the word was a thing in the world with the voice. Maybe certain animals could see words in the air, little animals, flies, insects. He said: Dad, dad, dad.

What do you want for god's sake?

Nothing . . . I'm thinking.

The father mumbled and dunked his hands in the sink. He said: Listen, if you don't scrub the table, it gets disgusting. Are you listening to me? I'm going to ask you a question, Salim: Who wants a disgusting table? No one. I'm going to ask you another question: Who wants to drink disgusting water? No one. Every time you leave a sponge in water, it sucks the water up. That's its job. Then you put the sponge in your hand and the hand washes. You have to wipe your hand over bags of rice, bags of sugar, and even vegetables, cabbage stalks, tomatoes. When sugar gets dirty, it's disgusting. Does anyone on Earth want disgusting sugar? No. Nobody, Salim. Nobody wants that.

The father kneeled against the wall and scrubbed the wall with the wall sponge. He scrubbed the baseboards with the baseboard sponge. The father had many, many sponges in cupboards, in basins, in the sink, on the edge of the bathtub, and in his pockets. Of every color and every material. He always had a sponge in his hand. A table sponge to make the table shine, a dust sponge to chase away the dust, a sponge for hard things, a sponge for soft things, an old sponge for broken objects, a new sponge for precious objects. And for cleaning the sponges, he had several sponges for sponges. A long sponge for long sponges, a short sponge for short sponges, sponges in pieces for pieces of sponge. The father would pick up his sponges, he would hold them.

Sometimes, the father imagined sponges inside of people. What if you could wipe down people's insides with a sponge? If you could wipe down lungs with a sponge? A lung sponge for people with sick lungs. If you could wipe down the stomach with a sponge? A brain sponge for people with sick brains, a sponge on a heart, gliding down a heart, into the arteries and behind the eyes. Wiping the slate clean with a sponge. Cleaning old days, old scenes. A sponge for cleaning looks, one for the kitchen, for the knives, for fights, a sponge for everything.

If sponges moved by themselves, they would slide over passersby, over their faces and the streets, over luggage, they would slide over their mouths, which would be smooth forever. The father scrubbed, he scrubbed, he said: I scrub the doors so they close. Think about it, Salim, if you don't scrub a door, it squeaks, and one day, it doesn't close anymore. Who wants a door like that? A door that doesn't close? And the light switches, you can't forget the light switches, Salim. If you forget the light switches, they get rusty, they fall off, one day, you're in the dark. And we'd be worse off in the dark. Now, Salim, think, if we don't wash the walls, guess what happens. It's bad. You have to take care of things, otherwise, they collapse.

The father got up on his stepladder to clean the ceiling with the ceiling sponge. He whistled and whistled, then he polished the corner of the wall, he leaned over and over, then he cleaned the floor with the floor sponge. He scrubbed Salim's chair with the chair sponge, he went up and up, and he wiped the sweater sponge over Salim's sweater and the ear sponge over the edge of his son's ears, he went down and down, and he wiped the sponge over his shoes, his pants, he went back up and up, and he wiped the sponge over his eyebrows and his cheeks. He said: I'm washing you, my son.

He wiped the neck sponge over his son's neck and the ankle sponge over his lower legs. This was his son, his grown-up son, and his affairs were his own. One day, children choose their affairs and these affairs belong to them. Salim didn't move, he was used to it, he touched his screen.

He zoomed in on the face of a man who'd just won 75 million in the lotto. This man didn't have eyebrows, his cheeks sagged. In the article, he said: The day I won, I felt afraid. I was afraid of losing the ticket. It was a formless fear. At home, I hid the ticket in a package of melba toasts. Who would steal melba toasts? Since then, I've slept poorly. In my dreams, every night, I lose the ticket. I lose it, and I never stop losing it.

The father was cleaning his son's hands as they held his phone. He said: If you keep leaning over that device, your organs are going to drop. They're going to come out of your mouth and you're going to vomit up your organs. You're all going to vomit up your organs. You'll watch the news one day and the announcers will say: They're losing their organs, they're vomiting them up.

The father wiped a sponge over the windows. He looked outside while he scrubbed, he was looking for the neighbor. She was always moving, she wandered through her large house, she spied on people. That was her life. Behind a curtain or on the garden wall, on her knees in the yard, lying down with her arms stretched out, in the dormer window or on the roof, her hair sticking out, behind a post, she was thin, all you had to do was wait, she'd show up. The father saw the neighbor sitting on the roof, looking through binoculars, she waved. From far away, her mouth was a hole. He tried to understand her. One day, she'd dropped off a letter for the father, it said:

> Sir, you look like a neighbor I had as a child. He was an old man when I was young, which means he's dead. May he rest in peace. Now it's a pleasure to watch your face LIKE IT'S MY JOB. It brings me back to my childhood body. Be kind, EYES ARE TAX FREE as far as I know, and there's no shortage of problems in the world. Please, grant your image to
>
> Your old neighbor.

Since then, from time to time, the father would try to see himself as a neighbor. He would try to get inside the mind of his neighbor to see himself as a neighbor.

In the mind of a neighbor, we're all neighbors. Our faces are the neighbor's face. If a neighbor runs into us on the opposite end of the globe, they run into their neighbor. They could run into us at sea, on an airplane, in the hospital, or on Neptune, they'd still be running into their neighbor. If our neighbor runs into us in a dream, they're running into their neighbor. We are a thing in their thoughts. From birth, we get inside other people's thoughts. The father had lived in other people's thoughts. He'd been looked at. People who are alive are looked at by other people who are alive. Children live in the thoughts of their parents and parents in the thoughts of their children. All the people on Earth have been seen, they've been looked at. When they were born, a doctor touched their stomachs, nurses measured their heads and their feet. A person who isn't looked at doesn't exist, cannot exist. People who aren't looked at don't exist. People who are blind look around like everyone else, through the power of their hands. Every person we run into has been looked at by their parents, their aunts, their cousins, by a horse, they've been looked at by their beloved one evening in the light, by their friends, by a deer, from up above by birds, or from the side by a lizard.

People resemble the traits we give them and thoughts transform into facial features, wrinkles, gestures. Every thought leaves a mark on a person, even hermits hidden away in their caves. They live in the thought of the word HERMIT, in the images of the word HERMIT in other people's thoughts. We don't know how other people see because we don't have their eyes, we don't have their nerves, we don't have their minds, we don't have their veins, but the father looked at his reflection in the windowpane, made an effort, and saw himself as a neighbor. A childhood neighbor, someone dead. And he said to himself: Hello, Sir, and answered himself: Hello. He wondered if the neighbor spied on him at night, maybe she didn't sleep. That poor, poor woman, her son was crazy.

The neighbor's son was a skinny boy. He walked the streets at night, his arms at his sides. Last year, she'd had to send him to a hospital because he was talking to aliens. He'd face the wall, and he'd talk to the inhabitants of other planets, he'd say: I'm waiting for you. At the hospital, the neighbor's son acted like the devil himself. He put pins in the surgeons' gloves and blocked the elevators. He cut the hair of people in comas and turned the lights out during operations. He was uncontrollable, the doctors had to tie him down. They had to do electroshock therapy for months. Was the neighbor's son sleeping now? The father didn't know. But at night, the father would put small objects on the table. Pots, utensils, he arranged them by size in his workspace. He'd take an object, dunk it into the dishwater, and it was as if the water spoke to him. It said: I am water, I am clean, I am long-lasting, I am calm, I am slippery.

The father would plunge his hands, his arms, and his elbows into the water and the water took him, it took him. If he could have, the father would have plunged his legs and his entire body into the water. From behind, the father looked like he was ramming things into his stomach. His elbows moved slowly as if he was moving a dagger around in his guts. He said: You guys think this stuff washes itself, but the house would fall apart if I weren't here. Your sister would fall apart and you would fall apart and your grandmother would fall apart. You would all fall apart if I weren't here. I had to ask them to give us this house, Salim. I got on my knees at the mayor's feet, he's the one who decides. All the trees you see in town, the mayor's the one who made them grow. We're lucky. Do you think we were the only ones who wanted the old school? This huge house, this huge school, this huge kitchen, these long hallways, your enormous bedrooms, are you listening to me? If you never leave the house, they're going to take it from us, Salim. We won't have a house anymore. You have to understand. Well . . . at least, if they come, they'll see that everything is clean. They might throw us out, but the house will be clean. I want to hear them say: These people are clean. And if there are any disasters—because disasters happen, there are always disasters—and if there are any disasters, we'll call the firemen, so the firemen will see the house is clean, they'll say: These people are dead, but they're clean. They might be dead, but they're clean. Try to wear clean underwear, Salim, always wear clean underwear. The social worker is going to come if you continue on like this, you know. They are going to take our house, we're going to lose everything. We'll look around and the walls will be gone. Take a good look at the walls and the ceiling. Now, imagine a life without walls or a ceiling.

The father's lips twisted. He scrubbed his own mouth with a sponge. He said: The social worker calls me every week. He turned around and said: At your age, you have to go out.

Salim liked two pictures on his phone. When he raised his head, his father was wiping the sponge over a bottle, his lips were twitching, his Adam's apple was going up and down. Could he swallow it? Was he going to swallow it? Salim wrote the words ADAM's and APPLE, then hit search. He found a sentence, he read: A laryngeal protuberance is a palpable lump on the anterior surface of the neck formed by the thyroid cartilage surrounding the larynx.

The father touched his neck. From all of the water, his nails had melted and his hands were soft. When he touched his body with his hands, it felt hard to him. He cleaned the big spoons and the forks, he cleaned the knives and the teaspoons, then he started all over again. He cleaned the spoons with the spoons and he cleaned the forks with the forks. When the father cleaned a spoon, it was as if he were cleaning all the spoons in the world since the dawn of time. He did it out of kindness, out of pure goodness. But while he was cleaning the big spoons, the little spoons got dusty, and while he cleaned the knives, the forks got dirty, so he'd start again, he'd go on for hours. One night, Salim found him with his head in the sink, the right half of his face underwater. Salim had said: What are you doing? and the father had straightened up with an expression on his face that couldn't be trusted. He'd said: I'm washing up.

Now, the father was silent. You could hear the drops of water between his hands. Salim took a picture of his back, the father turned around. Salim took a picture of his face. He sent the picture to Jonathan.

*

Jonathan turned his face to the sky and the sky was black.

He zoomed in on the back of the father's neck, he zoomed

in on his face, he wrote: Your father has heavy wrinkles. If you weighed his face and his wrinkles separately, his wrinkles would weigh more than his face. You ever thought of that? If you took the original weight of his face when he was young, the starting weight, and then you weighed his wrinkles, if you cut off all his wrinkles and weighed them, his wrinkles would be heavier than his face. Don't you think? I hope I have heavy wrinkles when I'm older. I want heavy wrinkles. When you have heavy wrinkles, you can hide things in them, little things like pills and crumbs. Old people carry things around in their faces, usually crumbs. All they have to do is open their wrinkles to find food. They can't starve to death anymore.

Children's clothes were drying on the lines, you could hear the sound of plates and cutlery through the windows. A dog was following him with his eyes from a second-floor balcony. Television voices floated all the way down to him, they were superimposed, they crossed. Serious voices and sweet voices, loud voices and soft voices, laughter and ringing. One voice rose above the others. Jonathan recognized an ad for spaghetti. He could see it in his mind, a woman singing in Italian. She had brown hair, crossed eyes, and big hands that she waved in front of her face.

He wondered how many images were engraved in his mind like that, how many ads, how many words, shapes, songs, smells, scenes, faces, how many thousands of clips lived like that in his mind, and how many more would get in without him realizing. He wondered if the scenes in his mind belonged to his mind or if they belonged to the world. Was he made of this combination of images and memories, some abstract, some clearer, in his mind? Did his memories make him, or did he make his memories? He locked his phone, he shuddered once.

The bathroom at the end of the courtyard was ugly, tiny, and warped, the door didn't close. In the shower, Jonathan thought: Someone invented this place. Someone imagined it. All the places Jonathan had ever seen, all those places had been designed, invented by a person. All those places had been born in the mind of a person. We're living in a person's drawing, in their mind. Architects transform their thoughts into images, and these images are transformed into rooms, buildings, houses, parks, cities, roads. You think you're walking down a street, but you're walking in the thoughts of a stranger. You think houses are built with stones, but houses are built with thoughts. You think plates have always existed, but someone invented the first plate. Someone invented combs, perfume, moustaches. You think things exist on their own, so you end up thinking they've always existed, however, someone invented speech, someone invented breathing, sleep, gestures. In the beginning, we probably didn't move at all, but someone moved one day for the first time. People invent gestures. One day, someone brushed their teeth for the first time. One day, someone thought: I'm going to stick a knife in someone walking by, and they invented crime.

Electrical cables hung from the ceiling, and the steam produced tiny drops around the filaments. Jonathan closed his eyes and imagined the electricity in his body as a flash of blue lightning. The lightning came out of the cables, entered through his skull, and went all the way down to his feet. Do people who die from a lightning strike have time to think? When a person is struck by lightning, the thought they're having stops, it freezes. The thought gets stuck, becomes a prisoner. No one else in the world will ever have this thought. He pulled on an old T-shirt. When he crossed the courtyard, the air surrounded his face. Then he went into his apartment, and he collapsed onto the couch.

The roommate was fiddling with a lighter shaped like an octopus, he was turning it between his fingers. He said: It's a rechargeable lighter, I plug it into my computer. The roommate leaned his head forward and lifted his eyes like a demon, he maliciously stirred his pasta, he put a lot of salt on it. His nails were bitten to the quick, he picked his skin to his finger bones, and his fingers were round. Jonathan said: How does your lighter work? You plug it in and the flame comes out?

The whole room smelled like mold. Huge black mushrooms grew along the walls. There was an enormous leak spreading across the ceiling. The leak had become the center of the apartment. A drop of water fell in the roommate's hair, he swiped at it with his thumb. He'd gotten so used to swiping at drops, it had become a tic. He spread it across his forehead, he didn't look up. He put a piece of pasta in his mouth and swallowed it without chewing. A drop fell on the plate, he said: If we had to understand everything we use, we wouldn't use anything. For example, do you understand your mouth? Do you understand the pronunciation of each letter in your mouth? We don't need to understand everything, we wouldn't be able to do anything if we understood things. We wouldn't be able to tie our shoes, we wouldn't be able to chew. Luckily, we don't understand and we can't explain. We don't understand fire, but fire is good, fire is beautiful. We can tell fire is beautiful. Did I tell you I've burned down houses with this lighter? But I prefer burning electrical appliances. I often buy small electrical appliances, I buy calculators and I burn them. Small cheap calculators from supermarkets, I buy them and I burn them. I burn batteries, I burn machines. I once set a fire inside a fridge, guess what happened.

It exploded?

How did you know? Have you been reading my emails?

Jonathan said: No.

How did you know then?

The roommate's eyes were two dry, black olives. He shrugged his shoulders almost up to his ears as if he were cold, he sniffed and he said: Before, I lived with this guy, and I burned his clothing. I didn't think twice. I burned his shoes and his boxers. Everything burns easily. Nothing has trouble burning. The guy had a photo of his parents in his room, and I burned it, no problem. I giggled while I burned it, I was giggling. His parents' faces twisted, they disappeared, and I was giggling, okay?

Jonathan locked his phone and he said: Okay.

I boiled his phone in milk. One day, I burned his leg hairs while he was sleeping, okay? What about you?

Jonathan scratched his cheek and felt a little scab, he pulled it off, he rolled it between his fingers, he flicked it away, he said: I might have burned a girl's hair at school with matches, but I'm not sure. Maybe it wasn't me. But I remember I got punished for it.

The roommate uncrossed his arms, made two gestures with his hands as if he were arranging things in the air, and he said: You're too nice. I have the same problem. One day in my old apartment, I found a robber. He was taking the couch, he was trying to take it apart. I explained to him that it was better to steal the computers. Don't you think? When you go into people's houses, it's better to steal the computers, right? They sell better, right?

Jonathan nodded, he had a gentle face. The roommate said: So, I showed him the computers, I said: This is what you should take, this is the stuff that sells. If you're a robber, you should steal things that are expensive and light, expensive and light, things that are easy to transport. So, the robber took the computers, it was the only option, it was logical. I like logic. When my roommate came back, I told him: Your computer isn't in your room anymore, but don't worry, a guy stole it because he was a robber. Jonathan was almost smiling, he ran his hand over his face looking for dead skin. The roommate said: I fight a lot.

Who do you fight?

I fight randomly, look. And he stuck his fork in his pasta. He pressed his lips together, his nose wrinkled, and his veins bulged on his temples, on his neck. He sent all the pasta flying, and in one sharp movement, he stuffed all of it in his mouth. He swallowed. All at once. All the pasta. He burped. He lowered his chin with a demonic smile, he said: What about you? Who do you fight?

Jonathan wished he could have filmed the scene, but the scene had disappeared. He said: I got into a fight when I was sixteen. It ended badly.

Is the guy dead?

No, his stomach got cut open.

From a sword?

No, from a window.

The roommate turned his plate, he placed his elbow in the middle, and he rested his face on his fist. He said: Tell me. Jonathan said: When I was little, I spent my vacations with my cousin. He had a swimming pool, and we would fight underwater, it was our game. The rules were simple, we punched each other underwater, we hit each other. Whoever put their head above water first, lost. It was simple. We had a good time. But one day, my cousin lost, he lost for a long time, he lost a lot, he lost ten times, twenty times, twenty-eight times. His luck was completely gone, there was nothing he could do. We played, he lost. He took it badly, I heard him shouting underwater. He got out of the pool with clenched fists, he kept saying: What the hell is this? What the hell is this? My cousin slipped, he fell against a window, and it broke. My cousin fell into the crack, and his stomach split open. I was in the water, I saw the blood, I got out. He was holding his intestines in his hands, I was looking at him. Drops of water from my hair were falling into his wound. I was standing in warm sticky blood on the ground.

The roommate threw his plate on the table and hit his own head. He said: That's not fighting. You have to breathe to fight, you can't just do whatever. You can't fight in water. I hope he's dead. Is your cousin dead? Jonathan swiped two fingers across his screen and showed him pictures of a fireman, he said: That's my cousin. The day he cut his stomach open, he knew he'd become a fireman. When the firemen were sewing him back up, he said: I'm going to be like you. The roommate said the letter P with a puff of air, he moved his head from right to left and then left to right, he said: You call putting flames out all day a real job? Aren't flames beautiful? Aren't they beautiful? Isn't a flame pretty? If you look at a flame, you know right away that it's beautiful, everyone knows it, even idiots, even children know it, even babies want to touch them. I don't understand firefighters, instead of saving fire, they destroy it. All that just to wear a helmet, all that just to have a truck, a hose, all that just so you can say: Hello, I'm a firefighter. It's repulsive.

Jonathan showed him his cousin's page. His kids were wearing shorts and smiling in the pictures, he said: My cousin has children, he does crossbow archery, he wins medals. He showed him pictures of targets with arrow marks right in the middle and the roommate looked away, he said: Have you noticed the kids upstairs? Have you noticed the neighbor's kids? I bet not. You didn't know he had kids? I didn't know either. There was no way of knowing, nobody could have known, but the neighbor has seven kids. You know why we don't hear them? It's because he hits them. One day, I got the wrong apartment, I got the wrong floor, and the neighbor opened his door, he clasped my hands, he said: Come in. He sat me in a chair, he was dressed like a Starbucks barista. He said: Welcome. They live in a studio, him, his wife, and their seven children. In a tiny studio. But since they have mirrored walls, it looks big, it looks almost infinite.

The roommate was crumbling tiny bits of bread between his fat round fingers. He moved his eyes more and more quickly, as if he were reading a text on his hands, he said: They were bald, the seven children, standing right up against the wall. I looked at the seven children against the wall, I saw how they were staring at each other in the mirrors. Each of them was staring at the back of another child in the mirror. It must have made up an entire body in their minds, their own head and the body of one of the other children. The neighbor told me: I have to shave them because of lice and I beat them every day. I have to keep them up against the wall, otherwise they take up space. They take up space and I don't have any space. You can plainly see I don't have enough space. He said: I love them. I even love the misshapen ones. One of my children has eleven fingers. He showed me, I counted, it was true. He said: I only hit them when they move a limb, that's it. If they don't move, I leave them alone. I said I understood. Then the neighbor gave me a nutty coffee with cinnamon, and another coffee from Ethiopia, and another coffee with coconut pearls, but after eight coffees, I wanted to fight someone, is that normal? I wanted to fight someone, seven children against the walls of a studio apartment, it was enough to get on my nerves. It got my nerves up. I could feel my nerves rising in the back of my neck, is that normal?

The roommate moved his hands, it was like they bothered him. He turned his plate over, and it cracked. Several drops of water fell on his head. They fell mournfully, with little bits of plaster.

He said: So, I lied, because I was nervous. Because of my

nerves, I said to the neighbor: Your daughter moved her foot. I pointed to the youngest, the smallest, I said: That one, she moved her legs. And the father struck. His hand smacked his daughter's face. When he hit her, something cracked inside my brain, I don't know, something sad, something big. The little girl looked at me tearfully in her reflection. It was like I was fighting without moving. I was fighting calmly. It gave me shivers, I yelled: She moved! When you were looking the other way, she jumped! She was taking up space, she was taking up the whole studio. She wasn't respecting anything, she wasn't respecting the other children. She wasn't respecting the space, I saw her, I saw her! Hit her! Hit her! And each time I cried out, the father hit her five times, once on the back of the neck, once on the forehead, once on her right knee, once on her left knee, and once on her larynx. He was methodical. The more I yelled, the more he hit. The little girl. The little girl lowered her gaze, she was ashamed, I didn't know that anyone could feel shame at such a young age. She was so small, but so full of shame. Isn't that funny? She was ashamed of feeling ashamed. She looked at me and she was ashamed of feeling ashamed in front of me. I saw her shame of feeling ashamed like a spiral in her eyes. Parallel tears ran down her cheeks like in manga. Her father said: Don't worry, she just feels sorry for herself. She isn't suffering much. She's not crying from the pain, she's crying because she's crying.

Then, he asked his children to line up, and he said: What do you think, which one of them will be happy later on? You know, I'd forgotten about this story, now I find it soothing. You know, it's soothing, this story soothes me, it's putting me to sleep, I feel sleepy, look, I'm sleeping now, I'm sleeping. I'm falling asleep, I'm going to fall asleep, I'm going to go to bed, I'm going to sleep, good night, dude.

A drop of water fell from the ceiling onto his forehead.

2

The female nurse and the male nurse take care of the grandmother with their gestures, with their voices, their hands rise and fall as if in a mirror. They wear blue scrubs, and when one of them speaks, the other says the same thing with their face. Their eyebrows answer each other, like the eyebrows of a dog looking at its master. They say: So, how are you feeling today? And the grandmother blinks twice.

They've put her on a hospital bed in the middle of the gymnasium of this former school. Lying there, surrounded by fabric, trays, stuffed animals—everything hurts her, the edge of each object. All objects have serrated edges, all of them, even water. When you look at skin under a microscope, you can see serrated edges shaped like swords, on any sort of skin, even ones that seem soft, like a maggot's, or even a snake's, the skin of a trout, the skin of a tadpole, the edges of a bodily organ. When you look at a cell under a microscope, you see spines, points. That's how objects are shaped, all objects, that's the shape of matter. Life is in the shape of a point, the shape of a big nail.

They spread lotion on her thighs and on the back of her neck. They put oil on her breasts and on her feet. They put powder on her back and on her ears. They prick her, turn her over, change her, wipe her, comb her hair, massage her, and all of it hurts. The bed, the covers, and even the air around each object. The air is a weight that she must bear.

They guide her hands, they put them on her heart, they smooth creams on her cheeks, her lips, and her buttocks, she is soft as larvae. When you crush a larva, it explodes. Its body becomes juice. When you crush a slug, it changes, its body becomes like glue. Slugs and larvae melt into the ground, they transform. But nobody crushes the grandmother, and her body remains in place, she slides, she swells, she's a ball. She is almost zero. Her body is molding from the inside, but it smells like cologne. She's fresh, her body is fresh, her folds are fresh because they wash them, she's been washed.

But they might as well stab her skin instead of covering it in ointments, they might as well use blades instead of oil, sabers instead of gloves. Her body is a blade that cuts itself. They might as well clean her neck with an axe. Her neck irritates her the way everything else does, it screams all day long. If the ceiling fell in, the grandmother wouldn't feel a thing, because her pain is heavier than the ceiling.

The grandmother sounds like a motor when she breathes. She produces a lot of phlegm in her old throat, between her old cracks, she makes a lot of lumps, her mouth is dry as stone, they wet it, and wet it, they practically hose it down. They put water in and around her mouth, but when she's alone, her mouth opens and the air rushes out. Her mouth becomes hard, her tongue turns gray, she starts to crumble. She's a crumb of tongue stuck to a crumb of tongue stuck to another crumb of tongue. After several hours, her tongue is replaced by light. The light replaces her limbs, it replaces the marrow of her bones, and the grandmother imagines the marrow like white and blue matter, something cold, frozen, vibrating.

She wonders if the insides of bones could be used as ice for picnic coolers to preserve eggs. The insides of bones frozen in refrigerators or in plastic bags to save ice.

The bed makes wounds and her skin opens.

When a wound appears, it stays. It learns. It progresses. It festers. The pain speaks. It says: You are in this world, you create ebbs and flows, you have no control. All sick people create shit, even some dying people. Even in their final hour, in the hospital, at home, the rich, the poor, the young, all sick people create shit. If you give flowers to sick people, they will make shit. If you give them pieces of wood, they will make pieces of shit.

The grandmother made shit with the corner of her mouth, with her nose, she made it from her neck to her legs. Everything leaked. We can make shit with every part of our bodies. When we leave eyes behind somewhere in nature, they turn into shit, that's their only option, like fruit, like meat. If you abandon a banana, it turns into rot.

She was heavy.

When they put her to bed on the first day, her body multiplied by two, she had four arms, four legs, and two heads. The next day, her body multiplied by four, she had eight arms, eight legs, and four heads. The day after that, her body multiplied by six, and then by eight, and by twelve. Each day, her body multiplies. Today, the grandmother has 21,170 arms, 21,170 legs, and 10,585 heads.

However, when her spirit rises up to the ceiling, she looks at herself, she sees herself in her bed, and the grandmother adds a sky over each thing. She looks at the objects, she looks around the whole room, and she adds a sky for each piece of furniture, a sky for the TV, a sky for the pieces of bread, a sky over the yogurts, a sky for each blanket, a sky for the floor, a sky over the gymnasium, a sky for each child, Salim, Sara, a sky over each of their heads, and a sky for each of their teeth, a sky for their foreheads, a sky for each lock of hair, and everything becomes lighter.

We can't put one eye directly in front of our other eye.

Our eyes look at other eyes, but they don't leave our heads. Our eyes can see substances, but they can't touch them. They caress nothing. Our eyes stay where they are.

If he could have, Salim would have put one of his eyes inside of his grandmother's eye. Every time he talked to her, his grandmother stared vacantly. Is it worth having eyes? What good are eyes when you're not looking at anything? He wished he could blow into her nostrils and wake her up. Put firecrackers around her bed to startle her and make her jump up. She would have said: How long have I been sleeping? And Salim would have said: You've been sleeping for 10,000 years, Grandma, now we're going to drink 10,000 liters of coffee.

When a person is sick, you want to help them. When you encourage this desire, you end up wanting to hit the person, slap them in the face, you want to say: Stop it, everyone is sick of this.

Salim wished he could put water in his grandmother's body with a syringe to dilute all her problems. You wash the bodies of sick people, but their insides are dirty. You don't clean the tendons, you don't wash the veins, you can't clean the muscles, the vessels. Their organs are brown, the color of shit, and their bones are dust, you can't clean them, it's a shame, a shame. Salim prefers dirtiness to death. He would prefer rot, he'd prefer rot by a long shot, rot would be much better than death, mold would be better, better dirty than dead. And if he'd had to lick mud, he'd have licked twenty tons of mud for 1,000 years rather than have his grandmother die. Swallow fifty kilograms of gravel rather than have her die. He would have swallowed screwdrivers and hammers rather than have her die. Remove pieces of his skull rather than have his grandmother die.

He said to her: I'm going to put you in a cradle, I'll cover you with leaves one day. I'm going to dive inside a healthy person, I'll take their stomach, I'll take their heart, their brain, I'll take everything. I'll give you new organs, brand-new, clean ones, I'll make you a new body. I'm going to boil your blood, Grandma, to restart your life. I'm going to make putty out of your bones and remodel you. You will be like a golden three-millimeter baby in my arms. And if someone wants to keep you from existing, I will break their fingers once a week. And when their fingers heal, I'll break them once a day until the end of time. I will put you in a stroller and I'll push you all over this strange world.

*

Hello everyone, today we meet again for a new video on the subject of people, meaning cells. Your parents carry you and you are born, a doctor takes you out and you open your eyes. Cells surround your body, but you don't see them. They have antennae, they absorb the vibrations of your life, and you don't even realize it. There are things you can't see, almost all things. In your room, in your house, when you breathe, cells cover everything. You can't feel them, but you are never alone and you don't think about it. You don't know it. You are cells surrounded by cells. But a cell knows you, it watches you, it understands you. You yourself are not a person, you are not a single person, you are cells.

He lowered his eyes, he typed the word CELL in his phone, he read: The cell is the smallest element forming all living organisms. A cell allows people to become enclosed and isolated. The cell is the basic unit of all organisms. But I'm going to tell you what isn't written down: Your cells understand your life, they know. If you don't understand your life, it's not a big deal, your cells understand. The cells surround you and they multiply. They don't sparkle, but they vibrate. One cell can help you, but it can also betray you, the same cell can betray and help you. Cells interpret your feelings, they know the contents of your chest. They act upon you because they are you. They understand your life better than your life understands itself because they are your life. Outside of your cells, your life is only the word LIFE.

Don't get up, don't think, stay in your room, and be quiet. I did it, I didn't understand, I couldn't think, I didn't know anything. Cells mock us because of our thoughts, they know our thoughts. One cell can become the lid on our coffin, it can become a teardrop, a pimple, a cold, or cancer. Cells giggle, cells hate. And to protect ourselves, we must be silent. When we're quiet, our cells calm down. Be quiet in your head. Thoughts are things that contract in your neurons, but neurons are cells in our nerves.

Now, I'm going to tell you something and you are going to write it down on your arm. Write this on your arm: If a feeling decides your life, you are like a shoe. A shoe needs a foot. A shoe can't move forward without a foot. But a foot doesn't need a shoe to move forward, a foot doesn't need a shoe to go out, it doesn't need shoes to walk. A foot exists and it's a foot. If there were no feet, there would be no shoes, but if there were no shoes, feet would still exist. If a feeling decides your life, things go through your body, and you need things to go through your body the way shoes need feet.

His room was large, his head was delicate. He brought his hands closer to the camera and said: Don't be afraid to wait. Everyone is waiting, that means everyone is praying, even people who don't believe. Look carefully, it's as if they had dirt inside, as if they were digging. Look in the streets, in the cars, in kebab shops, in parks, in middle schools, look at their mouths and look in their eyes, everyone is praying. And why do you think everyone is praying? Think about it, everyone prays to be a person. Everyone thinks: I am this person, I have this past, I have this story, I have this place, I am this person. When they eat, when they rest, in the metro, in the train, they think: I am a person. They wake up and they think:

I am a person, I am the person who lives at my house, I am one single person. Who is the opposite of God? It's a person. If there are problems, the problems aren't the person's, they belong to God. Who creates illness? It's not a person, it's nature. Everyone prays so they don't have to understand. From their right hand all the way to their left, everyone is praying. Cells assemble, they touch and they ask, they beg, you could say that they pray.

He moved his face close to the camera and said: Start the day without thinking, do an experiment. Let other things decide, let them choose your tastes, your problems, your movements. Stay at your house for an entire day, make the day last longer. Stay at your house an entire week, make the week last longer. Stay at your house an entire year, make the years last longer. Stay in your room. When I was a kid, I thought like a kid, I talked like a kid, then, at night, I slept like a kid, and everyone treated me like a kid. I had compassion for objects. When my parents got a new car, I felt bad for the old car. I felt pity for the papers in trash cans. Then I became a person and now I'm speaking to you. Sometimes, I don't know what I am trying to say. Start your sentences without thinking. Start a sentence and don't choose the end. I'm posting my poem A ZERO BETWEEN THE EYES, don't forget to like and share, ciao, bye, see you next time.

*

Hi who does God pray to?

Can you talk about life after death plz

Hi Salim, I understand what you're saying but I want to tell you a story. I've stopped eating. My parents give me soup, and I put it in the toilet, I pour it out, I put the bread in the toilet, I flush. Food is something that no longer concerns me. To me, nothing is edible. Eating doesn't exist, it doesn't affect me. When I see bread, I don't even think of eating it. It would be like eating a carafe, you don't eat carafes. For me, nothing is edible.

Your face is ugly

Most of the time, I talk about my body in the third person. Do you think we suffer when we die? I don't think so, I think we focus. I'm going to give you an example: someone gets eaten by wolves in the forest. He gets eaten and he thinks: Wolves have a smell unlike anything I've ever smelled, he focuses on the smell, that's one example

I hate people who give speeches about cells. Do you think you're some kind of imam? Do you think you're an imam, dude? You're like the retards we put in institutions, like my brother, you remind me of my brother, my idiot brother

Salim, I'm writing to you for a bit of advice. I have an illness that has left me with only one tooth, but it's a very beautiful tooth. People might think, poor guy, he only has one tooth, but I'm not poor, because my tooth is beautiful

Your mother should have swallowed you

The tooth I'm talking about is worth as much as the thirty-two teeth in anyone else's mouth. All the teeth of all the people in the world combined aren't worth as much as this tooth in my mouth. My dentist said: I've never seen anything like this. He said: It's the most beautiful tooth possi-

ble. He photographed it. He printed the picture. He put it on display in the waiting room, I'm proud. People think I've got less, but I've got this tooth. How can I let people know about it? I want them to notice it. I thought about pulling it out so I could show it to people in the street. I'd like to tell people: Look at this tooth. But my dentist advises against it, what about you?
What do you think?

Hi Salim, thank you for the video. Speaking of cells, I have brothers and sisters, but it's as if I were an only child. You see, when people ask if I have brothers or sisters, I say no. Obviously. No. I'm an only child. I don't understand the idea of having a brother or sister. I know you have a sister. But do you feel like you're her brother? To me, brothers and sisters don't exist. Everyone is an only child. I think my brother is an only child. I feel like my sister is an only child. Our parents didn't divide one person into multiple people. Our parents had children who are only children. I can't see it any other way

Hello Sweetheart, I request special consideration because this goes right to heart, It's about a sUM of 2,500,000 euros in millions, that I wish to offer as a GIFT to open a center for the destitute, in yYOUR area, contact this handle with CREDIT CARD NUMBER

Are you Sara's brother?

My parents' children are only children for example

You say that cells are all around us, but you could say cells surround the whole world, not just us

Hello Salim, is there another God above the regular God?

You have a soothing voice, I feel sleepy, I like how you move, can you whisper close to the mic next time?

Hello, I'm in love with my French teacher. I told her I wrote your poems. I don't think that's a problem, you said the poems didn't really come from you, that they were for everyone and they came from everyone. She took an interest in me, thanks. When she started to take an interest in me, I told her about my life. When I told her about my life, she complimented me. When she complimented me, that was the first time anyone had ever complimented me. I'm an ordinary girl. Every time she spoke to me, I wrote down the date and time in my notebook. I have her schedule stuck to the inside of my jacket. I wait for her by the doors. She's asked me to leave her alone, she doesn't want to say hello to me anymore, why?

She asked me to stop following her

Hi Salim, now I'm going to look at people and think they're praying

My teacher's name is Genesis

To the guy who writes the aggressive comments, what happened with your idiot brother?

It's an uncommon name

My brother is a mental retard. My parents put him in a center for mental retards. When they give him rice, my brother counts the grains. He counts everything, he counts everyone's fingers. I told him: Frédéric, everyone has ten fingers. Five fingers on each side. But he doesn't understand. He spends his days counting the walls in his room. I told him: Frédéric, there's always going to be four walls. He looks at me and says: One, one, one, he's counting my head.

I don't know anybody else named Genesis

Salim liked each comment, then he sat in silence for a moment. The objects in his room weren't saying anything. The objects around him weren't speaking, but he could feel them. And even when he wasn't looking at them, the objects were looking at him, they were giving off vibrations as if they were expanding. However, the objects weren't saying anything, so he closed his eyes. Objects are surrounded by the ideas of themselves. The object knife is surrounded by an idea-knife. A knife radiates the idea-knife up to six kilometers, up to ten kilometers. Maybe a blind man can sense a knife in a room. If you put a blind man and an object in a room, if the blind man concentrates, if he spends hours in the room, he might end up hearing the name of the object, he might end up seeing it. All things say their names, they basically introduce themselves. The moon radiates the idea-moon up to millions of kilometers. Salim imagined an experiment, he typed it up in his phone:

AN EXPERIMENT THAT PROVES OBJECTS SAY THEIR NAMES

1. You take a baby from his parents at birth.
2. You put the baby in a room filled with all possible objects.
3. You never speak to him.
4. You throw him bits of food through a trapdoor. He eats.
5. You throw him water. He drinks.

6. Twenty years later, you take him out of the room.
7. You ask him questions.
8. The former baby says a word. He says a few words. He says different words. He says the names of objects in different languages. He says the name of an object in German, the name of an object in Lingala, the name of an object in Bengali, the name of an object in Russian. He points to the objects. He knows them. He says their names in a language. He doesn't speak in sentences.
9. We learn that objects introduce themselves. Science proves that objects say their names.

Salim walked down the hall. He washed his hands in the bathroom. When you wash a hand, you're putting a smell on that hand, you're covering it. A dirty hand smells like work, that's the hand's smell. Salim got embarrassed looking at himself in the mirror, as if he existed too much, repeating. He put water on his face and the water was hot, he let it run. He wiped his hands, he wrote:

water has no center

He posted the sentence on the network and then looked up. He saw steam floating in the light. Suddenly, he felt like the world lived in a wave, the whole world in some sort of wave, a large, slow wave, a single motion, he wrote:

water has no style

He posted the sentence on the network, he readjusted the sleeves of his sweater, and he thought about clothing. Clothing is lonely, because clothing isn't a person, it surrounds a person. Sometimes a piece of clothing hates a person. The clothing doesn't like the body it covers, and you can tell. But clothing protects them, even a dirty, lousy piece of clothing. Clothing insulates, and the person remains inside. Clothing draws a circle, but the person is not the circle. Clothing beautifies, it adds something. We put different pieces of clothing together, they protect us, but no clothing can replace us. No piece of clothing can become a person. Clothing doesn't protect us from our smells, from our heads. Salim looked at the floor, he looked at the ceiling, he looked in the sink, his mouth almost open, he looked at his mouth in the reflection of his telephone, he lifted his left arm, he stretched it out, he bent his legs, his butt touched the ground. The lines of the tiles gave shape to the floor. They outlined the room. He saw eyes, tiny little gray eyes, thousands of eyes in the lines in the tile. We see eyes everywhere. You can see faces in yogurt or on a fingernail. Just look at a stone, wait, and you'll see a nose, eyes, and mouth. Look at one of your fingers and you'll see a head. A face like ours. We see each other. We can recognize ourselves in any surface. Napkins hanging like cadavers, toothbrushes, doors, faucets. Salim took a photo of himself, he looked at the image, he zoomed in on his eye. He posted the image. He lay down. He took a photo of his forehead, he posted the image. He wrote four lines:

my head
in water
my head
under a sheet

He posted the lines on the network. He added a wilted-rose emoji. He wrote the word: Careful. Then he looked up.

This is how it happened: he'd write the first word, then it was like he heard voices. He didn't hear voices, not really, but he translated them into a language. He waited with a stupid face, a dazed look. Then something like a mouth opened inside him. He wrote what he didn't know, as if things were writing themselves, like opening your eyes by shutting them. That was it. We're capable of writing words we don't know. In school, for essays, he'd written words he didn't know. If someone had asked him what these words meant, he wouldn't have known how to respond. The word pallid when he was eight. The word falter when he was ten. The word affable later on. Words he didn't know turned up in sentences. The words came from the sentence, they came from other words. The other words inserted them, they put them in the correct form where they belonged.

careful
if you drink
from the wrong glass
you might turn out
wrong

He posted the five lines on the network, he tapped the screen twice. Followers shared his words. Some followers left hearts. Some followers laughed. Some followers posted faces with a smile, faces with a teardrop, they posted faces with twisted eyebrows, with a tongue, red faces, black faces. He saw a hair on the floor. He'd lost it without realizing. Hair is a part of the body we can't control. He wrote to Jonathan: Nobody feels their hair. If hair could speak it wouldn't say anything. He wrote: Light is damp. When you look at it, you can tell it's damp. Jonathan replied: Yes, and he wrote: I feel like water forgives me when I drink it. Salim wrote: Yes.

*

Sara could drink lying down, she was always lying down, outside at night on the stairs, downtown, in the square, on the bus, she needed two seats, she stretched out her legs. On the floor, in her room, on her bed, on her brother's bed, in the hall, anywhere, it was her natural position. Her weight planted somewhere.

When we lie down, our mouths are on the same level as our feet. Our feet are on the same level as our hands. When we lie down, our organs are aligned. The father said: Sara, you're going to become flat like people who believe the Earth is flat. And she'd say: They aren't flat. The father sighed heavily, he said: Maybe not, but you're going to become flat like the Earth in their heads. You're going to get the floor dirty, I washed it. But the floor is going to get you dirty because it's not clean because it's the floor. You're not listening to me. You're going to get your back dirty, it's going to get disgusting. Does anyone want a disgusting back? Think about it. A back covered in dirt. Who wants dust on their back? Who? Well? Who in the world wants a gross back? Think about it. You turn around, people see your back, and they hate you. That's what happens. Who wants to be hated? Who'd rather be hated? Anyone? Who? You're going to carry dirt around on your back wherever you go. You're going to spread it all over the house and the house will be dirty in places we can't even imagine. Who wants a dirty house? I'm asking you, a big house like ours, a big dirty house, a huge dirty house. Who wants that? Who? A dirty old school? Who wants that? You're going to get sucked into the floor. Little by little, the floor will suck you up. You're stuck to it like glue. You'll see, if the floor sucks you up, you'll see where that gets you. Because nobody knows where that gets you. We don't know where that gets you, but you can explain it all to us once you're under the floor. You can tell us where it gets you then. Where that's gotten you and your brother, always lying down, always on the floor, always flat.

She rolled her eyes, she sighed, sometimes she fell asleep. She'd fallen asleep on the floor of the gymnasium. She dreamed there was a dead man in the house. The dead man moved without moving. His body slid forward as if on oil. She'd seen the dead man doing nothing in the fridge. She got up at night in the dream, she opened the fridge, the dead man was standing there. The sound of the fridge grew, it grew, it took up all the space. It locked her gaze to the gaze of the dead man. The scene went on for a long time. The dead man had a tender face. He took his eyes off her, he looked around as if it were a job, an activity. He diluted the house with his eyes and the house went soft. He looked at each thing and each thing softened. She'd felt love for the dead person in the dream. He tried to touch her. She tried to touch him. But they diluted each other. They pushed through the walls of the house, through the neighborhood. They wheeled their arms in the air, their ligaments dislocated. She wished the dead man could run his hand over her eyes. He smiled at her.

Sara opened an eye, the grandmother blinked. Salim came in and the female nurse caressed the grandmother's forehead, she said: She's not doing well, she's not going to hold out much longer. The male nurse said: A few days. The female nurse said: Her blood's the problem, and the grandmother burped. Salim said: Is there something we can do? The male nurse said: We can give her the blood of her child. Salim said: I can give her my blood. The female nurse said: No, she needs the blood of her child. You can't skip a generation. The body has rules. Sara said: Our mother isn't here anymore. The male nurse said: Her blood is rotting. Salim asked: How many more days? The male nurse said: Maybe a week. Salim said: Our mother is in town. Sara said: She won't give her anything. Salim lowered his head, he scratched his neck.

*

The father often sent emails to his children.

He gave them advice. He looked for sayings on the internet, proverbs. He copied them and arranged them. He gave them to his children so they could understand life.

> Sara, Salim, it's me, listen closely to what I'm about to tell you. You must know these ten things. Read carefully all the way to the end:
>
> 1. To God, nobody stinks.
> 2. When you cry, there will always be a wasp to sting your face. The sadder you are, the more you get stung, it's the law.
> 3. Lean on canes, never on people.
> 4. Every man blows his nose.
> 5. Everything looks like a nail when you're holding a hammer.
> 6. Bread bakes slowly when you're hungry.
> 7. People come into your life, then they disappear from your life for no special reason. Don't go looking for a special reason.
> 8. There will be miracles, it's inevitable.
> 9. During a flood, there is always one person stand-

ing on the roof of their house yelling: This place wasn't supposed to flood.

10. If you throw a cake in the forest, when you go back to the forest, you will find a cake. Share.

3

A long time ago, a man was slitting children's throats in the village. He'd drag them under a bridge, he'd cut their throats. A few years ago, when the grandmother could still speak, she said he'd killed birds. He took their warmth in his hands, he made them sleep. Then he pulled out their beaks. He always had beaks in his pockets, hundreds of beaks. He'd wiggle his fingernails in the beaks, you could hear the clicking.

He was a heavy man, he wore five or six jackets, four or five pairs of pants, eight pairs of socks. He didn't wash. He walked forward, he sighed, he was tall. Every day, he had a bird in his hand, a bird that was dead or dying, it depended on the time. People walked past him in the village, they said: Hello. And he would open his hand, he'd show them the cadaver. His face had no expression. Some people said he had died, killed by a guard at a labor camp, and then come back to life, but not completely, not all the way. So when children started disappearing, people suspected him. Some men followed him. One evening, they came upon him under a bridge, his eyes closed, a child in his arms. It's a shame, because the child was already dead, his throat cut. It's a shame, because the man could have just looked at his knife and looked at the children. It would have been enough just to mix the two images, he didn't need to actually cut them. If you really think about it, deep down, it's not worth it to kill or hit. If we're overtaken by the desire to kill or hit, it's not worth moving our hands, even lifting them. We look at the cheek. We look at the palm of our hand. We mix the two images. The mind quiets. When we think of heat, the body produces warmth. When we think about our sleepiness, our bodies rest. We look at an animal, we concentrate, we assume the rhythm of the animal's heart, we understand it. But dead animals no longer have heartbeats. We can no longer understand them.

A black smear glided in front of his face, he lowered his head in the video, he looked at the floor, he said: It's a bird. He took his camera, he filmed the bird, and he said: See, it's a bird, I think it's dead, it's a dead bird. That was the end of the video.

The bird was the size of a thumb, its beak open, it was warm, you could see its tongue, it stuck out, small and gray. He took it in his hands and pressed down. He pressed the round stomach to get the heart working again, liquid oozed from the beak, viscous, transparent, sad. Where did this bird come from? How was this possible? How could a bird fall from your bedroom ceiling? A dead bird. A little dead bird that falls from the ceiling. A dead bird fallen in his room.

Salim wrote: I don't know where to put it.

Jonathan wrote: You can't keep it, it'll get worms.

There aren't any worms at my house. It won't be able to get worms.

Jonathan wrote: The worms are going to come from the bird, because it's dead.

Maybe I'll keep it in oil. I'm going to put it in a jar with some olive oil, because oil doesn't rot.

Why would you do that?

To take care of it.

You shouldn't keep it.

Why?

Because it's going to give you all sorts of diseases. Put it in the ground.

And Salim stopped responding. After several minutes, he wrote:

For certain birds, the weight of their feathers is two times greater than the weight of their bones. The sword-billed hummingbird possesses a beak that is longer than its entire body. Some birds, like pigeons or greater flamingos, suckle their young, the milk doesn't come from mammary glands, but from the crop, a little pocket in the esophagus. The hummingbird lays the smallest eggs of any bird, the eggs are about one centimeter long. Birds sing before they're born, they communicate through the shell. The mother transmits a sort of password to her babies through the shell, and when they're born, they sing the password and she recognizes them. The pelican is the heaviest bird capable of flight, it weighs between ten and fourteen kilograms.

Jonathan wrote: It doesn't help to look up all these things about birds, you should just bury it. Ask your sister. Do you want me to come over? I can come.

Salim wrote: No.

He sent a message to Sara. One minute later, she came into his room. He opened his hands, she touched the bird. It was damp, she said: Did you put water on it? He said: No. My hands perspired around it. He showed her the video of the falling bird and she watched the video of the falling bird. She looked at the ceiling, she looked at her brother. He said: Can we put it in a jar of oil? She responded: No. We're going outside, we're going to bury it.

*

Outside, the light of the streetlamps didn't spill over with light. It stayed close to the light. The light was a bubble around the light, it didn't touch the ground. The streets were dark. Salim tried to walk straight, perfectly straight, he tried to have a normal, perfectly standard expression on his face. The grass on the edge of the sidewalk was in shadow. He said: In houses, you don't walk straight. Outside, you walk straight. In houses, you walk in a circle, I'm out of practice. There's air, isn't there? In the air. There's a lot of air, isn't there? Don't you think? Sara didn't respond. He said: Do you know the story of the man and the street light? She didn't respond.

One night, a man lost his keys in the street, he was looking for them under the street light. However, he knew that he'd lost them somewhere else. He was sure of it. But he was looking for them under the street light. Do you know why? She didn't say anything.

Because it's easier to see. What if we go back and put the bird in some salt and vinegar? Could we put it in the bath tub? I'll take care of it.

He was holding the bird lightly in his right hand, he said: I feel like I'm in front of us and following myself when we're walking. You know, like if I were farther up the road. Maybe there is a part of us that walks up ahead, an invisible part. It walks in front of us. We follow it. It's one millimeter in the future. One millimeter ahead. And we always follow it, don't you think? She said: No.

They were walking on a long road lined with chestnut trees. Leaves fell every now and then, everything was quiet. A bird flew off, and you could hear its wings. Salim said: I know we're not laughing right now, okay, we're not laughing, but every time someone laughs, I laugh. Even if it's not funny, if someone laughs, I laugh. When I send a smiley, my face smiles. When I think about it, I realize I'm smiling. It's like with vomit, if someone vomits in front of you, you vomit. It's like yawning, if someone yawns, you yawn. Mouths are weird, the mouth part I mean, isn't it a weird space? The mouth. It's like mouths imitate everything they see. Did you know that a rock explodes if you heat it up? She didn't respond.

Do you know what face you're supposed to make when you want to look normal? A normal face, you know what I mean? Salim's nose was leaking, he said: Try to see what I mean.

She gave him her scarf so he could wipe his nose, he put it on his head. He looked like a sainted woman bowing her head in the night. A flock of bats flew over the village, they were screeching. He said: There's a house in Mexico that cries blood, it cries drops of blood every day, I saw a video, do you think it's true? She said: Maybe.

They stopped in front of the church. Through the window, in the vestry, they saw the priest dressed like an ordinary man. A candle lit his table. He was scratching lotto tickets, but he wasn't scratching with his fingernail, he was scratching with his hand, with his whole hand, like an animal. She said: Do you think he's winning? Salim said: Yes.

Then they left the main road, the ground became dry. Their feet kicked up clods of earth. In the park, she said: We're going to put it here. He slowly placed the bird on the ground at the foot of a little tree. He touched the earth, it was warm, they made a hole. Mist enveloped their hands. They covered the little thing with its open beak. They covered it with earth, and Salim said: Burials are slow. It's slow, I'd never thought about it. Nobody runs during a burial, nobody moves fast, even the words are slow in burials. Everyone speaks slowly. We're going back now, okay? And as he spoke, it almost felt like the fresh smell was coming from his mouth and face rather than the grass.

They were kneeling. Sara tapped her phone screen, a rapper sang:

> Oh, my brother, my brother,
> Keep my eyes far from this situation

Free me from my stress through visions, oh
Free me from my stress through bitches, oh, my brother,
Hundreds of dollars will rain on our graves
Rain on our graves
Rain on our graves
Rain on our graves
My brother, my brother, oh please
Free me from my stress through bitches
Free me from my stress through visions, oh
Bring my hand closer to the light
Bring my hand closer, my brother
Your crab head, my brother, free me from my stress through bitches
Free me from my stress through visions, oh
Hundreds of dollars will rain
Rain on our graves
Rain on our graves
Rain on our graves
Yeah, yeah, yeah, yeah, oh
Your crab head, my brother,
Oh, oh, oh, oh, oh, yeah, yeah
Free me from stress, oh
Your crab head, please, please, oh

They were silent for a bit, and Salim wished for the earth to be good, for it to be good and light for this bird and other creatures. For them to be like pearls scattered underground. For the earth to be good to the bird, for it to be his blanket, for it to be discreet, an earth that's discreet and good and kind. For the bird's body to rest under a canopy of cream, wool, and soft animals. For the earth to turn and return him. For the earth to swallow him whole.

The earth swallows the dead, it breaks the dead, it breaks their bones. Let the bones of the dead crack. Let the earth make joints for them, draw them down, and shatter them into confetti. Into dead-person confetti. Let it pull them into the crust inside of continents, then under the continents, then all the way down to the Earth's core. May all the dead descend, and let them descend. Let the earth break their arms into twenty pieces of arm, let it break their legs into twenty pieces of dead leg. Let the earth multiply them. Let it multiply the dead and help them. And may the trees grow, let them be the dead for our eyes, for us, for our living eyes. The dead grown just for us. Pieces of their bodies. Their dead-person bodies. Their legs broken into 1,000 pieces. Their arms broken into 1,000 pieces. Let them form buds, boughs, and branches.

The magpies were chattering in the park. Salim shook the tree. The tree's parts were like the broken arms of a child. The broken legs of a dead child, its little broken arms, frozen in the tree. Salim looked for a stone or some wood, but he could only find a can, he stuck it in the ground like a cross. Sara pointed out something in the distance. It was a man, rising in the dark, on a swing in a corner of the park. She said: Look, it's the neighbor's son, the electroshock one.

What's he doing?

He's swinging.

*

In front of the middle school, Salim coughed.

The middle school was a cold thing in the village. The sky seemed darker around it. Every day, a few years ago, Salim had to wake up before the sun, splash his face with water, and get dressed. He had to go inside of this large building, and he had to sit in an ugly room. They said his name, and he had to say the word: Here.

Every day, he had to contain his face so his face didn't come out of his face. Every day, he locked himself in the restroom so he could become horrible. He stretched out his mouth to become horrible. His nostrils, his eyes. All alone in the bathroom, he deformed his face. He made his lips bleed, he flushed the toilet, he spit in the water. He spit, he came out, he thought about it, he said: Have I done anything wrong? I haven't done anything wrong.

Still, in the winter, every morning, the white lights went on in the classroom, and everyone squinted their eyes as if in a nightmare. Was the world crazy?

The parents were crazy, sick people who sent their children to a gray building. Every day, sick, crazy people sent their children to gray buildings. Every day, on the best days, the best days of their lives, the best seasons. The parents gave away their children's best days as if it were normal. The parents had given away their own best days, and they gave away the best days of their children as if it meant nothing. Salim repeated the word: Punished, in his head, he repeated the words: Punished, graded, seated, and he saw the parents as people who were punished, punished regularly, born punished, and punishing themselves. They punished their children who would punish their own children to spread unhappiness on Earth. Adults were so weird. Sometimes the teachers stopped moving, they looked at the floor, they looked at nothing, they said words, their heads like wax. The Spanish teacher wore makeup like a clown, the red went far beyond the outline of her mouth. The music teacher never smiled. The PE teacher had skin that was almost green.

One day, Salim said to his father: I don't understand why I have to go there. And the father scrubbed something, maybe a fork, in silence.

In this middle school, like in other middle schools, everyone spit on one child at recess. In the cafeteria, in the halls, in the locker rooms, he got hit with mucus, that was his life. Every morning when Salim was walking to school, he'd gather saliva in his mouth to spit on his face, in his hair, in his ears. It was normal.

He'd arrive with his mouth full, all that was left to do was spit, and he spat. The boy laughed. Everyone spit on him, and he laughed. He spit on himself and he laughed. He never cleaned off the mucus, so it dried out, it gave him white clumps of hair.

Everyone would form a circle around him and abuse him. They put sand in his mouth. They rubbed their knuckles back to front and front to back on his head. They'd stab their compasses in his back, they'd roll him around on the ground.

His cheeks had tread marks on them. His skin was always cut at the elbows, the knees, and the temples. Red was the color of his body. They stuck his head in the toilet bowl, they kicked him in the teeth, he bled. Salim hit his forehead with the corners of books.

They put gravel in his eyes, they threw him down the staircase, he picked himself back up. They pulled down his pants in the hallways, they tugged on his privates and yelled: DING-DONG, and they laughed, they laughed, he laughed, everyone laughed, he laughed, he hit himself, he laughed while hitting himself, he punched himself in the head, in the legs, in the stomach, he laughed, he hit, he said: Ha ha, I hate myself too, guys, I just hate myself.

They walked on his fingers and he didn't say anything because he was hittable and he was beaten, like something to do, like tying your shoes. Sometimes he'd take a break in the infirmary, but he annoyed the nurses with his big eyes, his damp look, with his kindness. They ended up locking him in the closet where they kept the chemicals that cause cancer. People often called him Little Shit, but he was quiet. When the teachers walked near his body, they had to hold their hands still to keep them from flying into his face. In class, one teacher wrote on the board: I want to make him suffer. But he caught himself and changed it to: Find the complement of the direct object.

They taped insults to his back, and when he found them, he laughed. They posted pictures of him on all the networks, pictures of his face getting beaten, pictures of his face all red, of his head in puddles, and his butt in the hallways. When he saw them, he liked them, he shared them, he left a heart, a comment, a laughing smiley. He assimilated.

When there was no more room on his face, they spit in his hood. They pissed in cups and dumped them out on his head. He laughed, he laughed, he cried from laughing, he said: Nice, you really got me.

On the street by the middle school, the neighbors came out of their houses to insult him. They flipped him off from their yards. Everyone laughed, the students, the teachers, the hall monitors, and even the cats in the streets looked on in a participatory way. From time to time, an explosion of laughter covered the school. The principal burst out laughing, he said: That'll teach you about life, little man, ha ha. Life isn't easy, little man, you have to know how to defend yourself in this life. And the principal of the middle school patted his head, but his veins were bulging, they were bulging and he had to pull his arm back so he wouldn't strangle him, so he wouldn't hit him, so he wouldn't yank out his cute, tiny, immaculate teeth, so he wouldn't smash him on the ground.

One day, things went further. They put his eyes out.

When Salim saw the blood, his mouth opened, it spit. His mouth spit three times into the boy's eyes. His mouth spit fat loogies into his bloody eyes. His feet kicked the body in the blood. They kicked the body lying in the boy's blood.

No one punished him.

The firemen took the boy away. Classes started again.

After that, Salim never wanted to leave the house. It was as if the outside world had ended there.

*

The father rushed outside in his bathrobe and he started yelling: What the hell are you two doing? Why did he go out? You're both crazy! Sara, why did you take your brother out of the house? He's not prepared! He needed to be prepared! Years without leaving the house, years, he needs some preparation! You're both going to make him even crazier, you're going to make him even weirder! Sara, you have to take care of your brother, you need to look after him. I feel like I'm dreaming, is this a dream or what? Is this a dream that looks like real life?

Salim looked at his father. This man had once been a few centimeters long, he'd once been a few millimeters long, he'd lived in a stomach in the form of a fetus. One day, he was born, they'd cut his cord, and that creature had become his father. He imagined the birth of his father and the birth of his mother. They were born. His sister was also born. And even his grandmother. Old people were born once, they were born babies.

The father yelled: Why is Salim outside? Why? Is this normal? Am I dreaming? Sara and Salim didn't have any particular expression on their faces. They didn't say anything. They looked at this father in his bathrobe in the street, shaking all over, his hair dry and his hands twitching. He said: You're going to get even sicker, Salim! You need to take people's advice, important advice! The social worker said: Go slowly. Go slowly with this child. She said:

Little by little, the little-by-little method, go little by little, tell me why you're in the street. I feel like I'm dreaming, maybe I'm dreaming. Am I dreaming? Am I dreaming, Salim?

He found a dead bird.

A dead bird? Where would he find a dead bird? In his room? Do you two think I'm an idiot? Maybe a bird just fell from his ceiling. A bird just fell out of nowhere, is that it? A dead one?

Yes, that's what happened, a dead bird fell from his ceiling. We just buried it. The father started yelling again, he yelled for a while, he repeated the sentences: Quit getting on my nerves, you two really need to quit getting on my nerves, you're testing my nervous system, you're messing with my internal systems, you know that? This behavior isn't normal, children who behave this badly aren't normal. You're taking bad behavior to a whole new level! There aren't any birds in the ceilings, stop, stop it right now, stop all of this, these stories won't get you anywhere good, you're not supposed to lie to your father. You're not supposed to lie.

The neighbor was spying from her yard. He turned to her, yelling: Are you seeing this? I brought these children into the world, I brought children into the world who lie to me, do you see them? They just lied. Look at their faces. You should be ashamed, Sara, you're both hiding things from me. I look out the window, and what do I see? I see you and I think I'm dreaming, is this normal or am I dreaming? Am I dreaming? Sara, am I dreaming?

She said: It's possible. We might be living in a simulation created by aliens.

Salim said: And the blood?

The father said: What blood?

Sara said: You know which.

You know she's old.

And?

It's nature, Sara, what are we supposed to do? There's nothing we can do. And because we can't do anything, we won't do anything. What are we supposed to do when we can't do anything? Everyone has to die, right? Everyone has to die, yes or no? Go back inside right now. Go, get back inside. I'm cleaning the house, I'm cleaning, go back inside!

He pushed his children. The neighbor quickly repositioned her binoculars, like a flicking tongue. The father slammed the door.

Salim said: You have to find her.

The father pulled a sponge from his pocket, he cleaned the tops of his hands and under his nails. This sponge left yellow and gray bits behind, it was old and irritating. He flipped it over, he scrubbed with the green side.

He said: Listen, Salim, don't talk to me about your mother. Am I dreaming or are you talking about your mother? Don't talk to me about your mother. We don't even know who that woman is anymore. She was a person we knew once, but she's no longer that person. It was a long time ago. We knew the way she spoke and the way she thought, but these ways no longer exist. That's it, they no longer exist. That's all. Don't you understand? You'll see later on, you'll see, you're going to meet people, and those people will change, that's it. They will become other people. They will become strangers, do you understand? Strangers. They'll run into you in the street, they'll no longer say hello and you'll no longer say hello and you won't mind. That's it. One day, you won't mind. You'll wait for that day to come and when it comes, you won't even be able to remember the old person. You'll look at photos, but they won't help. You'll ask yourselves questions, you'll wonder where the people from the past go. Everyone wonders that, and you'll wonder too. But who will you ask about it? Nobody, because nobody knows. History moves forward, that's it. We look back and all we know is that people disappear. Wash your hands, that's the important thing. Keep yourself clean, that's it, that's the important thing. You don't realize it in the beginning, and when you're old, you don't know anything, but you notice, you notice that you don't know anything. That's all. People travel to the past, but you can't see the past. You can't see the past because you can't see time. We say the word TIME, but we can't see time, we can't draw it. We can't see time because we can't measure it. We use numbers, but we aren't measuring anything because we don't know where the beginning or the end is. Where is the beginning and where is the end, Salim? Where is the end and where is the beginning, Sara? We measure a part of time, a small part, we measure a century, a millennium, we measure tens of millions of years, but we're measuring a part. It's a part, but we don't even know which one. Which part are we in? Which part of time are we in, Sara? Are we at the beginning or the end? Are we in the middle? We don't know. It's almost like cleanliness, you can't know how clean the floor really is, you clean the floor, but it's already dirty. We can't measure cleanliness, what does it mean to be dirty? You clean the floor, but are the molecules in the floor clean? We can't know, we can't know everything, we can't clean everything. For everything to be clean, it would have to disappear. We can't measure time because past time exists in the past, but where does the past exist? It doesn't exist where we can see it. We can't measure the future, it's like the past. How long is the future? Do you know? No. And you Salim, do you know? No. You don't know, my children. We know that people disappear. That's all. That's all we know, Salim, that's all we know.

That has nothing to do with this.

I told you to quit getting on my nerves. I've had it! When you were six, you were a person, right? When you were seven you were a person, right? And today, you are another person. Your mother no longer exists, the mother you knew no longer exists, that's it, she doesn't exist!

Sara said: You're letting Grandma die?

The father said: Yes.

Salim said: I'll go and I'll find her.

Oh, you're really testing my whole nervous system the two of you. You're killing me, you're going to wreck my immune system, and I'm going to get sick. What will you do if I get sick? What will happen to you, and what will happen to the house, if I get sick? Salim, you're going to stay in the house, and little by little, you'll return to school, little by little, you hear me? Little by little. Do you want us to lose the house? What would we do, living on the streets with your grandmother? Make videos in the rain, is that it? Is that what you want? She has to die, it's normal. We don't need anyone. Your mother is like a ghost, exactly like a ghost, if you think of her, you catch a whiff of ghost in your mind.

Sara said: She wouldn't want to give her anything anyway. The father said: Who? And Sara said: Our mother. And the father yelled: Who are you talking about? Who is this person? I just explained that she no longer exists. And Salim said: I'll go. The father yelled: I just explained that she doesn't exist anymore! Where will you go? Are you going to look for a ghost? She doesn't exist! He was still yelling, he yelled: She doesn't exist anymore! And his voice broke on the first syllable of the word exist. It broke as if the casing around his words had just cracked. The father's sentence was like a collection of soft little balls that overlap, like interlocking snake eggs. If you could see it, it would have looked like this in the air:

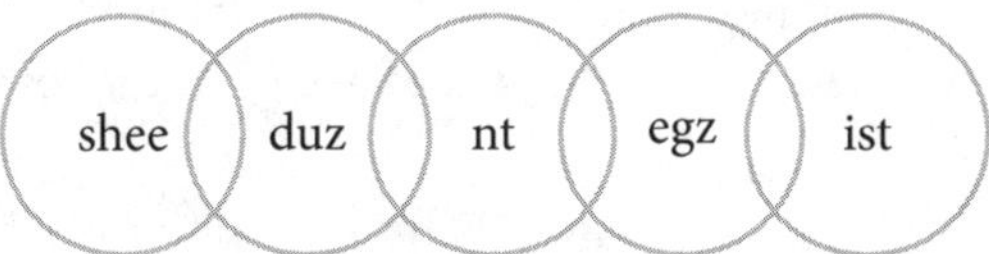

One of these balls just cracked in the father's throat, it was very clear, almost palpable. The membrane just broke apart on the second syllable of the word exist. His voice had broken.

Sarah remembered it breaking that way before one night. They were on vacation in an apartment near the sea, it was hot, the windows were open, and the curtains moved gently in the dark. Her father and mother had yelled, they'd slapped each other. The mother had slapped the father. The father had slapped the mother. The mother had started bleeding near her eyebrow. The father had yelled: I was sleeping. His voice shouted in a whisper, but his whispers contained screams: You woke me up so we could fight. It's your fault, you always want something to be wrong. And the mother had said: Look at our children, you're making them cry. My eyebrow is bleeding. Is this the first time you've made me bleed? Is this the first time you've made the children cry? And the father yelled: I was sleeping and you hit me, I was asleep, why would you make me hit you? And the mother had said: Look at your hands. Look at what you've done with your hands. Your huge, heavy hands, your big mason hands with your heavy fingers. And the father had felt the mark of the slap in his hand. He'd said: I was sleeping. And the mother said: Hitting is always a choice. You're making us cry. You want to know why I hit you when you're sleeping? Just look at your hands, you use them for hitting, they're heavy. Just look at our vacation, look at our children. You're making your children cry. The children, they're children, they're still children.

But I was sleeping.

Listen, do you hear that? It's the sound of our children's tears falling on the tiles. Do you think you take good care of your children?

But I was sleeping, you hit me on the head, you slapped me. You hit my head, I had to defend myself.

They fought, they yelled, they talked, and when the parents fought, Sara felt splashed, bits of their fight exploded onto her face. The mother had said: You're making our son cry, you're making our daughter cry, look at them, do you see them in the dark? Take a close look at their eyes, you're making our children cry. They're going to be unhappy when they're older.

But I was sleeping, I was sleeping.

And the father's voice had broken on the second syllable of the word sleeping. The cover had broken. The outer layer surrounding it had burst.

In Sara's mind, her father's voice was the shape of a slug sliced in half by a box cutter.

*

Salim posted his dreams on the network.

Dream #572:

A mechanic is waving at me, he points to a door. I go inside, it's a garage. My grandmother is sitting in an iron chair. She's surrounded by floating feathers and skulls. My grandmother's stomach is transparent. It's full of cables and chargers that move in her guts. She's smiling. She asks me what time it is.

I say: I don't know.

She says: Ask that lady.

A woman touches my arm. Her hair is shining because it's dirty. She has pink lips. I ask her what time it is, I say: It's for my grandmother.

The woman pulls me onto her lap, she tells me her life story.

She says: I'm German. One evening, I was in a hotel with my husband. He jumped from the thirteenth floor. But right before that, he'd said: My God, we're so happy.

She shows me the video of her life on her telephone.

Then I think it would be nice to see the film of my life or the lives of my family members. It would be nice to see summaries so I could understand people better. Maybe one day there will be videos of everyone's lives on their phones, videos that are easy to watch. You'd just have to show the video, and then you'd be understood.

And that's what the woman is doing. She's showing me the video of her husband jumping out the window. She says: My husband hid his bald spot under a combover.

I watch her life. I watch how she became crazy. She says: They put me in a psychiatric hospital. I stayed there for sixteen years.

After that, she lived in a train station. Because she was crazy, she cut off her left breast with a piece of glass in the restroom.

I say: I don't want to see that. Don't show me these images.

She says: I know what time it is.

My grandmother is watching.

My grandmother giggles.

*

It was raining, Salim and Sara were touching their screens on the bed. Sara turned her face toward her brother, she said: What are you doing? Salim was moving his thumbs, he said: I'm writing. Sara pressed her browbone against the sheet and her eyelid folded. She said: Read me the last line.

The snow is alone, goodbye, my head is leaving my shoulders.

She looked at her brother's reflection in the bedroom mirror. Maybe they did look alike, maybe their faces were similar. She said: Why do you always talk about snow? He looked at his sister in the reflection, he didn't respond. She made spit bubbles while placing her finger on the photo of an American rapper on her phone. She said: Which do you like more, people or pizza? He wrote something and swiped his thumb down. He saw a medical drawing. It was a diagram of the human body. He zoomed. He showed his sister. He said: Look, if you take all the veins in your body and you line them up, you die. If you line up all the veins horizontally, vertically, diagonally, you're dead. If our bodies were symmetrical, we'd be dead. If we align our bodies, we die. If we line them up, we die. If we straighten them up, we die. Can you imagine if everybody was dead? Just imagine, you wake up, you look around, and everybody's gone. There are no more websites, there are no more names, no more pictures. Everyone else has disappeared.

He balanced his phone on his forehead and lifted his legs in the air. He said: Do you think we'll be able to screenshot our dreams one day? Do you think we'll have internet when we're dead? Do dead people have internet? How many dead people do you think there are online? In a few years, there will be more dead people than living people on the internet. Where do you think the internet was before? Before it arrived on Earth? He was tapping a beat on his screen. She hit him to make him stop. He said: Before, people looked at the internet in their hands. They sat down, they opened their hands, and they watched. Or else, it used to be on the ceiling, on surfaces, a sheet, the sea, people looked at the internet everywhere, out the window, on their neighbors, trees. One day, they'll put the internet under our eyelids. Then, they'll put the internet in our brains. After that, they'll grow the internet inside of fetuses, inside of the stomach like an organ. Before, people didn't have paper, they had to write things down on rocks, they carved them. It was tiring, it was difficult, they exhausted their bodies to make sure they never forgot a sentence, an idea. At that time, people used their bodies for everything. A long time ago, things didn't have names, rivers, lakes, fruit, foxes, feet, night, grass. Teeth were just hard things in your mouth, they didn't have a name. You had to remember objects, their shape, how they look, without giving them a name. Don't you think furniture looks clever? I mean, don't you think pieces of furniture make faces that watch us with a clever look in their eyes? A clever look, you know? He looked around the room. Do you think a retina can fall off an eye?

She said: Yes. And she lay down, she rolled.

He said: It's too bad we don't live inside the internet. We'd see things better. Our eyes can't travel to other planets, like Saturn, if we look at Saturn in real life, we see a white spot. At night, we see a little white ball. But on the internet, when you look at Saturn, you see Saturn. You zoom in, you see its color, you can find out about its size, its age, its bumps. You turn it, you can open it, you can see its layers, its core. You can see people better too. You can see what they like or what they do. You can look at their faces for a long time. You look at their faces, you can look at their clothes, parts of their bodies. You can change them, you can modify them, you can add a mustache, a hat, a smile. One day, everything will be in our eyes. All people, all the possible people, all objects, each planet, everything, we'll stay in one place, we'll have everything. What are you doing?

I'm rubbing my belly button.

Do you think there will be drugs for robots one day? The person who invents robot drugs will be the most powerful person in the world. He closed his eyes and he said: When I close my eyes, they open, I think I'm dead, but they open, and even when I sleep, they open. I sleep for a long time and my eyes open, do you see what I mean?

Sara imagined a bomb and she said the word: Bomb.

Salim typed the word BOMB in his phone.

They looked at images of bombs together. They exploded, people ran, they screamed. Salim saw his eye in the reflection, he placed his finger on it, he tried to press on the circle. Nothing happened, he pressed again, he said: Look, do you see me? If I didn't carry my eyes in my head, they'd fall out. If I didn't carry my cheeks on my face, they'd slide off. They wouldn't be cheeks anymore. There would be cheeks on the ground, crushed, in the rain, blackened and burned cheeks, bits of skin. I hold on to my face, I hold on to the ground. You also hold on to the ground. If there weren't any people, the ground wouldn't be the ground anymore. We hold on to our hands, we hold on to our faces. Everyone is behind their faces, we can sit, we can stand, lie on our sides, we can turn our heads.

She looked at her brother with a closed expression. She touched his shoulder, and Salim touched his sister's hand on his shoulder. She rested her forehead on her arm, she whispered: You're going to do what you said.

Not right now.

Yes, you're going to do it, he's waiting for you.

No, I'll go later, he'll leave.

No, you're going. You're going to do it. She poked her brother in the eye. She said: You'd better. He moved away, he hid his eye with his right hand, but she got up, she said: I'm going to rip out your eyelashes, I swear.

But why don't you go?

He came to get you, so you're going. It was your idea, you're leaving, if you don't, I'll twist your fingers. And I promise they'll stay twisted. You'll have twisted fingers your whole life. You're going.

I don't want him to look at me directly.

You are going out, today, you are going outside. Today is the day. You were almost out in the world already. Do you think messages don't leave the house? You think videos don't leave the house? Everything leaves the house. You're already out of the house, you just have to change your location. You're out and you're going. She pushed, he got up, she hit him, he protected his face, he said: Stop, why are you doing that?

I swear I'm going to make you leave. I'm going to make you cry, or I'm going to make you leave. I swear you are leaving the house today. This is the day you leave the house, you decided, you're going to do it, that's it. She poked her brother in his other eye. He screamed: You're going to cut my eye skin. You're scratching my eye. She dug her finger in and she said: I'm going to take you outside like when we buried the bird. It'll be just like that. You'll walk. You won't be alone. We'll meet at the square, we'll meet there.

He backed away, then they looked at each other as if they knew one another completely. She came closer, she hit him on the mouth. He put one hand over his mouth, the other hand over his eye. He looked at himself in the mirror. He wasn't bleeding, he was red. She took her brother by the shoulders, she pushed him into the hallway. They went downstairs, one in front of the other. She held two fingers to his back like a gun.

She said: Keep moving. He kept moving. She opened the door. She pushed.

*

The night made vapor around everything. They walked and they walked. Jonathan had skinny arms like twigs growing from his sides. His phone lit up his hand, everything else around him was dark. He was wearing a white tracksuit, a baseball hat, and sneakers full of holes. He said: We're going to take the bus, it's over there. The air smelled like dirt. They walked, they walked. Little stones rolled under their feet, gravel. Near the forest, twigs snapped. The vapor rose along the tree bark, the leaves crackled, drops of water trembled in the foliage. As they moved forward, they went further into the world, everything became opaque, they crossed thickets and the trees rustled as if each tree were saying: Look at me. Then they went down an even darker road, and Salim said: The ground is heavy. It's weird because the weight is under our bodies. Still, when you walk on the ground, you can tell the Earth is heavy. And Jonathan said: Yes.

Do you feel like the ground is breathing under our feet? Do you feel like it's digesting? Do you feel the ground digesting something under our feet? Something is chewing under our feet, do you feel it? And Jonathan said: Yes.

Did you feel that way before? And Jonathan said: No.

Do you think we can put our impressions in other people's minds? Do you think it's easy? Do you think it's enough to say words or write them down to put your impressions into another person's mind?

Jonathan said: Yes.

Under the bus shelter, Jonathan gave Salim his jacket. They watched videos of animals escaping death. Deer, donkeys, cats. They avoided accidents, falls, missiles.

The clouds were gone. The sky and the earth merged. They formed one single texture in the dark. Salim pinched a bit of dirt between his fingers, he said: Look, do you see this dirt, it's earth. And Jonathan said: Yes. Salim said: Even when we're dead, when there aren't any more humans, there will always be earth. Even if there aren't any more animals, there will be earth. Even if the next humans become robots, if they're robots, when we're all robots, there will always be earth. There will always be earth beneath the factories and beneath the roads. There will always be an earth smell somewhere. When we dig, we'll find earth, it will make us smile. When people laugh, don't you think they make a noise like a swarm of flies? When people laugh as a group, I mean. I was thinking about it yesterday. Do you see what I mean? A swarm of flies, like a group of flies when people laugh. Do you see what I mean?

Jonathan said: Yes. And he looked at Salim's face. His eyes filled with things. He wished he could say the opposite of the word moron. But he didn't say anything. His thoughts sped up and slowed down. A leaf fell calmly into a puddle. Thoughts don't know which direction they're going in. They're never going anywhere. Thoughts begin, but they don't go anywhere. They don't have a destination. Each thought forms a road and the roads form a map inside a person. Some roads cross and others overlap, but they don't lead anywhere. The roads have no end because the world is a circle and people make circles, little circles on the earth. Nobody can say: That's it, I finished a thought.

*

A ZERO BETWEEN THE EYES

thin horses one night near a river
you can touch the ceiling with
your hands
if you get on a chair
but you can't take care of the dead

as for me
I grew like garlic
every time I find a gnat
I think it's asking me questions

who invented truth?
I don't know
does god have a favorite
language in the world?
I don't know
as though I've always had a zero
between my eyes
I don't know

but if the rain breaks the windows of my house
I don't know where I'm going
my limbs my back
age they become
a single piece
of ash
open my eyes

you can move a body from boiling water to ice water
and wait for the skin to come off
you can move a body from ice water to boiling water

but the skin
won't reattach
as for me
I wanted to be a liquid I kept
my eyes in the air
so people could see
I was alive

but
the ground cried when I walked
the 37,000 billion cells in my body
are happy
but
god gives coffins to his children

TO EXPRESS CHEERFULNESS THROUGH A MOVEMENT OF THE MOUTH ACCOMPANIED BY IRREGULAR EXHALATIONS THAT ARE MORE OR LESS LOUD

1

We go to the black earth in the end.

Everyone goes into the earth and the earth is black for everyone.

Is anyone buried in white earth? No, it's always black earth. The worms in this earth love anyone and anything. They like women, apples, claws, rabbits, sick people, crazy people, old people, children, they like people who bought and people who sold, they like people who cooked and people who ate, they like doctors and patients, terrorists and victims, they have an appetite for every life in the universe.

When he worked at construction sites, the father dug up the earth. Sometimes, he found bones in it. He took them in his hands. The bones had been people in the past, but the people were now a bone in the father's hand. Back then, when he went home at night, the father had dust in his nostrils and powder in his eyelashes. The mother said: You're turning into a wall, and the father laughed and the mother laughed. She called him my wall, my little wall, rampart, facade, or my sweet partition. The father liked it.

He liked the walls, the construction sites, all the different bricks, he respected them. On Sunday, when he went for a walk with his children, he touched the walls in the streets, the houses, the churches, he patted the stones with his big hands, he said: That's beautiful work, that's some beautiful work, that's hard to do and it's well done. The father loved work. He bent over his work, he always started by kneeling. He lowered his head as if in prayer, and he laid foundations, slabs, and binder, then the wall rose, it rose, and when the father stood up, the wall existed.

The father constructed brick walls and cement walls, cinderblock walls and concrete walls, load-bearing walls and dividing walls, enclosing walls and wooden walls. Everything that stands upright leans on a wall. There are walls for everything in nature. Just look at trees. Trunks are circular walls. Just look at a mountain. In any shape, in any object, if you look, you find a wall. Beds contain several walls. A lateral wall, little vertical walls, a wall for resting your head. Fridges are walls, six walls for one box, the top wall, the bottom wall, the right wall, the left, the front, and the back. Offices are walls. Books are walls and so are machines. Each machine has internal walls, and so do people. The spine is a wall in the middle of a person. Everyone has their wall. Without a wall, we can't live. Wherever you look, walls are rising, that's nature. They're born, they prosper, they evolve, but certain walls don't exist, they can't exist, they commit suicide. And there's nothing we can do. There are walls we can't build. We make the slabs, the foundations, we work on them, but they fall. It can't be helped.

One winter, the father's crew was building a house for a dying family. The son, the daughter, the parents, all sick, gravely, mortally ill, a condemned family. Skinny, yellowed, with tubes in their throats. They moved through the construction site with their breathing machines, they said: Is it going to take long? Tell me, is the construction progressing? And the boss said: We'll go fast, don't worry.

Everyone had their assignments. The father had to build a wall between the parents' bedroom and the children's bedroom. First, he put the wall up the way he usually did, but the wall crumbled because of the ground, maybe, because of the climate. It was the first day. The father remade the wall. He fortified it with wedges and bolts, a solid, intelligent, and reliable system. The wall crumbled, nobody understood why. Maybe it was the air, maybe the balance. It was the second day. Next, the father built two walls next to each other so they'd hold each other up, so they'd support each other, but the walls fell. Immediately. They crumbled, nobody ever knew why. Maybe it was the material, maybe the cement. It was the third day. Then the father said: I'm going to make a traditional wall, robust, with a rock base. And the father left for the mountains. The fourth day, he collected stones, he dug forty centimeters into the earth, he spread the mortar, added the iron bars and the concrete. He put the longest stones on the bottom, the smallest stones in the center, and the squarest stones at the corners, it was the fifth day. The father added some dirt and cement with a trowel, thirty-seven centimeters thick. The days passed, the work was long, his head was aching, he was dizzy. He clutched at his ribs with his hand, he coughed. A hump appeared on his back, his fingers were cut and two nails came off. It took ten days, but the wall was magnificent, vivid, and powerful. An ideal wall. All the guys on the team were impressed, they took pictures. They wanted to baptize it. When the bottle struck the wall, it fell apart. Nobody was surprised. They knew. It wasn't meant to exist. There was nothing they could do. The parents, the children, they would have to die in the same room.

For other walls, it's the opposite, they grow on their own. On construction sites, if you turn around you find a wall. Nobody built it. You see things on constructions sites, certain phenomena. The scaffolding hovering a few centimeters, it floats, it's common. Nobody can explain why. But in the evening, the father stuck his hands in flour and closed his eyes. He was sleepy. The flour healed him, it calmed him, it filled in his holes. One day, the father had his hands in the flour, and he noticed that his wife didn't love her children anymore, she didn't love her family anymore. She looked at the children, she looked at the father, and she didn't have any more love for them. When the children were in front of her, she went the other way. When they entered the room, she sighed. She looked at them with a blind eye, without her eyes, she no longer looked at them. She saw everything they were not. She wished they were different, that they had a talent, that they sang, that they danced, she wished they had different voices, different faces, a different skin texture. She showed them pictures of children on the internet, saying: Like that. But the children didn't change, they didn't do anything, they didn't have ideas, they didn't have gifts. She asked them to leave, but Salim and Sara were children, they said: Where do you want us to go? They rode around the town on their bikes, they rode to the grandmother's house. She gave them ice cream, she told them stories about people on TV, then they left. One day, a scooter knocked Salim over, his knee got cut, they never told anyone. Salim, Sara, they lived all alone by themselves.

The father built walls in prisons, in schools, in apartment buildings, the walls of temples, a dozen walls per day, sometimes forty or even one hundred. High walls, walls in towers, in the wind, after work, just for fun, in the forest. He'd head off into the woods, he'd stay the whole night. One morning, when he came home, the mother was no longer there. That was it.

At first, the father had scabies in his eyes. His eyes burned all the way down to his chest, it felt like starting to die. Then he missed work, he started dusting in the corners, under covers, in light switches. He used putty to get the dust from crevices. He bought a lot of putty.

In the evening, the children ate chips dipped in cans of beans. People saw them walking through the town, house keys around their necks. Then the grandmother got sick, she came to live with them. Sometimes, the father brought his lips close to her ears, he said: Die, Grandma. And the grandmother blinked.

*

It was dark. There was only silence around their skinny bodies. Sitting at the main square, Salim and Jonathan looked at a website. Emojis laughed on a pink background, tears sprang from their eyes. Two emojis bounced. Their movements, their bodies, the emotions they expressed, their size, their whole lives came from numbers, letters written on pages. The emojis achieved their mission. Every pixel in every emoji represented the perfection of success. They only succeeded. Emojis succeeded with excitement, without anger, without fatigue. Jonathan refreshed the page on the joke website. He showed his screen to Salim. Jonathan activated the speech function for the visually impaired, the phone said the words: Face crying with laughter.

Salim was trying to produce a normal smile on his face. People who meet or gather laugh and smile. Laughing and smiling are signs of sympathy, celebration, and kindness. People who laugh and smile have a higher chance of being appreciated than people who do not smile or laugh. He'd read about it. Is the person who smiles the hardest the most appreciated? Is the rate of sympathy in the human world proportional to the size of a smile? Salim was trying to widen his smile into a laugh on his face. He tried to produce tears of laughter in his eyes by lifting his lips with his hand. Sometimes, for days at a time, Salim didn't laugh, he didn't smile, his face forgot about laughing and smiling. For his face, laughing and smiling were rare, surprising movements.

With a rigid expression, he typed the world LAUGH in his phone. He read: Laughter is a reflex involving a series of small, irregular exhalations accompanied by inarticulate vocalizations that are more or less loud. The upper part of the cheek and the cheekbones rise, they push on the nose and the lower eyelids, that is why the eyes sink into the face. For some people, the eyes disappear entirely. Jonathan said: It's true. His voice echoed all over the square. Shadows moved in the distance. Salim looked for a short definition of the word LAUGH, he read: To express cheerfulness through a movement of the mouth accompanied by irregular exhalations that are more or less loud.

Emojis bounced in Jonathan's hand. Their teeth were a straight, white line. If you looked at them long enough, you couldn't tell anymore if they were crying or laughing. Their faces seemed pained. Salim imagined a laugh that went on forever, and he felt pain. He said: Do you know the story of the man who died from laughing? Jonathan said: No, and he swallowed several pills.

Salim said: It's a video I watched one night. I was researching how to make people laugh, because at school, I wanted to make people laugh. I didn't have any friends, but I wanted to make people laugh, and I often did make other people laugh. When I spoke, other kids would often laugh, but I didn't understand why then. So I did some research on making people laugh to understand it better. That's when I found the story of this man.

It's the story of a man on his couch. He'd worked a lot, he was resting. He was watching a comedy show without words. The characters were fighting, they tricked each other, they fell into traps and they got out, they fell again, they did somersaults, they slipped, they got back up. The man was watching this and he loved it, he was laughing. He loved their gestures, he loved the scenes, he loved the characters, their reactions, their adventures. It made him laugh, but he couldn't stop laughing. It went on for fifteen minutes. His muscles didn't have enough oxygen. His lungs were tensing up. The nerves in his face slackened. His face changed color, he became purple. Tears fell from his eyes, his nose, his cheeks, his moustache, his entire body. It made him laugh, he kept laughing, he didn't stop. In fact, he couldn't stop, he couldn't keep himself from laughing, you know why? Jonathan leaned toward Salim's face with a mysterious, drugged expression. He said: I don't know. His eyebrows seemed permanently arched on his forehead, he said: Why?

Because his laugh made him laugh. He made himself laugh. It's as if he were fighting himself, as if he were hitting himself. It's a physical reflex, you know, he got infected. He got stuck in a loop, he was self-destructing. In fact, he was killing himself. His temperature rose, he couldn't breathe, he couldn't control himself, all his liquids came out, he became dry inside. In the end, his heart exploded. He died.

Jonathan asked if the story was true, then he looked in a different direction as if he'd just forgotten his own question. He tapped on an emoji, he read:

No Reason, Crazy, and Nobody are on a boat. Nobody falls in the water. No Reason tells Crazy to call the coastguard. Crazy calls the coastguard and says: Help, I'm Crazy, I'm calling for No Reason, because Nobody fell in the water.

Salim didn't laugh. Jonathan didn't laugh. They were silent. They looked at the emojis. Salim read:

What is all red in a corner?

Jonathan didn't respond. Salim said: A baby playing with a scalpel.

Salim didn't laugh. Jonathan didn't laugh.

Their faces didn't have any particular expression. The night was calm. Jonathan read: A guy with a wig kills himself by jumping from the top of the Eiffel Tower. They find him at the bottom of the Eiffel Tower, but his wig is still miraculously attached to his head, why? Salim didn't respond. Jonathan read, exaggerating each word: He washed it with a shampoo that prevents hair loss.

Salim didn't change his expression and Jonathan didn't smile.

Salim leaned his head over until the right side of it touched the wall. He tried to remember the dead bird in his room.

How much time does it take to become a skeleton? And after that, how much time does it take for a skeleton to become dust? Why aren't dead humans placed directly in the ground the way the bird was? Why don't people all have the same kind of blood? Why do blood types exist even though everyone's blood looks the same? If we don't swallow anything red, why does blood stay red? He typed the word BLOOD and hit search. He found a list of expressions containing the word BLOOD. He copied six of them, and he ordered the words into lines. He posted it on his page:

blue-blooded
animal
runs cold having bad
blood
clot of
blood from
a stone in cold
blood

They he searched for the origin of the word BLOOD. He copied everything, he pasted everything:

/ˈbləd/ the fluid that circulates in the heart, arteries, capillaries, and veins of a vertebrate animal. lifeblood. to bleed (a person). to spill one's blood, to give one's life. Chide him for his faults, and do it reverently, / When you perceive his blood inclined to mirth, William Shakespeare.

He searched ANIMAL BLOOD and he looked at animal bloods. Horse blood looks like horse blood. Horse blood looks like chicken blood. Chicken blood looks like frog blood. Frog blood looks like cat blood. Cat blood looks like human blood. Human blood looks like the grandmother's blood. There are types of blood. There are rare types and common types. There's blood everywhere. Every person carries their blood around. All passersby, dogs, skinny people, idiots, each of them carries their blood around, even people who don't know it, even newborns, even people in a coma. Even asleep, we carry our blood.

We draw blood, we give blood, we inject it, we store it, we classify it, we put it in tubes, we index it. We construct categories for blood, for things. There are things around us, we look at a thing, we store it, here is the thing, we give it a name, we say the word blood, here is the blood. We say: Here is the blood. We think we see a thing, but there are so many nuances in a single thing, there are so many varieties. Nuance divides the varieties into such specific groups that categories can no longer exist. Varieties are divided into subvarieties that are divided into subvarieties to infinity. If we take the word LINE, if we examine the category, we see that it doesn't exist. Some lines are as wide as the sea, some are as fine as an atom, and others are wider than the entire universe. Categories are like water divided into pools, divided into casks, divided into bottles, divided into glasses, divided into pipettes, into drops, into microdroplets, into nanodroplets, into water particles, but water is still water, it's a single thing, a single material, a single image, a single idea. It's like nature is trying things out. Like nature is trying out different forms. Salim had thought of the differences between each thing. He'd thought of the differences between each planet. He'd thought of the differences between each illness. He'd thought of the differences between each idea. He'd thought of the differences between each person, the varieties of hair, the varieties of skin, the shapes of fingernails, the sizes of eyes, the muscles, the lengths of muscles, the lengths of bones, senses of smell and hearing, vision that changes from one person to the next. We say: Look at this blue object, but we don't see the same color, we don't see the same shape, we don't see the same object. A color doesn't exist. Blue doesn't exist. It can't exist.

The emojis bounced in his phone. Jonathan was smiling with his eyes closed. They read forty-two jokes like that on the stairs, without laughing, without speaking.

In the morning, a man came up to them, he had pink skin and he said: I've created a religion. Salim asked which one, and the man replied: That's a secret I keep to myself. Salim asked why, and the man replied: Because it's too famous, it's one of the major religions. Salim said: I'm looking for my mother. And the man said: What does she look like? Salim described his mother and Jonathan said words that were impossible to understand. Salim wished Jonathan would go back to sleep because he was drooling and he was talking like his mind had been divided into different pieces of mind. Every time he opened his mouth, a small piece of his mind expressed itself in a sad and solitary way. The man said: Why are you sitting outside and not going anywhere? Salim said: I don't know. The man went away, he walked straight ahead.

Salim looked at Jonathan, he wondered: Can an image hurt us? He typed HURTING YOURSELF WITH IMAGES, he hit search. He found a video of a man. His eyes were gray and his lips were colorless. A camera followed him through a hallway. He whispered, he said: I was hurt by an image. I saw an accident, a car ran into a scooter. I was on the sidewalk and I saw everything. It wasn't my accident, but I saw it. It hurt me. I clenched my teeth so tightly they broke into millions of pieces and fell down my throat. They cut my esophagus. Now I don't have any more teeth, I have throat problems, I've almost completely lost my voice. I whisper, I whisper, that was fifteen years ago. I can't get over it. You know, the people on the scooter and in the car weren't injured. They shook hands and they went back home. But for me, all it took was seeing the accident. Please be careful with images. Look away.

Then Salim looked at Jonathan's profile photos, and he looked at the real Jonathan sleeping on the stairs. He brought his phone close to Jonathan's face and he compared the two images. Jonathan's face looked like Jonathan's face, but it wasn't like Jonathan's face. He wished he could write to Jonathan, but Jonathan was there. He tried to strengthen the real image of Jonathan, the image became more solid as he watched him. He'd written things to him every day and now Jonathan was there like a real person. There was no other Jonathan. There was no other person than the physical person in front of him.

*

They'd met a few years ago under a video of a whale. The whale was jumping above the sea as if particles were lifting its body. The image of the whale was moving in the world, but it vibrated in a way that ran parallel to the world. It was slow. Salim wondered if the whale's heart beat more slowly than his. Did the whale's heart beat once per minute? One huge beat per minute, a big, heavy beat. Maybe there was a big animal, bigger than whales, an enormous animal the size of cities, the size of a country, whose heart beat only once in a lifetime. One big, calm beat, one tremendous beat, a long, heavy beat. Was it the opposite for little, fast animals? Did little hearts beat 1,000 times per second? Does the heart determine our appearance? One day, Salim had put his ear up to the stomach of a cat, its heart beat so fast, he thought that it would die, but it was purring, it squinted its eyes. That was its rhythm and its way.

Under the video of the whale, he wrote:

> Do you think you see the world differently if your heart beats faster? Do you think you see the world more quickly when your heart beats faster?

The whale rose and fell like a bomb in the sea. Jonathan was drinking wine from a large bowl, he'd read the question and he'd done some research. He'd copied and pasted sentences under the video of the whale:

> The heart of an elephant beats 30 times per minute.
> The heart of a horse beats 35 times per minute.
> The heart of a human beats 70 times per minute.
> The heart of a goat beats 100 times per minute.
> The heart of a dog beats 140 times per minute.
> The heart of a wolf beats 90 times per minute.
> The heart of a rat beats 300 times per minute.
> The heart of a hedgehog beats between 5 to 280 times per minute.

The heart of a dolphin beats between 50 and 110 times per minute.
The heart of a pig beats 100 times per minute.
The heart of a rhinoceros beats 146 times per minute.

And Salim had responded: We see a whale jumping, but for the whale, it feels like a long time. The whale is flying. We only see two seconds of it. For the whale, it's like an hour. A whale is a bird to a whale. Then he'd copied other things, and he pasted the information under the video of the whale, under Jonathan's sentences:

As William Harvey states in his book *On the Motion of the Heart and Blood in Animals*: I have also observed that almost all animals have truly a heart, not the larger creatures only, and those that have red blood, but the smaller, and pale-blooded ones also, such as slugs, snails, scallops, shrimps, crabs, crayfish, and many others; nay, even in wasps, hornets, and flies, I have, with the aid of a magnifying glass, and at the upper part of what is called the tail, both seen the heart pulsating myself, and shown it to many others.

We can see a heart beating, but the heart can't enter our minds. Things can't enter our minds, they remain on the outside. We cannot understand the outside. We cannot understand another person, an animal, or pain.

A woman cuts her hand, she suffers, she says: It hurts. But we cannot know her pain, we can only imagine it. She says: Please understand, I'm in pain, but we cannot understand it. Someone burns themselves, we think we know their pain, but we only know our own. We see our pain. We see the memory of our burns, we say: I know how much you're suffering, I've also suffered, but we don't know what it's like, we can't understand. The person suffering doesn't understand themselves over time. They can't understand a past pain. They can't know a future pain. We don't feel pain the same way when we're eight or forty-eight. The two pains are like two different species of animal. If a forty-eight-year-old man had to feel the pain of his eight-year-old self, he'd die on the spot. If we move a pain from the past to the present, it kills. We could die from a shiver or a cramp.

Salim had written:

Nobody has the same face as everybody else.

He'd looked at his own face in his phone camera and he'd tried to see a simple shape covered in skin. Everything that touches a person touches their skin. You can only touch a person's skin, you can't touch a person anywhere else. You can't touch an object or a stone in order to touch someone. To touch someone, you must touch someone. Babies don't have a lot of surface area, they have practically no skin. Salim had searched, he'd found, he'd copied, he'd put the words into lines, he'd pasted:

Newborns have a surface area
of 0.24 m
on average
and
adults
have a skin
surface area of
1.9 m
on average

Salim and Jonathan's conversation was posted vertically under the video of the whale. The sentences aligned. They each reread them several times. Later, Salim had written private messages to Jonathan to tell him that Greenland sharks could live to be four hundred years old. He'd written: At one hundred years old, a Greenland shark is at the beginning of its life. Some Greenland sharks were born in the seventeenth century. Jonathan had looked up pictures of Greenland sharks and sent Salim the most beautiful pictures of Greenland sharks. Their bodies were smooth and gray, surrounded by the sea.

The next day, they'd sent each other videos of people with rare bodies.

In a video called CONJOINED TWINS STUDY LAW, brothers in a single body rolled over themselves horizontally through the halls of a university. They wore a specially fitted suit and glasses. In class, they lay down in the first row, and they placed their computers on their single stomach. When they pronounced the letter J, their lips rose up to their noses. They said: When we eat, when we sleep, we time each other. We're organized, we time our trips and our conversations. Maybe we'll die on the same day, in fact, that's almost certain. Normally, you can't predict which people will die in the same instant, but we can guess: we'll likely die aligned, aligned to each other, aligned in time. Every morning, we look at each other and find ourselves handsome. We talk to each other in our thoughts, but at night, we sleep. We don't dream.

Then Salim had sent Jonathan a video called A WOMAN WITH AN EYE ON HER TONGUE. In the video, the woman wasn't blind, but she had only one eye on her tongue. She didn't speak, she opened her mouth to look at her son. She stuck out her tongue and the baby laughed. He patted his mother's tongue. She smiled the way dogs do. Her child moved his fingers across her tongue. The video was quiet, wordless. The mother and son were in a park. The baby crawled in the grass. The mother sometimes closed her mouth the way you'd blink your eyes. When the baby cried out, the mother widened her eye. It was green with eyelashes.

Then Salim and Jonathan had sent each other videos of jumping robots and videos of falling robots and videos of robot interviews. Salim wrote: I feel like the bones in my face don't think about anything even when I'm thinking.

*

At Jonathan's house, water was dripping. The roommate had installed a system of oilcloths connected to basins. Pieces of the ceiling were falling, white crumbs like confetti. The walls made little sounds as if they were creaking. The roommate lit three cigarettes and smoked them. He didn't smoke them all at once, but took turns, alternating, one puff at a time. Salim didn't say anything, his hands were resting on his thighs. Jonathan was taking pictures of himself silently. He leaned his head to one side and drops ran through his hair. He saw himself in his screen, he recognized himself, but deep down, he didn't understand how this appearance could correspond to the sense he had of himself. When you're a child, you don't imagine your adult face. If someone had asked him as a child to imagine an old version of himself, Jonathan would have glued his child face onto a larger face. He would have imagined his face inside of an adult face, a basic face, a soldier's face. He took twelve photos of himself smiling, half-smiling, looking pensive, looking ahead, to the right, down, his hand in front of his eyes. In these images, he saw himself as real and non-real, it was both normal and impossible, like when you see two groups of birds crossing paths in the sky and they don't run into each other. The birds should run into each other, but they don't. Reality should have hit them, but it didn't. It's almost not normal, it's almost not real, but we see it. On our phones, we look at our pasts, and even when we look at ourselves in the mirror, we're looking at ourselves in the past. We can't see ourselves in the present. The mirror gives us an old image of ourselves. We always see ourselves later. You will never be able to see yourself in the present. The mirror adds an image on an image. You can't touch the hand of the person in the mirror. A doctor can't examine a person in the mirror. The mirror produces the inverse of the person, it reflects an opposite, but the opposite resembles the person, it looks more like the person than anyone else. It resembles itself, but without being itself.

Jonathan chose one photo of himself out of the thirty-seven photos of himself. He added a filter and he posted the image. Salim liked it. Jonathan said: Thanks. The roommate said: You're both ridiculous. You're weak, the exact opposite of a castle. When I was a kid, I had three mothers and four fathers, we lived in a castle at the base of the mountain. Have you heard of it? I lived in a castle, are you listening to me? Jonathan said: I've never been inside a castle. The roommate said: Oh, are we talking about you? No. I'm talking about me, I started speaking to talk about myself, not you. We're not talking about your life, we're talking about my life, I'm talking about myself right now.

He showed them an image on his phone, he said: This was our castle. They demolished it because we were supposedly a cult, supposedly because I was born in a cult, supposedly because everyone in the cult committed suicide, my whole family, my brothers, my sisters, my mothers, my fathers, my uncles, my aunts, my cousins. Supposedly I'm the sole survivor, supposedly because they forgot about me. They forgot to have me commit suicide, supposedly, but that would really surprise me. All the people in my family were perfect. There's no other way to describe it. No complaints. They were like the people in The Bible, do you know The Bible?

Jonathan said: A little. Salim said: Yes.

The roommate continued: I had an uncle who was continuing The Bible. He put it on a podium in the middle of the living room, my uncle did, and day and night, he wrote his magnum opus. And we watched.

What was his name?

Who?

Your uncle.

What? You want to know my uncle's name? Is that it? You want to know his name? Did I hear you correctly? Am I dreaming? Do you think I remember? Do you think I keep a log of every name? I had a lot of uncles, I told you, it was a huge family, I just said that. I can't remember all my uncles, I can't remember everyone. Do you think I do memory competitions on the weekend? That I think it's fun? Do I look like someone with a passion? A passion for memory? Do you think I go to memory clubs and do memory competitions with all my friends? I don't have any friends. If I had friends, they wouldn't like memorizing things, not one bit. I don't do memory competitions, but you think I spend my days training to remember random people's names, is that it? You think I remember the names of everyone in my family? Do you think people remember the names of all the people in their families? Their uncles? Their aunts? Everyone forgets things, it's our duty. We can't hoard names in our brains like idiots. It takes up space for no reason. Knowing your uncle's name serves no purpose. It serves no purpose in life. Who uses it? When is that useful? People who know their uncle's name never use it. Just ask them, it serves no purpose. I don't like it when people ask me questions.

Jonathan made a gesture at Salim, as if he'd placed his hand in the air and it slipped, which could have meant either: Be quiet, or: Don't worry about it.

The roommate said: We lived together in the castle and we baptized each other. We baptized each other every morning. We splashed water in our hair, on our foreheads, on our ears, do you know about The Baptism? Every morning, before breakfast, we baptized each other. I baptized my mother and my father and another mother and another father that I had. Then, I baptized my uncle, a brother, and an aunt I had who was in a wheelchair and often my aunt stood up because of The Miracle. Do you know about The Miracle? We applauded when The Miracle happened, we always applauded. But it's mostly for dead people, The Miracle I mean, it's mostly for dead people. Do you know about death? I personally didn't know that people died, I'd never heard the word dead, I learned about it late. Do you know that word? Salim nodded.

The roommate said: We had three or four Miracles per day. The blind could see, the lame bounded like deer over the grounds. We baptized every creature, we baptized animals, especially slugs, beetles, lizards, we baptized a lot, especially in summer. Certain animals would drown for the glory of the Earth, do you know about The Glory of the Word? You don't? We made dried plants rise from the dead, you know, those dried roses people put on walls, we gathered them, we made them rise from the dead. That was The Miracle and The Glory of the Word.

Salim asked: Did you ever experience any miracles yourself?

The roommate pointed at himself and said: Me? You're talking about me? You mean my body? Miracles in my own body, is that what you mean? Do you have a problem or what? Do you have a problem with me or what? What is your problem with me? You can't ask that. You can't ask me that, it's just not done, it's private. I'm not going to start telling you about my personal miracles. Do you think people who have been miraculously saved talk about their miracles? Their personal miracles? The miraculously saved do not talk about their miracles, the true miraculously saved don't talk about their miracles, miracles happen in silence, it's between you and God, do you know about God? If the miraculously saved talked about their miracles, the miracles would get canceled, everybody knows that. You can't brag about miracles, do you want my miracles to get canceled? Would you like it if my miracles got canceled? You want my miracles to get canceled, is that it? If you want to fight, we can fight, I don't care. You're the one who hasn't left your house for four years, right? You're looking for your mother, right?

Salim said: Yes.

The roommate said: I know about people who disappear. I'm kind of an expert. I read a lot of random things all day on the internet, ask Jonathan. Once I've read something, I read it again, that's what I do. I've read all the lessons for FBI agents searching for people who've disappeared. I've read them fifty times, 2,000 times. The classified X-files, I've read them, I've read everything, I know all that by heart. I'm going to give you three pieces of advice: First, don't look under her real name, she's changed her name. Look for her under names you've made up, change the name frequently, type random names into the networks, ask around. There are a lot of names, you'll see. Then ask anybody questions, listen to everyone. Among all the people in the world, somebody knows something. Finally, remember what she used to eat and look near food. If she ate meat, she's near animals. If she ate mashed potatoes, look near potatoes. If she chewed gum, she's close to a supermarket checkout line. The roommate turned toward Jonathan, he said: And you? Do you have a religion other than looking at yourself? Do you actually have a religion, other than taking pictures of yourself, do you have a religion? Did you have a religion when you were little?

Sort of, yes.

What was it?

I ran. My mother and I lived close to a forest. I got up before my mother, I ran naked in the forest. That was my religion, I think.

The roommate said: That's not a religion. You think that's a religion? Do you have any respect for religion? Are you really comparing that to The Bible? You're comparing that to The Baptism? To The Miracle? You're comparing that to God? Listen carefully, there's almost nothing worth respecting. When you think about it for a minute, there's nothing worth respecting. Everything around us is there for no reason. There's nothing worth respecting, almost nothing, we don't have to respect anything. Respecting nature isn't worth the trouble. Why respect the planet? There's no reason to respect whatever it is. We don't need to respect people. We don't have to respect ourselves, there's nothing worth respecting, almost nothing. Respect doesn't even deserve our respect. And you don't respect the one thing worth respecting? You're comparing running to a religion. But it's not a religion, it wasn't your religion. You think that's religion?

That's how it felt to me. I didn't pray to anyone, but sometimes, I prayed for a while. I prayed while I ran in the forest, that was my religion. I know this isn't anyone's religion, but I didn't have a personality. You have to understand, I didn't have a personality. I did everything the way everyone else did, I didn't have any ideas.

If I had to choose, I chose the same thing as everyone else. I said: Me too. I said: The same for me. When people asked me what I wanted to do when I grew up, I responded: A job. When people asked me what game I liked to play, I responded: Playing. When people asked me what I like to eat, I said: Eating. I never wanted anything special, but running in the morning, naked in the forest, that was the thing I did. I decided. Nobody knew about it, it was my religion. My body and my spirit relied on speed. I ran on the outside, but on the inside, I wasn't moving, I was inside the speed. I think I was praying.

Salim said: I believe you.

The roommate said: Man, you believe anything anyone tells you. It's obvious. As soon as I saw you, I knew it, it's written all over you, like you were born yesterday. Do you think there's another sun behind the sun? Do you believe anyone? Neither of you know anything about anything, do you know what religion is? You know what it is? No, you don't. But I know. I know it by heart. It was my life, it was my religion. Look, I'm going to show you religion. Look closely. The roommate emptied the ashtray into his mouth and stuck out his tongue. It was black, covered in cigarette butts.

He said: That's it.

2

Oh, so you got your nose done, you got lip injections, and you, we haven't seen you for a while, where were you? What are you hiding? You haven't slept, I can tell, what were you up to? Do you have problems? What kind of problems do you have? Is it because of your children? Is it because of money? Is it because of your boss? She was speaking to the faces inside of her brain, she said: You're old, you're too animated for your age, you overreact, you talk loudly, that's not normal, are you snorting something? Are you? I can tell, I have an eye for these things. And you, you're really worried about something, it's obvious from the line on your forehead, I read: Worry. Is it because of your husband? He's mean at home, is that it? He comes home and he's mean in the bedroom, is that it?

She knew their names, their voices, their laughs, all the voices, there were so many voices, it didn't matter what they said, they touched something invisible inside the grandmother. She felt them. She watched these people grow old, their faces changed, their places on set changed, they went from the center to the side, and from the side to the center, they became different characters. Over the months, singers became judges, fat people became thin, hosts became commentators, bullies became the bullied, the bullied became judges, and everyone laughed. Athletes became commentators or presenters, Michelin-starred chefs became health inspectors, they rummaged through kitchen drawers, there was a timeline, there was order. She watched television like a long frieze, like a mystery in the mystery of human life. These people never went anywhere, they aged onscreen, they almost never moved. They were available. You could count on them.

A robot was singing on the TV, it was holding a microphone in its iron hands, people were applauding. The judges jumped with surprise, they opened their mouths, and their eyebrows rose, they jumped with joy. The camera turned toward the audience. And people put their hands in front of their mouths, someone yelled the sound: Wooah. The robot arranged expressions on its face. Its skin stretched automatically, it was pale, pink and blue. It had stiff hair, all plastic, combed for eternity. The grandmother thought: We'd save time if our hair didn't move, like people who tattoo makeup to their eyelids, it saves minutes. When you add up the minutes, you save weeks. People would save time with fake clothes stuck to their bodies, with fake hair. They'd save time if they didn't change, if they were robots. People would save time if they were machines. At the end of the song, the robot produced one superb tear. It slid along a pale path down its smooth cheek, it sparkled. The grandmother thought: Illness has kept me away from everyday hardships, I don't know how to cry anymore. A mechanism activated lights inside of the tear and everyone applauded. The grandmother applauded in her brain. The robot smiled, it said: Thank you very much. The judges got up, they put their hands on their heads, their mouths formed empty circles at the bottom of their faces.

The grandmother liked TV shows with judges because of the faces they made. The judges looked worried, happy, they yelled and they hated each other, they loved each other. The camera lingered over an emotional face for a long time. The face changed. It expressed gratitude, the judge would say: Thank you. Sometimes, the grandmother imagined all those faces covered in wood. She tried to see those faces like ancient tribal masks, she lined the masks up in a room, and in her mind, she was walking in the room. She wasn't thinking anything.

Every week, the grandmother watched a show where women gave birth. The women would lie down in front of the judges, they lifted their skirts. The judges took notes, they observed the insides of these women with a magnifying glass. The women spread their legs, they pushed, the babies were born. If the baby was dead, the mother lost a point. If the baby was blue or red, she lost a point. If the cord was strangling it, she lost a point. But if the baby was beautiful, she won a point. If the baby had hair, she won a point. If it wasn't sticky, she won a point, if the baby was smiling, everyone applauded. The mothers prepared for the show months in advance, they would speak to the fetuses through their stomachs, the mothers asked them to smile and be healthy, to move their legs. If the baby had a proportional, standard body, the mother won a point. The president of the jury would announce: The adventure continues. If the baby cried, that made sense, but it wasn't recommended. It was tolerated. If the baby cried for a long time, that was a point off, they'd cut the microphone. A deep voice would say the word: Goodbye. If the mother was beautiful, if she wore makeup, if her hair was done, she got a point. The judges would congratulate her, they would give her compliments, they would look at the camera and say: She understood the goal of the show. If the mother smiled while she pushed, if she laughed while she pushed, if she pushed without sweating, if she pushed without yelling, if she pushed without crying, she could stay. Someone would say: The adventure continues. When the mother was ugly, no one applauded, no one applauded for anything, not her, not the baby. The judges would look embarrassed and sorrowful. Their mouths would point toward the bottom of their faces and they would eliminate her. The audience booed. If the mother died, she lost a point, they stopped filming her, they stopped filming the child. Even if the child was alive, they didn't film it. It had lost everything. The camera focused on the judges. They were emotional, someone brought them tissues that they patted against their cheeks. High-pitched piano notes accompanied the scene. A judge would say: We must go on. They used the expression: Never give up. And the song THE SHOW MUST GO ON played in the background. The judges hugged each other, then they danced. They raised their fists in the air and the audience stretched their arms toward the light. If the father was there, that was a point. If the mother was a lesbian and the other mother was present, that was a huge point. The judges used the word: Diversity and the expression: Like everyone else. The lead judge would congratulate the parents: The adventure continues. If the father or the other mother kissed the mother giving birth, everyone applauded. The judges leaned their heads to the right or to the left as a sign of endearment. Their faces were filmed with bells playing in the background and everyone smiled. Everyone touched everyone else's hands. Everyone patted everyone else's shoulders and backs. If the father or other mother was absent, that was a point for or against, it depended on the mother, it depended on her hairstyle, her outfit, her appearance. Was the other parent right to have left her? Could we sympathize? The judges decided. The judges wrote things down on their tablets, then they drew a big circle and showed the point awarded in the middle of the screen. When the placenta came out, that was a point, everyone applauded. When the placenta stayed in the stomach, a point was lost because of complications, because of the metal objects they had to use. The scene wasn't interesting then, it was too long, too complicated. They'd cut the microphone and announce what happens next. If the mother caressed her child, that was a point, the judges applauded, they nodded. The lead judge used the expressions: Life event and: Bonding. If the mother looked at her baby and thought it was ugly, if you could see it on her face, that was a point off. People booed at ugly babies. There were mothers who didn't like their babies sometimes. People would throw shoes and point their thumbs down while booing. One day, a baby came out of its mother's stomach almost dead. Its eyes were open, but it wasn't moving. A judge picked it up, he said: Do you want to live or not? Yes or no? We need to know, but the baby didn't respond. The mother cried without smiling. Then the judges each made their trademark grimace according to their face type. They moved their heads, and the lead judge turned to the mother: Suicide is the leading cause of death for women during the first year after giving birth, be careful, it's a statistic.

Sometimes, the grandmother closed her eyes. The male nurse muted the sound. The female nurse raised her head. She inclined the bed. The male nurse held the pillow. He pulled back the sheets. He lifted the covers. He opened her shirt. The female nurse washed her neck. She washed her breasts and the grandmother would sweat. The female nurse rubbed the glove over her sides, into the folds, on the back of her neck. The male nurse pulled up her arms, he washed her stomach. He changed the diaper, he scrubbed her thighs. They spread cream on her legs and on her back. They turned her over. The female nurse bent her legs eight times while holding her knees. The male nurse bent her arms eight times while holding her elbows. They asked: Does that hurt? And the grandmother blinked twice. Then they put her shirt on, they said other words, they combed her hair. The male nurse would take her blood pressure, it wasn't good, he'd say: That's not good. The female nurse would listen to her heart, she'd say: That's not good. It's getting less and less good. And the female nurse listened to her own heart and said: I'm fine. She listened to the heart of the male nurse, she said: You're fine. They covered the grandmother. Cars drove silently past the house. They caressed her hair. They sang things to her. Their voices overlapped and the grandmother fell asleep.

*

People who are almost dead are almost somewhere else, they're almost alone, they make almost no noise, they almost never move, they take up almost no space, they almost don't have a name. Sara was sitting near the grandmother, she took off her shoes so she wouldn't get the sheets dirty. She pointed her toes, she grabbed the tip of her sock, she made a knot, she untied the knot, she put her shoe back on, she took it off, she looked at her phone, she locked her phone. She took her grandmother's hand, like a handful of bees around a flower. She moved the grandmother's fingers, she pulled them up, they fell back down, they didn't have any direction. She looked at her grandmother's fingers, they'd become weights. She talked about their hands, she said anything that came to mind. The grandmother's eyes moved, Sara spoke, she said everything. She wasn't really sure if she was speaking with her mouth or if the words never left her head, she said: Your hands are heavy. Look how soft they are, it's like touching cake. They're heavier than a baby rat, heavier than a baby tuna fish, you know, your hands are heavier than a maggot, Grandma. They're heavier than mine, much heavier than a seed. Your hands are heavier than a roll of paper, but your hands are lighter than a house. They're lighter than a cellar, they're lighter than a church. You know, Grandma, things are always heavier or lighter. Not just hands, planets, buildings, things are always heavier or lighter, we're always between the two, we always have a place in the world. Your hands are lighter than a head, lighter than a barrel. Look, the thumb and the little finger, they're separated by three fingers, look at them. The little finger and the pointer finger are separated by two fingers. There aren't any fingers between your pointer and middle fingers, but some people do have a finger between the pointer and middle fingers. An extra finger between the thumb and the pointer, between the pinkie and the ring finger, between the ring and middle finger. Each finger has a name, what do you call an extra finger? I don't know, but it might have a name. My mother told me that, the day I was born, when you saw me for the first time, you didn't look at my face, you counted my fingers, my fingers and my toes. You said I was normal, Grandma. Some people don't have a pointer finger, other people don't have fingers at all. We don't know what's real, but I could break your hand. Your hands are very heavy, but they're yellow. They're thicker than a screwdriver, but they're thinner than a crate. Your hands don't have any more strength, they're not as delicate as a fly, but they are more delicate than a mattress. To have fingernails you have to have fingers, but your fingers are twisted. You have veins, lots of veins, old people are covered in veins on their hands, on their legs, on their noses, on their arms, on their chins, on everything. Veins multiply on old people. Maybe the word old comes from the word cold. We don't know, Grandma, but if I pinch you, your skin lowers, it's slow. If I pinch you, your skin stays up in the air for two seconds, then it goes down, and I can see it going down. You're wearing a ring, but why, Grandma, for your husband? But he's dead, Grandma. Are you engaged to a dead man? You're going to get married in a black dress, Grandma, to a zombie, Grandma. You have crumbs under your nails, wet crumbs the way babies do, mashed potatoes under your nails, you store wet bread under your nails the way three-year-old children do, Grandma. Old people are like babies. Old people are like three-year-old children. I'm holding your hand, Grandma. I'm holding your hand, my four fingers under your hand, my thumb on top. You can do it all by yourself. You can hold your own hand. I'm putting your hand in your hand and I'm leaving. Try to believe I'm still here.

*

The father thought about it, he was sure of it: nobody runs in their sleep.

Everybody is like a dead person in their sleep. Sleep gives us a certain appearance, the form of death, but we don't become this form. We fall asleep, we're asleep, but we wake up, we're still a person. When we sleep, we can no longer move, we remain stuck as if inside a snake that's digesting us. But certain people don't sleep. The father was one of these people. He watched his own outstretched palm, he watched documentaries on his phone, short or long videos about people who don't sleep.

In Vietnam, for example, there is a man who hasn't slept for forty-three years. Doctors are studying him, ten cameras have been placed around his house. His name is Thai Ngoc. The doctors put soporifics in his food, but he won't sleep. They try to make him fall asleep by injecting liquid anesthetic intravenously, but he won't sleep. He can't sleep because his body has forgotten how to sleep. He's a quiet man, he works, he goes into the fields. Because he works night and day, he receives two salaries, it's as if he were living twice, but with only one life. In the video, Thai Ngoc says: I'm starting to feel like a plant without water. I lose pieces of skin that regrow, then I lose them again and they regrow, and then I lose them again. I'm comfortable, because fatigue has its heart in the right place, it has a lot of layers. If sleep overcame me, I'm sure it would kill me.

At night, Thai Ngoc's children sleep, his children's days are separated by nights that set them apart from each other. Every morning, their alarm clocks ring-in something new. The scenes of the new day push aside the scenes from the day before. Each day is separated from the previous one by a dark scene we call sleep.

In the video, Thai Ngoc says: Night disgusts me. When I think about it, it's like I'm always eating the same food. You know, the night goes by fast, but it goes by non-fast. Night isn't normal, it isn't logical. When you stop sleeping, you watch time. Believe me, time isn't really cut up, it has no measurements. Believe me, time can't be cut up, it doesn't think that way. For time, units don't exist, time is not a line and days do not exist. This is a myth that comes from humans. We can't single out a day, one day, a day doesn't exist. A day is not the day after a day. A day is not the day before the following day. Days are linked together like a chain, but in a circle. There's only one chain, there's only this chain, and days do not exist. When you don't sleep, the days lose their color, in the end, you can tell they don't exist. The sequence of a person's days is called their life, but hours don't exist, I can tell, I don't sleep. Unlike you, I never step outside of time.

Thai Ngoc's eyes are black, he says: My eyes run and I eat my tears, the present has no length. When did time start to become time? I wonder about it, but you won't have an answer for me. You won't be able to tell me because there's no separation between seconds. You can go mad, that's for sure, but you can't decide to go mad. You can wait for it to happen, but you can't decide. You wait and when the night arrives, a great peace falls over the trees around the house, and I watch it. That's it, I watch it.

Thai Ngoc takes short pauses to drink herbal tea. He pours water over herbs, and he says: A night changes a person, I see it in my children. It changes the edges of their faces. The present is a point, but what is the size of this point? A second, an hour, a minute? You can't tell me.

The cameraman turns around Thai Ngoc's face. His small sharp eyes look at the lens, he says: We change from year to year, we change from week to week, we change from day to day, we change from hour to hour, so we change from minute to minute, but minutes don't exist. Have you ever seen a minute? You can't hold a minute in your hand. You can't see a minute around you or in front of you. You can't describe it. Believe me, time is just one huge block and days don't exist.

The father watched the video while vacuuming in front of his feet. He was eating sunflower seeds while sitting in a chair. He crunched the shells, he spit them out, then he vacuumed them up. He could no longer even try to sleep, he could no longer close his eyes.

When he closed his eyes, he saw a shadow through his eyelids, a hard shadow. Every time he closed his eyes, a bad, hard shadow approached his head, he could feel it. So the father opened his eyes, and his eyelids jumped as if from fear. And yet, his fear wasn't tied to the world, it didn't engage with the world. His fear was a string that left him and came back to him without touching the world at all.

A few years earlier, the father had consulted an eye specialist to take care of this problem. The doctor had said: If you aren't sleeping, it's because you aren't closing your eyes. And the father had responded: My eyes don't close. And when the doctor asked him to close his eyes, the father said that he couldn't.

The doctor yelled: I saw you blink. You can close your eyes. Close them now. Close your eyes, sir!

My eyes blink, but they don't close.

If you blink them, you're closing them, it's unavoidable!

No, I can't.

So the doctor took the father's chin between his fingers and he said: Eyelids blink twenty times per minute. 28,800 times per day,

10,512 million times per year. You spend ten percent of your life with your eyes closed, that's thirty-six days per year. You can't tell me: My eyes don't close. I don't want to hear this type of talk in my office! Is that understood?

The father didn't move.

Do you understand? Your brain rests when you blink, it's a vital and instantaneous movement! If you didn't close your eyes, you'd be crazy, sir. You'd be delirious. We'd have to tie you up.

Then the father had explained that his body felt like a hotel, and the doctor said: That's an entirely different story. That's not my area of expertise.

The father put his vacuum to the side without turning it off, and in the noise of the machine he saw something like images. He saw his son outside, searching for his mother. He lay down under the table, he crossed his arms behind his head, the table calmed the father. It covered him. Things were written under the table, measurements, initials, it was an old table. His eyes landed on a red letter, he stared at it for a long time, and it started to swarm. It became blue, then he saw the sea and black dots in the sea, two small black dots, his two children, his son, his daughter, Salim, Sara. The father was on a beach in swimming trunks, his hands on his hips, and he yelled: Don't go too far out. Be careful, it's dangerous! And the children swam, they didn't listen to him, they were laughing, the father yelled: I told you to be careful. Don't go too far, Sara, Salim, this is serious, listen to me. You can die at any time. But the children dove, they came to the surface, they held their noses, they spit water toward the sky, they swam, they sank, the father yelled: You're not listening to me. Salim, you're not listening to me. Salim, I don't like to wash my hands of people, but if I'm giving you advice, and you're not listening to me, my hands are going to wash themselves, do you hear me? The children swam farther and farther out, faster and faster, they swam backwards. They looked at the father, they sank into the sea, always straight, like arrows. The father pointed at them, he intercepted an old, tan woman, almost nude, on the beach, he said: Look, those are my children. The old woman replied: I understand the feeling, I have a child myself, I like it when people look at him. He was born with wrinkles on his face, not baby wrinkles, but old-person wrinkles. And the father said: Really? He said: Really? Really?

Sara came into the kitchen, she turned off the vacuum. She asked the father what he was doing under the table. He said: I'm resting. She told him not to worry, because Salim was fine.

Later on, while the father was watching his son's latest video, the phone rang. It was the social worker. The father needed to come to her office the next day to discuss his son, his problems, his absences, his situation, his documentations, his dysfunction, to discuss the house, the past, the future, and Sara. The social worker no longer had an office because of budget cuts. She would send an email to tell him where to meet.

*

Everyone was always lying down in this house because everyone lies down in every house. Everyone lies down eventually, because that's the natural tendency in every home. Rooms are designed for bodies lying down, like the body of the grandmother, always horizontal. It would make sense if water formed a puddle in our backs every time we lay down, that would be logical. We drink water, we're made of water. Water should form a pond in our backs, in our bodies, when we lie down, but water descends, and even when we're lying down, water moves toward our feet. Substances go down, that's their way, their natural direction. If you put a piece of wood in your mouth, it will go down. A piece of iron, a piece of cement, both would go down. You could even put human body parts in your mouth and they would eventually go down. In truth, food should stay stuck in our throats, but our bodies force it down. When we lie down, liquids don't follow the laws of physics, they follow the laws of the body: descend, descend. The sun makes heat and humans make things go down inside themselves. A spoon goes in. A spoon goes out. The row of top teeth works with the row of bottom teeth, just as the top lip works with the bottom lip, just as the left eye works with the right eye, and the lungs between themselves, like ovaries do and ears do, as if we were two. Two people who don't look at each other, who don't know each other, who never meet. Every person contains multiple people, at least two people, at least two eyes, at least two legs. When two people meet, it's really a group of people meeting. The left eye doesn't look at the right eye. The right eye doesn't know the left. If they don't see each other, they can't look at each other, it's not because of their position, it's because the brain has made a choice. The grandmother had heard on the radio: We always see our noses, but we aren't aware of it. Our brains cancel out the image of our noses. Our brains make a choice. Our brains hide things from us that are in plain sight.

They sat the grandmother up to feed her oil and sugar. When she finished a yogurt, they said: Bravo. They applauded close to her face. The children, the father, they put food in her mouth, apple, broccoli, tomato, milk, and carrots.

They clean the edges of my plate with Camembert, they put it in my mouth with spinach, with mashed potatoes, I eat it. She bathed her mouth in food, she coated her mouth, she swallowed her own mouth. She no longer felt like she was biting down so much as falling. She let her mouth fall into substances. They give me broth with lettuce, they give me peas, beans, zucchini, dead fish. When you eat a lot, the food all tastes the same, the food becomes a ball, the eating ball, a ball called eating. They give me rice with bread and butter, banana, breadcrumbs, almonds, hazelnuts, and dead baby cow. They give me cinnamon with a dead quail. They put it in coriander for me, with pickle and squash, a dead crab. They give me cream and watercress, turmeric, and curry with a dead turkey. They ram me full of shallots and endives and spelt, tarragon and ginger, redcurrants, a dead herring. What if every animal appeared. If all the animals gathered around me. If they looked at me. All the animals I've put in my mouth. What if all the animals formed a circle around my bed and looked at me. If all the animals that fly, lay eggs, swim, run, all the hard animals with a shell, with pincers, with hair, with feathers, with scales, with spikes, with fleece. All the animals I gave to my children. The animals I gave myself. All the animals I was given. All the dead animals. What if all the animals looked at me in silence. And all the other animals, all the animals I've known, the ones I've pet, the animals that have licked my hand. I've seen animals on TV, they put them in a cylinder, they came out sausages. And I tell myself: You eat, you eat, but if you eat, someone else gets eaten. That's the order in the world. When you get fatter, someone else gets thinner. Every time you go to sleep, someone else wakes up. Maybe a pheasant, maybe a baby. Every time you wake up, someone falls asleep. Every time you stay silent, someone else in the world speaks. They talk and talk, that's nature. Each time you lose weight, someone takes on that weight because weight is displaced, it never disappears. When someone dies, the weight from their body makes algae and nails grow, it contributes to nests and rivers. Oil sits above water. Water sits under oil. Weight places us somewhere. Every time you get angry, someone else calms down in the world. You can't destroy anything. You can't change anything. Every time someone insults you, someone else in the world says they're sorry on their knees, they ask for forgiveness. Someone cuts their arm while someone else is getting stitches. You can't inhale and exhale at once, but while you're inhaling, someone else is exhaling. Everything that happens to us is within the order of the world. Everyone works for the order of the world and even people who are sleeping or even people who reject the world order work for the order of this world. You can't change anything, you can't produce anything. You can't produce a substance. We use things the way they exist, they transform, they proceed to other forms. Accidents, torture, illness, explosions, meals, legs, a muscle, someone taking a bath, mist, a puppy coming out of its mother's stomach, the smell of heat and horses, all these things occur. We participate, it can't be helped. When we empty our trash, someone in the world fills theirs. Our gestures are linked. Every time someone takes a piss, someone drinks in the world. Every time we eat, someone dies of hunger. When I throw up, someone fills their stomach, and when I'm hungry someone else in the world eats. When I open my eyes, someone closes them. When I close them, someone opens them. The whole universe is ordered, and everyone participates. Any gesture is part of any other gesture. All acts, all thoughts are part of the history of the world. And the history of the world is part of the history of the universe. The history of the universe is part of the history of all the universes. When I move my tongue, my gesture is part of the history of all universes. Every crumb of bread from all the bread from every era is part of the history of all universes. Every insect, speck, and every bone of every creature. There are directions inside my head, I move. I go into my knees, I put my mind inside my knees, I wait, I go everywhere. I go out, I fly over the house, over the town, I go inside a lock of hair on the head of my grandson, Salim, Salim, he's walking in the town, then inside the cheek of my granddaughter, Sara, Sara, she's singing, she's singing on the steps, I go into a rag, I wait, I wait, I stay.

The female nurse tosses a packet of tissues onto the grandmother's stomach. It bounces, it hits the ceiling. She throws a sponge onto the huge stomach. The sponge bounces, it flies through the room. The nurse throws other objects, gloves, cables, a phone. The male nurse throws his wallet, he throws a folded drawing from his children. The things bounce, they play, they aim for targets on the gymnasium ceiling, old traces of paint. They score, they win, they count the points. The female nurse says: Her veins are about to go. Look at her, she's almost out of blood. She's so soft, like rotten cheese. Eventually, her skin is going to split. We'll be able to hear it give way. The male nurse says: She's full. We're emptying her, and they're filling her back up. She's going to croak. The female nurse says: It's always the same with the families. They think they're prolonging the person's life by feeding them. They stuff sick people. They push the sick person in the wrong direction, they stretch them out. The bed becomes too small, the person suffocates, the blood can't handle it. The female nurse says: She was thin when she was young.

How do you know?

She told me. She talks during REM sleep. The neurovascular units redirect the occluded artery through intravenous thrombolysis, which provokes temporary, parasympathetic recovery of language abilities, and she describes herself as a young woman. I've heard her say: I was young and pretty, passionate about the occult. I was a delicate woman, they called me The Wire.

The male nurse nods slowly, slowly, he pulls the sheet back up to the grandmother's shoulders. And the grandmother blinks twice.

*

If someone puts on makeup, if they paint their own face directly onto their own face, if they use the right technique, the right colors, if they paint their own mouth onto their own mouth, their own cheeks onto their own cheeks, if they paint dark rings under their eyes onto the dark rings under their eyes, then they're hiding their face with their face. They're wearing a mask of themselves.

On the network, people have a form in the form of their faces. They have an appearance over their appearance. The image of their bodies masks the form of their bodies. The form of their lives masks the form of their lives. They place a form on their food in the form of their food. A form of their family and friends in the form of their family and friends. A form of what they like in the form of what they like. A form of what they believe in the form of what they believe. In fresh, assorted colors, the forms stand out. Sometimes, the forms are stolen, accounts are hacked, appearances are taken. Then our form operates under another name, in another country, with other friends, in other conversations, our form has left us. We send complaints to the network, we say: It's me, I'm this person, it's my identity, but it's our form, it's just moved on.

For the video, Sara chose a sixties-style filter, an echo filter for her voice, another filter to make her eyes larger, and another filter to make the outline of her head sparkle. It was dark outside, the square was empty. She was wearing a jacket with a black hood. She was holding out her arm while lying down on the steps, she was looking at the camera. She sang: Let me die one second, one second in your arms, one second in your arms, let me die, the moon is so dirty because we walked on it, because we walked on it. Her voice lingered, it was slow. Her voice slipped by as if it were on a candle-lit slide. Because we walked on it, let me die on the moon, we walked on the moon like sad dogs, sad, sad dogs, like sad dogs. Her voice was a long thick line. Sad, sad, sad dogs, sad, sad dogs, sad, sad, dogs, yeah yeah yeah, yeah yeah yeah. Her voice was like an ancient caramel, almost black, surrounded by light colors. She wasn't singing loudly. She turned her phone toward the square, she zoomed in on the light of a streetlamp. She was shaking, so the light jumped. She turned the phone again, she filmed her own mouth, which sang: Let me play with your dead body, one second with your dead body, boo hoo, dead body, boo hoo, like sad dogs, we laugh like sad dogs, oh, sad, sad dogs on the moon, on the moon, on the dirty, dirty moon, dirty dirty, dirty dirty dirty dirty moon. She turned the camera and, by accident, filmed a woman sitting on the steps a few centimeters away from her. The woman smiled horribly with her rotten teeth. She was missing a lot of them. She said: You have a beautiful voice, it makes me want to caress your glottis. And she burst out laughing with threads of spit between her lips.

Sara locked her phone and her nostrils contracted. She insulted the woman, she told her to get the hell out of here, to go get some teeth, to go to a special place for trash like her, to stop talking, to take a bath, to brush her hair, to apologize, she'd ruined the video, she said: People were watching me. She unlocked her phone and she showed her the number of subscribers. She said: All these people were watching me. The woman responded: Oh really? That's not that many people. All those people are each just one person as far as I know. Each person is just one single person, right? One person each, one person isn't several people, right? In reality, only one person is watching you. That's not a lot of people. Her large lips were gray and dry. She said: My name is Catherine, I'm gullible, don't be angry with me. Anger doesn't work on me. It doesn't help, I don't notice, I don't have a normal level of intelligence. I see things my way, I'm direct, that's all, like animals. I know the world of humans is indirect. I know that's a problem. She looked at Sara's forehead, she said: Anyone can make me believe anything. I believed there was sperm in beans until I was twenty-six years old.

Who told you that?

My parents.

And she made a sound with her throat like a clock that's about to strike. Her parents had made her believe all cars contained monkeys that pedaled under the hood, she'd believed that until she was twenty-eight years old. Her parents had told her that, in certain countries, the inhabitants had legs in their ears, little legs that served no purpose, she'd believed that until she was twenty-five years old. When she discovered sex in her adolescence, they'd made her believe that brothers and sisters shared orgasms and that, when a brother orgasms, his sister does too, no matter where she is, and vice versa. As a joke, her mother would cry out at the table, she'd say: I have news from my brother. Catherine had believed her until last month. Her mother had made her believe that movies in the theater weren't really movies, but real scenes that were taking place in the basement. For almost her entire life, Catherine had believed that humans didn't shit, and that she was the only one who produced those black things, like a disgusting beast. Her father said she was like a beast. And every time Catherine went to the bathroom, her father said: That's right, squeeze it out, you little beast! Catherine believed that each person's genitals had a different shape, some in a shaft, others in a spiral, and others in the shape of a flower or a triangle. Her parents laughed. They looked at her genitals when she was little in the bathtub, they said: Yours don't look like anything. They laughed, then they looked at each other while raising their eyebrows. At school, Catherine believed the teachers were robots controlled by her parents. That's what they said, and she believed anything. In her family, she was called The Idiot. She said: I can't be mad at them, you have to do something to pass the time . . . I had problems with food, I hid so I could eat huge quantities of it, and I was overweight. Do you know what my parents called me?

Sara didn't say anything.

Catherine said: Overweight.

Then she rubbed her nose the way thumb-sucking babies do, with the tip of her index finger. Her hair was thin, you could see her scalp. She said: Even now, anyone can make me believe anything. I believed tap water was elephant saliva, I believed that until last week. Honestly, I don't understand anything in life, I don't understand anything. I don't understand why some things are possible and others aren't. I don't understand. Impossible things seem just as possible as possible things, right? Possible things seem just as impossible as impossible things. I don't understand the logic. Every time I think about it, I realize I don't understand anything. Everyone seems to understand, but I don't understand anything. Sara replied: I don't give a fuck.

I just wanted to watch.

It annoys me. You're bothering me.

Okay, but I'm going to keep doing it.

You think I'm some kind of show?

Yes.

You ruined my video, people were watching me.

What about me?

You're just there, you stink, you won't stop talking, are you drunk?

The expression on Catherine's face didn't really come from her face, but rose up from the inside, from underneath her face, as if her face were dead and life came from far away, from somewhere in the depths. Her eyelids fell, her eyes were the shape of a vulva.

Sara said: I don't like alcoholics, they make me want to vomit. Poor people like you who're alcoholics, with your ugly clothes, you depress me, you all age the same way, you all end up with the same face, it disgusts me, you're disgusting.

Catherine laughed with a kindly dribble. She said: Oh, my dear girl, oh no. I'm not really an alcoholic, I wouldn't go that far. It takes years to become an alcoholic, my dear, it takes many years. I'm still far off, I'm a novice, it's only been a few years. It takes patience, you don't just become an alcoholic overnight, it requires time and commitment, my dear, time and commitment. You don't just become an alcoholic by drinking, it's deeper than that, more difficult.

She pulled a lock of hair behind her ear, but the hair stayed in her hand. She said: There are very few alcoholics on Earth, it's rare. Rarer than pandas. Sara was looking at her phone. Pandas are almost extinct, did you know that? There are only about 1,000, no more. To become an alcoholic, it takes at least ten years, but often twenty or thirty, even a hundred. You need to work at it every day and drink every day. People don't realize, you have to work tirelessly.

Between each sentence, Catherine would suck her lips into her mouth. She said: I'm chasing a feeling. A few years ago, I was watching a show on alcoholism. It was so well done, it made me want to drink. I'd never drank before, but I found my way. Many people stop, I understand, they undergo treatment. Who can blame them? They can't keep going, I understand. They start but . . . I understand. Most people don't have the strength, as for me . . . I've often thought . . . Many times . . . I think about it, but I don't throw up, that's what saves me. I have cirrhosis of the liver, but I don't throw up. My body got stronger, it got used to alcohol. At night, I don't have to wake up anymore, my body drinks in my sleep. My body opens a bottle, it drinks it, it knocks it back, and I just sleep. I worked hard to get to that point, my dear, I worked, but there's still a long way for me to go. A long, shit-filled way. It feels longest during the day. Sometimes, I feel lonely, it's true, but that has nothing to do with other people. Other people don't interest me. None of that interests me. I'm all alone with myself, but without myself. How can I explain it . . . I don't have my own company . . . That's it, I'm looking for myself, but I can't find myself. You wouldn't understand. I'm looking for myself, I'm looking, I'm working . . . It's a lot of work . . . Even for beginners . . . It's constant work. Alcoholics drink eighty-nine percent of the alcohol in the world.

Sara looked up, she said: How do you know?

Oh, I read about it, my dear. I read about it because I know how to read. I've lived my life the way you have, and I learned how to read. You know, if you were me, you'd be me. People often tell me: Catherine, if I were you, I'd do this, I'd do that. But if other people were me, they'd be me, that's it. And if I were other people, I'd be someone else.

What do you do all day?

I feed the cats in vacant lots. Have you ever seen people feeding cats in vacant lots?

Maybe.

Of course, my dear, of course. And that's entirely normal, because everyone has seen us. Everyone runs into us. You can find us in every city, you'll see. In every neighborhood, everywhere in the world, we walk funny, we feed cats in vacant lots. We know each other, we limp, we're family. We try to be alcoholics, but the days are long, so we feed cats the way other people go to mass, as a sign of belonging.

Oh, I didn't know that.

Unless you've lived it, you can't really know. You know, the dogs in vacant lots, we also find dogs in vacant lots, they're very skinny and dirty, the cats are missing eyes, but the dogs are dirty, skinny, and covered in fleas, do you see those dogs? They're trying to look like me.

Why would they want to look like you?

Oh, my dear, I don't know, I don't have the faintest idea. But there is one moment in time when I know everything, there's an instant, one second, when I drink, an instant, when I'm drunk, not too drunk, almost too drunk, but not very drunk, there's a moment when I know everything. I understand everything and I forgive everyone. I forgive you. I forgive myself, but I forget, that's the problem. Don't you think this city's boring? Everything's for sale here, the pharmacies, the corner stores, nobody wants them, nobody's buying. And this theater, it's always closed, these steps and this sad square. When buildings are destroyed, new buildings are built and these buildings are put up for sale, but it doesn't matter, nobody buys them, I speak, I go on, this morning, I woke up with a magnificent wad of spit on my face, alcohol spit, I often drink white spirit, do you know it? White spirit.

How old are you?

Would you say I'm sixty?

Yes.

I'm thirty-five, my dear.

Catherine's dark lips smiled, she said: And you?

Nineteen.

What are you doing in this square then if you don't drink? What do people who don't drink do anyway?

I'm recording myself.

Oh yes, that's true, I saw you just now. I don't like that style at all, I think it's shit, those lyrics, those tunes, it's pure shit.

She said it with a sweet smile, like a compliment. She sucked her lips into her mouth with a sucking noise. The sound must have reminded her of babies, because she said: Every time I meet a man, I get pregnant, but thanks to alcohol, I lose the fetus, hallelujah.

My brother writes poems.

Oh, my dear, I don't give a fuck. I'm not interested in other people.

Do you want me to read one?

Why not.

because it's the end of the planet
they left the world
they carried their eyes away in a bag

Catherine said: That's shit.

these days a fish replaces
its scales with a black dot
if I had insect tears
I'd give them to other animals like little pieces of jewelry

And Catherine said: That's shit, my dear, total shit.

put your hand in the darkness
it spreads

Catherine said: Like shit.

I'm stopping.

No, finish.

Sara looked at Catherine and she said: I don't want to anymore.

How many lines are left?

One line.

One piece of shit. Come on, finish it. Finish it please.

accelerating sadness

Catherine applauded in an asymmetrical way. Her hands didn't touch. She was smiling. Her lips creased over her black gums. Sara said: Why did you come up to me? Why do all the crazy people talk to me?

Oh, my dear, that's obvious. You're lying on the steps in an empty square at night, of course people are going to talk to you, we know what we're supposed to do. Everyone has their job in the world.

Sara didn't say anything and, suddenly, Catherine got bored. She was sighing like a madwoman with her old, gray, pursing mouth. Her lips came out of her mouth like a mollusk. Sara showed her things on her phone, music videos from an American singer, and Catherine thought it was shit. She showed her videos of people who climb on the roofs of apartment buildings and don't fall, and Catherine said it was shit. She showed her Salim's videos and videos of people eating spicy Chinese noodles, and Catherine thought it was all shit. She showed her videos of trees and flowers growing at an accelerated speed, Catherine thought that was shitty and she smiled. She smiled and rain started to fall. She looked at the sky and yelled: Go on, squeeze it out!

*

My children, there are ten things you must know:

1. You sharpen a knife with a knife.
2. The wind might not have hands, but it shakes the trees.
3. There are two kinds of people. First, there are people who behave toward you the way they would behave toward anyone. Sometimes they are agreeable and sometimes they are disagreeable, that's normal. Then there are the others, people who are afraid of bothering you. They're very attentive, they pay you compliments, but fear them, for they will change. If they were good, they'll become bad. If they were polite, they will become rude. If they flattered you, they will wound you. It won't be normal.
4. Smile at people you don't like but without your eyes. Don't force your eyes to produce a smile.
5. Everything that heats up becomes hard, like mud, for example. And everything that heats up becomes soft, like gold, for example. That's how it is, my children.
6. Often those with no legs to stand on don't like shoes.
7. Cook something before you get hungry.
8. Maybe the world was created by people and they forgot. It's possible, honestly, it's possible.
9. Everyone deserves pity.
10. God gives nuts to those who have no teeth.

3

The social worker wasn't a woman, but a man with a high-pitched voice.

His bald head shone in the sun. He did nothing to welcome the father. Still, he had a sweetness to his face, like a man who runs to pick up children who've fallen on the playground. He said: I have a huge forehead. You're looking at my forehead, aren't you? The father tried to smile, but his face made a grimace. The social worker said: You weren't looking at my forehead? Oh, yes, well, I thought you were looking at my forehead. Have you brought the receipt?

The father said: What receipt?

The receipt that demonstrates your presence.

I'm here.

I see that, but do you have the receipt?

The social worker's voice made his teeth hurt. The father said: No.

The social worker sighed. He held out a folding chair to the father who unfolded it. He said: I'll get straight to the point, you're in a bad way. Let's talk about it. The father said: I brought all the papers. He pulled out a fat mauve envelope and took out some documents: gray and black records, photos of his children, the grandmother's medical records, a divorce certificate. The social worker yawned with his mouth closed. He said: Yes, well . . . As you know, we are looking at several years of school absences concerning your son, Salim. Is that correct? Just say yes or no, we don't want to waste any time. The social worker was addressing the papers in the father's hands. The father responded: Yes.

The social worker said: It's a rather classic case. The first thing you should know is that the well-being of students takes precedence over legal matters in my department. There are formalities, frameworks, and criteria that we must respect, however, the well-being of individuals, particularly that of minors, takes precedence over administrative issues regarding national cooperation with the Office of Family Affairs. In addition, as a senior social worker, I'm particularly invested in improving the development of students in distress across sectors, and always in partnership with families. It's a collaborative partnership, a form of co-creation. We work hand in hand, sir. Your hand in mine. And my hand in yours. That's our policy.

He looked like a toy. His skin shone. He said: School absences are generally due to complex family situations or a lack of commitment on the part of one or both parents, depending on the case. I know you benefit from social housing assigned to you by the mayor of your municipality. As I'm sure you are aware, the mayor is a natural person representing municipal authority. Hence, we must respect him. I also know that your wife hates you. It is also possible that she hates her children, which may seem rare and dramatic, however, it's rather common, mothers who hate their children, I mean, it's rather common. According to the information I have at hand, these are the factors that led to her disappearance. Have at hand in a manner of speaking, because I am not physically holding the documents in my hands, as you can plainly see. He twiddled his thumbs as if to support what he was saying.

The father tried to smile. He said the word: Yes.

The social worker continued: Listen, sir, you have to understand that the future of your son is at stake, and the future of a child is the future of a municipality and the future of the planet, given the globalized world we live in. Our wish at the Office of Family Affairs, our sole wish, can be summed up by the following image, listen carefully: children holding hands and molding the world of tomorrow. Don't you agree? The father said: Yes.

The social worker said: I must ask you to repeat that back to me, sir.

The father said: Children holding hands and molding the world of tomorrow. The social worker came closer to the father, and he said: Do you understand the depth of this sentence? I repeat: Children holding hands and molding the world of tomorrow. The social worker made incomprehensible gestures in front of his face with his fingers. He said: Think about it. Tomorrow. Two hands. Out of two hands. The world made out of two hands. And what do they do with two hands? What do they do with the world? Do you follow?

The father couldn't keep his mind still, it went from the man's nails to his nose to the landscape, as if the things around him existed only for him, as if a scene had been set for the father alone. A world created for no purpose, a world the social worker was part of just like anything else. The father articulated the word: Yes.

The social worker said: Listen, when I say the future of your son is at stake, it's a manner of speaking, sir, because the future is an undefinable notion, and therefore purely speculative. The social worker typed the word FUTURE into his phone. He showed the screen to the father, and he read out loud: Time to come (opposite of the past).

The father nodded.

The social worker said: As you can see, these terms are too vague for the job at hand. However, we can visualize your son's future together. Close your eyes, sir. This isn't my area of expertise, but let's give it a try. Visualize your son's future. Visualize your son as an adult, working, imagine your son working, okay? Do you see him? Very good. My colleague will add this information to your file. Now, open your eyes. I know you are taking care of your ex-wife's mother and that she's dying. This is indicated in your file. But your son's disappearance from school isn't legal. The methods of distinguishing between individuals belonging to a single community, whether scholastic or familial, encourages me to remind you five to seven times per day by phone. And I must inform you of the following: I can take away your house, which will complicate an already complex situation, and nobody wants that to happen, sir, least of all me, least of all you, and vice versa. I assist my team with all operational and strategic activities, and I started to notice my old age by looking at my hands, the back of my hands. Additionally, your financial state worries our offices. Are you aware of that? The father said: Yes.

All documents related to dependents were filled out by my superior in a white office on an enormous computer. A brand-new, impersonalized office, on an enormous computer. I personally aided in the information unification procedure. The situation is alarming, sir, in a manner of speaking of course, because alarming doesn't mean that an alarm is going to go off in your house, make no mistake. Alarming means that things aren't going well, however, no alarms will actually go off. We haven't placed any alarms on the premises of your place of residence, however, the situation remains alarming, even without an alarm. Have I made myself clear?

The father said: Yes.

The social worker said: I'm going to ask you to repeat what I've just said.

The father said: The situation remains alarming.

The social worker said: Even without an alarm?

The father said: Yes.

The social worker continued: Very good. Among other things, I'm also concerned about your daughter who is out of school, unemployed, out collecting donations online through her singing videos. I myself am subscribed to her channel and I take great pleasure in listening to her. Pleasure, yes, that's the word. Especially at night, with headphones. Yes, pleasure. You know, my mother studied fine arts, so I know when something is artistically fine. Additionally, my thesis was about the acquisition of the concept of beauty in children ages zero to three, so I know what I'm talking about. I've managed cultural projects across the country, and getting back to your daughter, to your family, to your life, to your problems, your children's videos are evidence I could use against you at any moment. I'm warning you, sir, poverty doesn't rule out the most severe consequences. In effect, like dead trees caught in a storm, one by one, the poorest homes, too, become subject to eviction. When it rains, it often pours. We can take everything from you, and there's nothing you can do to dispute it. Is that clear?

The father said: It's clear.

The social worker said: You are surely aware of the fact that work pays. I'd like to know what kind of legal and labor example you hope to set for your two dependents under the age of twenty-five. So, the father talked about the walls he'd built for more than twenty years. And the social worker said: Oh, look over there. And he pointed to a low mountain covered in grass. Two dogs were running in the mist, they were white. The social worker said: I love them, they're twins, I'm very proud of them. I think of them as my children. I know that you have children. Sir, as a man with children, you can understand me. And vice versa. In spite of the formality my job requires. He yelled: Aucassin! Nicolette!

The dogs made a sign with their muzzles in the air. The social worker said: Did you see? That's a trick I taught them. At night, I put bulbs on their muzzles, and they write my name in the air with light. Isn't that amazing? Amazing. I love dogs. I try not to compare them to humans, but I can't help myself. I try not to, but I can't help myself. When I think about it, I almost feel sorry for myself, I'm just like you, I do what I can. Oh, look over there. He pointed to a black spot near the mountain. He said: That's a small, unmanned, remote-controlled or programmable airplane. My team and I have commissioned these little vehicles all over the region. These marvelous devices allow us to track the movements of dysfunctional families like yours whenever they venture beyond their domiciles. Progress makes me shiver in the lower half of my body. The social worker pointed to the lower half of his body. The father didn't know which expression to put on his face. He felt an enormous desire to frown. The dogs ran in the distance. The social worker said: I see you're thin. Do you work a lot with your hands? They're worn out. Look at your hands, please.

The father looked at his hands. The social worker said: They're not in good shape. I'm using basic words so you can understand me. Your face isn't in good shape. Your hands aren't in good shape. When I see you, I think: this is a man who's given up. I've read your CV, I noticed you haven't worked for a long time. A very long time. A long period of time. A hole in a life. And that's a problem, I'm telling you honestly. That's what we call a black mark on your record in the administrative field. We talk about BLACK MARKS! A BLACK MARK! We shout it. It's a joke between colleagues: BLACK MARK! We pass around casefiles and yell: BLACK MARK! In the hallways, we roll on our chairs and yell: BLACK MARK! The social worker laughed and choked. The father also choked a little to be polite. His chin quivered. The social worker took out a large, black marker. He wrote: NOT GOOD on the father's envelope, the marker squeaked. The father tried to say a sentence, but he spluttered.

The social worker said: I will message you regarding next steps. If your son doesn't return to the real world, I'll take everything away from you and you might cry, it's possible, it's happened before. But tears are necessary for keeping your eyes moist. Tears contain proteins and other substances that keep your eyes healthy. They fight off infection. It's interesting. Evolutionarily speaking, scientists argue that humans cry to signal their distress without producing any sound. We can therefore imagine a selective pressure that would have driven humans to develop a system of signals that doesn't let predators know they are poor vulnerable creatures. Whatever it may be, I'll let the secretary of the assistant at my school office know, and she will keep you up to date by email or I will call you directly. Now, give me back my chair. Quickly now. Let's get up. I like to get up quickly to feel a little dizzy. Do you feel it? And the father said: Yes.

*

He'd placed his phone in front of his face to protect himself from the sun. The shadow formed a rectangle around his eyes. He yawned, he touched the screen: a man had carried his mother's head, cut into three-by-three-centimeter cubes, in a pink briefcase for over twenty years. He touched the screen: bodies jumped from the impact of bullets in a far-off country, they rose and fell on dry ground. Dust surrounded them. He touched the screen: a soldier photographed his own death. In the image, you could see big red and blue flames, nothing more. He touched the screen: during his trial, an adolescent serial killer stated: I wish everything were worse, I wish I'd killed more people, I wanted more drama and for all of you to cry. His parents spoke in front of the camera. The father said: We lost him a long time ago, we felt like he was lost from the beginning. When my wife got pregnant, we understood that we were losing him. He touched the screen: dead fish, belly-up in a murky lake. A lake of dead fish. The images disturbed him. He touched the screen: chemical products were burning in a factory fire. A tunnel of smoke spit black clouds across the sky. Specialists said not to worry, they used the word: Excessively. He touched the screen: a multibillionaire was having an eight-kilometer-long slide built through his forest. He unveiled his private attraction by cutting a red string with golden scissors. He said: I like sliding.

Jonathan's eyes were shining. He'd gone out, he'd been drinking, that's for sure. Salim might have followed him to the bar. Jonathan found three pills in his sock, he chewed them. He might have taken something. He could hear the blood in his temples. He touched the screen: collections of phrases appeared in blue rectangles. The phrases of the day and the phrases of the day before. He saw the rectangles as paintings, perfect and still. He liked the rectangles without reading the phrases. He left a heart under a random rectangle. He touched the screen and he learned that dwarf elephants the size of pigs had lived on the islands of the Mediterranean in prehistoric times up until 5000 BCE. He sent the article to Salim who didn't say anything. Sara, who was lying on the stairs, didn't say anything either.

There they were, all three of them, in the morning, not saying anything.

Jonathan scrolled through other pages. He looked at the pages of unknown artists. He touched the screen here and there, there were so many artists, in every city, on every street, so many unknown artists. He looked at their faces, their hair. Before, unknown artists were unknown artists, now unknown artists are known, they have their pages, their galleries, their followers. An unknown artist recorded her husband brushing his teeth, she said: I'll watch these videos when he dies, it'll be nice. I sense that he'll die before me, it's okay, we're artists, it's a feeling. On another unknown artist's page, he learned there were fifty ways to say the word snow in some people's language somewhere in the world. He copied and pasted images of white mountains on Salim's page. He copied and pasted igloos and holes in ice, then he lowered his phone.

Sara was chewing blackcurrant gum, and the smell was bothering him. He cracked his jaw, he asked for some water. No one had any. There were colors on the objects around him, but the objects didn't have any color, he could understand that. On the other side of the square, water was running in a fountain shaped like a saucer, as if it had been placed here by aliens. He said the word FOUNTAIN without making a sound. He typed the word FOUNTAIN into his phone and he touched the screen. He looked at images of fountains, they spouted water, clear and docile. They never stopped being born. He imagined a long fountain that flowed and flowed, it flowed above the world, in the sky, above the universe, it flowed above everything and he opened his mouth. All he had to do was open his mouth. He touched his screen several times in random places and he put his phone down, he got up, he crossed the square.

He walked slowly and the world vibrated in an irregular, irritating way. The faces of passersby quivered in the middle, around the nostrils, everything was wide, the faces were long, they curved. People could have walked through him, through his chest, through his face because he didn't really exist, not 100 percent, he could feel it. Reality felt malicious, evil, he muttered: Mean, really mean. And he plunged his hands in the fountain, then his arms, then he lay down in the fountain, on his back, eyes open, fully clothed, mouth open, and he flowed, flowed, he sucked in, he swallowed, his body filled in the fountain. Underwater, he imagined crabs in the dark, crazy, neon crab-scientists wearing glasses, crabs around his body, smiling crabs, crabs in clothes eating him, they were swallowing him. He forgot to breathe. Finally, he remembered.

When he stuck his head out, an old man was leaning on the edge of the fountain. He didn't have eyebrows, but bristles, like hay. He said: Luckily the air doesn't have a face.

What?

Luckily the air doesn't have a face. A face like yours or mine, I mean. Luckily it doesn't have one. We're lucky, right? You and me, we're lucky.

Jonathan said: What do you mean? And the old man replied: Luckily, the air doesn't do faces. That's what I was getting at. Air doesn't have a face, right? The old man threw a coin in the fountain, he said: Superstitions are an eternal feeling of the soul, but if the air had a face, we'd be miserable, I'd kill myself, you know? We'd be crazy, it would be unbearable, and I'd end up killing myself.

Jonathan didn't say anything. Water flowed over his shoulders.

Everything is made the way it should be, right? Don't you think? Just imagine, you open your eyes, and you realize the air has a face. Awful, right? How horrible. An eternal horror, always the same face, always the same horror, for our entire lives. We'd look up, we'd see this face, the air's face, always the same. If the air had a face, we'd see this face from birth to death, continuously, just imagine, in front of us, just imagine if the air had a mug, a kisser, a visage, a pie . . .

Yeah, yeah, I got the idea.

The old man moved his eyebrows like a wave from left to right. He rested his cane against the fountain, and he said: I'm old. Then he tried to take off his jacket, but his body was dry. He said: I'm old, look at my hands, you see them, they hurt, just like my back does, my legs, my ankles, my low back creaks, can you hear it? It's impossible for me to get this jacket off. I'm stiff, see for yourself, I'm an old piece of bread, bread from 1802, an ancient baguette. That's what I've become, an old piece of myself, an old, dried-out, hardened piece, my poor lad. And if someone offered to help me, I wouldn't say no, oh, I'd say the opposite, young man, I'd say just the opposite. Yes, the opposite of no. Do you understand? The opposite, you see? He gestured to Jonathan who got up with a sound like a wave. He tried to help the old man, he touched him, he touched his jacket. He put his hands on his back, he manipulated his arms, he grabbed him by the elbow, he tugged on his jacket, and the man cracked. It was a definitive cracking.

He said: It's my left arm. You just broke it, but don't worry, it's not important. You really hurt me, but it's nothing, it doesn't matter. I'm not a wimp. The bones you just broke will never be able to regrow, but that's not important. I wasn't that attached to them. Besides, I have to admit, I never liked that arm, I've been suspicious of it since I was a child. It's one arm too many, as they say, one arm too many.

He spoke without moving, his body stuck in his jacket, his arms twisted, his elbows close to his head. Jonathan said: I'm sorry. I didn't mean to. And he tried to pull on the fabric, he folded the jacket back, it got harder and harder, as if the jacket were shrinking. It clung to the old man, it was glued to him. He suggested borrowing scissors from a bar to cut it. The old man refused firmly: Out of the question, my good fellow, it's my jacket and I'm attached to it. I don't have any memories without it, you wouldn't understand. I keep my objects close, I'm very attached to them. I used the same plastic bag for over thirty years. I always had it with me. I took it everywhere. It fell to pieces, completely to pieces, over the years, to pieces, and I still keep a few of those pieces in my jacket. I think about it every day. About the bag, I mean. What time is it, my good fellow? Don't answer that, I'm going to unwind myself. And like a flash, the old man shook out his body, he shook it with great flexibility, he spread his arms in the air like two doves. He arranged his jacket, which slid like oil. He leaned over and touched his toes nimbly, with grace. He made chaotic gestures with ease and beauty. He multiplied his positions, raising his legs, turning his head, and Jonathan blinked. He creased his forehead, he couldn't follow all of it. The old man capered then did a cartwheel on the edge of the fountain, he folded in on himself, his heels touched his thighs, and his knees touched his nose. He took off, as if he were flying, then he stopped dead, and he once again became old, very old. He lowered his head. He coughed several times with his dry mouth, and he almost choked.

Jonathan asked him if he was sick, and the man replied: I'm fit as a fiddle. He squinted his eyes. Then, he took his cane, he grabbed Jonathan's arm as if it were part of a merry-go-round, and he said: Onward.

Jonathan felt this fragile body on his arm. He leaned slightly to be the same height, he curved his back and neck. He tried to smile and the old man gripped his arm with his old hand. Jonathan moved forward at his pace, in his pace. He paid close attention to each step, as if his steps were new people, small people who were short, weak, breakable. He calibrated his entire body to the body of the old man, and then, his own body started to weigh on him, his strength bothered him, his youth burdened him, it was too big, too heavy on the old man's arm. He felt too strong, capable of killing.

*

On the steps, the old man didn't say anything, Salim and Sara didn't say anything. Why weren't they saying anything, why wasn't anybody saying anything? The Earth deformed around his body, his clothing soaked the ground, the cement. The ground is like cement, the sky too, the sky is like cement, he saw it, he felt it, Sara's face was expressionless. Salim was looking at his phone with his face tilted, maybe sad, and the old man was moving his dry mouth, he muttered, then he spoke. He said: I'm wondering what you're doing on these steps. Are you beggars? He emphasized the B, he repeated: Beggars? Are you begging? Then he patted his abdomen. He said: I don't have much in my jacket, maybe a banana. I'd give it to you, but it's an old friend, I've had it for years, yes, for years, it will give you warts on your tongue. They are very painful, the warts, they explode, if truth be told, the taste isn't very nice. Of the warts, I mean, I have them every morning. They pop, every morning, in my mouth, every hour. Have you ever tasted moldy lemon? Have you ever tasted it? Are you familiar with moldy lemon, lemons green with mold, rotten lemons? Have you ever seen lemons white with rot? Lemons covered in white fuzz, does that ring a bell? The warts in my mouth taste the same, it's almost the same taste.

Sara sneezed and her eyes brightened, she looked all around like someone just waking up. She pulled out her earbuds, it was a shock, the light, the people, the sounds, the old man, his face, she went from one thing to the next, the way you always do, unprepared. So many times in a day, all throughout the day, we go from one thing to the next thing. When we sleep, we wake up. And when we aren't sleeping, we go from one image to another, one impression to another. Every time we walk, we go forward, we go from one step to another. Every time we speak, we go from one word to another. Every time we cry, we go from one tear to another, we forget the previous tear, here comes the next tear. Every time we make gestures, every time we blow our noses, we go from one substance to another, one texture to another, one frown to another, and one wrinkle to another unprepared. We look at people, we go from one skin to the next, one eye to the next, one forehead to the next, one behavior to the next and one voice to the next. Every time we scream, every time we fight, we go from one sentence to the next, one wound to the next, one sting to the next. Every time we walk in a forest or in a park, we go from one tree to the next, one trunk to the next, one mushroom to the next. In maternity wards, every day, people go from one newborn to the next, one birth to the next, one bracelet to the next, one nurse to the next, one stretcher to the next always unprepared. Every time we learn, we go from one idea to the next, one thought to the next, one discovery to the next, one year to the next, we go from one season to the next, one piece of clothing to the next, we go from one flower to the next, one lawn to the next, and on the highway, from one accident to the next, from one car to the next, from one gear to the next always unprepared, one color to the next, one person to the next. We shift our eyes but our eyes have already shifted. We absorb things, but our eyes are absorbed.

Jonathan said: Let me introduce you to this man, we've just met. I met him in the fountain. The old man said: Nice to meet you. Yes, nice to meet you. But, if I may, you two look alike. In a negative sense. You have what we call a common deformity. It's in your nature, the way a triangle has three angles. You are like two plums from the same plum tree. A plum tree crawling with parasites.

Sara didn't say anything, she looked straight ahead. With his old, twisted index finger, the old man pointed at Salim. He was close by, so he was almost touching his cheek, he said: This young man here, this one, is he disabled? Is he with you? He's disabled, I think. He looks like the girl. They must be brother and sister, are they disabled? Him especially, he's disabled, I presume?

No, he's looking for his mother.

Oh really? Maybe. Maybe he's looking for his mother, but I think he's disabled. He looks disabled to me. Why doesn't he ever look up? Can't he hear us? Hi, hello there! Can you hear us? Say something! See, he doesn't react. If I were his mother, I would have abandoned him too.

He repeated: I would have abandoned him. Abandoned him straight away.

Salim slid his thumb across the screen and the old man stared at him with contempt across the upper half of his face. He said: Look at this. Look at this young man, this boy, this young man, god, he's ugly, he's so ugly, his mother, his mother has a problem, I guess, I imagine, I suppose, I've deduced this systematically by analogy. And thus, if he has a problem, I imagine that his mother has a problem, that's how I work. I've always relied on another object to construct my thoughts, that's my way of doing things, I create links, I construct thoughts. I don't know what the first thought in the world was. But if we found out, we'd never have to think again, right? The first thought contains all the others. I've never really thought, I've never thought for myself, I only link ideas to ideas that have already existed for millennia. I admit it, though, I don't mind admitting it, I'm modest. Is his mother crazy? Is your mother crazy, my disabled friend? Boo hoo, is your mother crazy? The old man turned his old head toward Jonathan. He said: You know that crazy people aren't crazy. They're not any crazier than other people, they just don't do things at the right time, that's all. You know that. I can see in your eyes that you know this, my good fellow. Your mother was also crazy, I suppose, like all mothers, of course. When a creature comes out of your stomach, when it comes out from between your legs, what happens to you? You become crazy. If you weren't already, you become crazy then, that's nature.

Yes, it was true, Jonathan's mother was crazy, but his mother was dead. Jonathan's mother used to clean, she cleaned fast food restaurants before they opened. And at night, Jonathan's mother kissed the big screen in their living room, on the mouth of a singer. She was in love with the singer, he was like a member of the family, he was like a member of her life. On screen, in pictures, she loved him, she talked to him, she talked to the screen, she closed her eyes, she talked to the singer. She said: I love you, I'm your biggest fan, your biggest fan. Every Sunday, the mother printed pictures of the singer. She glued them everywhere, she covered the walls, she wallpapered the apartment, the doors, the hot water tank, the radiators, the refrigerator, she covered everything. Sometimes, when Jonathan was sleeping, she glued a picture of the singer to his head or his hands. In middle school, in high school, Jonathan often arrived with a picture of the singer stuck to his neck or his back, his mother did it, she made an effort. She measured, the pictures made sense, she didn't go overboard. On bananas, she pasted pictures of the singer in a yellow sweater. On packages of mashed potatoes, pictures of the singer dressed in white. On the stove, pictures of the singer posing in flames. On the radiators, pictures of the singer skiing while wearing a scarf. On her son's forehead, a picture of the singer as a young man, and on her own nails, she glued tiny pictures of the singer sprinkled with glitter.

One evening, they were eating artichokes. Jonathan and his mother weren't speaking, they never spoke. Jonathan was pulling the leaves off the vegetable, layer by layer, but the two of them weren't speaking. They were eating. They dipped the leaves in vinaigrette, they put the leaves in their mouths, they licked, they bit, the leaves became more and more tender, thinner and thinner, and they said nothing, their fingers shined. And then, in the heart of the artichoke, Jonathan found a picture of the singer, miniscule and precise. The mother said: Please, do it for me. And Jonathan put it in his mouth. He ate it.

Later on, in a big city, the mother spent fourteen days on a sidewalk in front of a concert hall. The mother drew green lines and black lines on her face like a soldier. Every day, she sent pictures to her son. In the photos, she smiled with her mouth open as if she were screaming. She was wearing a baseball hat with a picture of the singer and a T-shirt with a picture of the singer. She was surrounded by people like her, covered in pictures of the singer. The night of the concert, the mother was in the front row and the singer threw his shirt. The mother fought, she lost her earlobes. The mother came home with a piece of the shirt.

From then on, every morning, the mother kissed the piece of shirt. The mother fell asleep every night on the piece of shirt, she spoke to it, she whispered. Jonathan saw her crying in her bed with the piece of shirt, she said: I live for you.

In the beginning, Jonathan couldn't stand his mother anymore, she drank, she talked to the shirt, she didn't have earlobes, she hung around in bed, she kissed the screen. She was crazy.

But he slowly understood that things were just not where they should be, they were out of sync, displaced, they weren't in the right spot. They were true, but they weren't in the right place. You just had to shift things to understand them. You just had to shift things for them to seem right.

If a child kills someone to defend themselves, we can understand it. If they kill a random person ten years later, we don't understand it anymore. If someone is hurt, they should shout, if they shout two years later, nobody will understand. You have to be punctual. Cry when things are sad, tremble when it's cold. It was the same thing with the mother and the shirt. There was a time, there were scenes, but she messed up the location and it wasn't a big deal. Her name was Monique. Maybe she was crazy.

One evening at a casino, it was raining, a woman entered, she was tall, bald, wet, she came up to her, she said: Monique? She moved her hand toward the mother's forehead, she said: Monique, is that you? The mother replied: No. She wasn't lying, she was far away, out of sync.

Everyone tells the truth, that's all they can say. People don't always tell the truth in the right place, but they always tell the truth. When the mother told the shirt that she loved it, it was true. Nobody understood, but it was a love as good as any other. And then one day, the mother died of a common illness.

*

Jonathan swallowed two pills because the sun was white.

He swallowed two more because it was bright, and his legs were shaking. He said: Why won't you talk? Can you tell us something, can you tell us something, please? Can you tell us a story from your life? Can you tell us any story from your life, please?

The old man cast sideways glances, his eyelids laughed, he crossed his arms. He said: Why not. Why not, my good fellow. Of course, I can tell you my life story, if you insist, if it helps you relax. Because you seem anxious, don't you? About to explode. There are life stories that aren't worth telling, the vast majority, to be honest. However, mine is worth telling. He emphasized the M, he repeated: Mine is worth telling. Note this diachrony: things take a long time to tell, but take a short time to live through. When we're living them, we aren't telling the story. In reality, things take place. If we had to tell the whole story, if we wanted to tell the story as it took place, honestly, to be accurate, we would need a language for each thing, yes, a language for each thing, for each situation. For example, a language for greeting, a language for asking for forgiveness, a language for giving compliments, and a language for my life, of course. I would need a whole language for my life, but that's okay, I'll tell you the story in our common tongue. Here we go: I was born to a quiet family, my parents were mute. At the age of thirteen, I discovered language through a priest in my village. I realized I was different, that I am divine. When I was younger, I saw the future in fields of grain, wheat, rice, oats. Even today, if you give me some spelt, I can tell you the day you will die. And so, back then, I read misfortunes in the barley and the rye. Tragedy strikes all the time, it always will, but I knew what would happen, I saw it, I read it, and people ran from me, they said: He's the one who makes death come. But I was innocent. And I can prove it: in the countryside, there is a lot of grain. Wherever I looked, it was misfortune, misfortune, misfortune. Every second, I could read disaster. I had to leave my village. One morning, I moved into the city and I got into singing.

The old man squinted his eyes until they became as small as sesame seeds, then he fell silent. Jonathan said: You were a singer?

Not at all, my good fellow, I invented rap.

Oh, you were a musician?

The old man smiled strangely, he said: No, not at all, my good fellow. When I say I invented rap, I mean that I invented rap. I don't like innuendo or subtlety. When I say something, that's the thing I'm saying, I invented rap. The old man was quiet for a moment. He seemed to be collecting his memories in his mind. Finally, he said: I was a building manager. One night, in the basement, I came upon some rats, a whole group of rats, a community, very beautiful, very elegant, and very organized. Of course, being an aesthete, I was seized by a passion for their athleticism, their souls, their bodies, what bodies, those bodies, did you know that a rat stores its memories in its feet?

Salim put down his phone.

Everything they touch turns into a memory in their feet. It's like they're reading a map. When rats rub their paws together, they're reading their memories. Does that interest you, my disabled friend? I knew it, you love life, I could tell. Their body is their brain, each part of their body is a part of their brain, you weren't aware of this I suppose, nobody is aware of this. Their teeth never stop growing. They can weigh as much as twenty-two kilograms. They keep their heads very clean, they wash them eight times an hour, because they're cleaners, cleaners by nature. In a city like Paris, rats devour 800 tons of garbage every day. Unfortunately, those who clean are perceived to be dirty, it's dreadful. That's what humanity is, ignorance. Accusing rats of uncleanliness is like accusing florists of growing in the ground, it's idiotic, people confuse everything, anyway . . . three out of four insects in the world have disappeared, did you know? Anyway, back to the rats, they're a beautiful species, very pure, very friendly, we became close, the rats and I, very close. And I was overjoyed, I was honored, they stuck their tongues out at me, that's a sign of tenderness, friendship, affection, sympathy, feeling. And the old man stuck his tongue out. It was delicate, shiny, and pink. A rat tongue. Jonathan wanted to take a photo. Too late.

The old man said: Oh, yes, my friends, what a joy it was. What a joy in my life. I spent my time with my rats and when they saw me, they wiggled their wieners. That's the lower part of their bodies, it's called a wiener, or a ween, depending on the size. They wiggled them with joy. I gave them everything, a bit of everything, crumbs, plants, wine, jewelry, peels. In the evening, I put my armchair in the basement, and it was . . . It was . . . It was . . . He closed his eyes and a thin string of drool trickled onto his jacket, he muttered the sound: Mmmmm. And he remained for several seconds in this strange state, then he said: Magnificent . . . But one night, the rats kneeled before me, they prayed to me, do you understand? A long prayer, an exceptional rat prayer, in the language of rats. They were asking me for something, but what? I didn't understand. I pondered, I thought, then I figured it out. The old man looked at Sara, he said: Don't you want to know what they wanted?

Who?

The rats.

Sara didn't say anything.

Salim asked: What did they want?

Rap.

Jonathan took a photo.

The old man said: So I rapped. Rap came out of my mouth. At first, I rapped simple words, because spoken language was new to these gray creatures. I said: Wind, I said: Sky, mountain, branch, gums, I said: Coat, salad, flame, I said: Fireplace, breast, sleep, baby, mouth, hug, grain, house, roof, call, bother, shut, caress, bury, scratch, bite, death, birth, worry, gnaw, treat, live, pregnant, thin, abandoned, born, dead. I listed out all the colors, I listed objects in a kitchen, I listed countries, plants, furniture, basic words, I rapped them, they loved it: Kitchen, road, globe, cup, page, nice, cloth, pencil, etc. I pulled out all the stops. First names, seas, planets, winds, cars, one word called up another, illnesses, continents, drugs, lakes, religions, they loved it, they wiggled their weens until the doors rattled. They loved my lyrics, they loved language, they loved rhythm, have you ever seen rats applaud?

No.

Oh no, my disabled friend? I hope you can see it one day. They jump, they whirl around. The more I rapped, the more they jumped. Joy surfed on their fur. Imagine a sea of rats, 10,000 rats that rise and fall to the rhythm of the lyrics, my lyrics, your lyrics, our human lyrics. A horde of rats. They reveled. I saw the ground cry with love, a crowd of rats rising and falling like a bellows, like a bellows, like a . . . He closed his eyes, and he started to drool. He muttered the sound: Mmmmm. He remained for a few seconds in this strange state. Then he said: Amazing . . . Of course, I did my best, I widened the span of my arpeggios. I became meticulous, like a manicurist painting the nails of a baby. No, the nails of an embryo, that's it, like a manicurist painting the nails of an embryo. During the day, I trained, and, at night, I rapped. To be totally honest, it became my life, the center of my rhythm. I had a splendid and enjoyable goal. Listen to that word carefully: enjoyable. An enjoyable life. The rats waited for me every night the way people wait for Christ, the way people wait for Michael Jackson at a Michael Jackson concert. When I arrived, they cheered for me. Tears circled around their eye sockets. I gave all I had, I invented tales, I told life stories, the lives of people, I rapped them, the lives of people from my childhood, the life of the priest, the life of my stepbrother who was crushed by a tractor, the life of my virgin aunt, the life of my stammering uncle. Sometimes, I told the story of future lives with my gift, I told them what will happen next, when everything is destroyed. I told them about the end.

Jonathan wrote: The father of rap, and he posted the photo of the old man on the network. But the old man said: You're so obnoxious with your machines, with your chins bent toward your hearts, you're ugly. Honestly, I don't understand what you're doing on these steps. Instead of begging, you'd be better off progressing from one point to the next. Select a point and reach it. Then choose another point and so on, like everyone does. Actually, no, that's false. I retract my sentence. I retract it. You can't really move, nobody moves. You can't move because in order to move you have to go from one point to another. Yet, when we're walking in the street, the street is located on the Earth and the Earth moves. It turns around the sun. The sun moves, it turns inside the galaxy. The galaxy moves, it moves in the universe. That means that if I'm walking, if I'm moving in the street, I'm moving in the universe, but am I really moving? Nothing could be more uncertain.

Salim said: You really think so?

Yes, of course, my good fellow, you'll note that everything moves in relation to something else, but what do I move in relation to? We walk in a street on Earth, the Earth turns around the sun, the sun moves in the galaxy, the galaxy moves in the universe, but the universe has no end. Imagine if the universe were completely empty. Just imagine. Imagine a person in the emptiness of the universe. They're floating. Now, give this person a rock. The person throws the rock. Because there's no air, because there are no obstacles, the rock goes straight, it moves farther away. Now, remove the person from the scene. That just leaves the rock. Is the rock moving? Who is the rock moving away from? If the person is gone, who is the rock moving away from in the universe? It's moving away from nothing. Because the universe has no end, since it has no bounds, it's approaching nothing. When you're moving away from nothing and moving toward nothing, you aren't moving. We might be alone in the universe. We think we're moving, but we're not moving. What is the universe moving in relation to? Maybe the universe isn't moving. Maybe we aren't in the process of moving. We are like this rock, but we're a pretentious rock. All right. The old man grabbed the straps of his own overalls and he pulled, he was relying on his own strength, all the strength he had. He said: I'm trying to get up, can't you tell? Maybe you can't tell. You're not seeing this right now? Good grief, help me, I'm old. Maybe you can't tell. Good grief, the sun is roasting your brains, the sun will end up roasting all of our brains!

Jonathan got up and he gave his hands to the old man who put his head against his neck. He sniffed him with his eyes still closed, he said: You smell like a dog, poor boy, you make me sad. You're breaking my heart, all three of you. Wait, I've changed my mind, I'm changing my mind, I'm staying. Put me down. Your smell calmed me.

Jonathan put the man down and said: I think I'm going to vomit.

The old man replied: I knew it, you're thirsty, don't forget, I sense things.

He pulled a bottle out of his jacket, it was blue and cylindrical. He placed it in front of his face, and the bottle distorted him. The old man's eyes tripled. He spoke through the bottle. He said: The word THIRST represents the three stages of thirst. In the word THIRST, first there's the TH, it's sneaky because it sounds soft and pillowy. That's the first stage. Then the word suddenly lengthens, it takes up space in the body with the IR, it stretches throughout the body, it touches every area, it's a long, slow stage. In the end, the word THIRST kills, that's the third stage. The ST hisses like a snake, it sands your body, you're done. Drink now, my good fellow.

The old man held the bottle out to Jonathan. His veins were beating under his face, something opened behind his eyes, he drank and drank.

The old man said: That's enough, you're going to blow a gasket. Poor thing, oh, poor child, poor soul, did you know you look like a rat? I imagine you know already, I imagine people have often told you, you look like a rat or a frog, can I call you frog? Frog. Batrachian. I'm going to call you The Batrachian. It's in your facial features, you can tell the frog is one of our ancestors.

And the old man tenderly ran his hand through Jonathan's hair, and Jonathan pushed him away. The man's face changed, he jumped up, he started yelling: You broke my hand! You broke my hand!

I just moved your arm off me.

And then, you little shit stirrer? And then? You broke my hand. I'm fragile, haven't you noticed? Do I not look fragile? Don't I look fragile? The old man called out to passersby, he yelled: Look at me, do I not look fragile? Ladies and gentlemen, do you find me fragile? The answer is yes, your answer would be yes. You think I'm fragile. Everyone thinks I'm fragile because I'm fragile. I'm fragile and I'm old from my head to my phalanges. And you, The Batrachian, I'm giving you an F, an F out of pure kindness, an F, and I hope a terrible misfortune befalls you, oh yes, a terrible misfortune, you piece of shit, a misfortune longer than the distance separating us from the farthest planet in the biggest universe of misfortunes. I hope you choke on a wooden stake you little spitwad, you decapitated my hand. You know what I wish for a lazy pissant like you? I hope you're imprisoned, banished, dragged, roasted, burned, dismembered, silenced, oh, you're a worthless hole, oh yes, from the beginning, I knew it, you piece of gangrene, you wad of cum, I saw you, you ball of pus, you pile of manure, I knew it, you give people the runs. I had you pegged the moment I laid eyes on you. I always knew there was something criminal in your face, you lazy pissant, such a sad, sick boy, you and your disabled friends. You're a gang of moldy sperm. Moldy sperm. Useless sperm, that's what you are.

Jonathan looked at the sky, and his hands moved. He was whistling the hit song by his mother's singer. He trembled while he whistled and his ears buzzed. Something horrible came over him. He said: Stop. Stop it right now. That's not what happened, that's not what happened, this can't be real, this can't be real, I just moved your arm.

Oh really? Oh really, you little shit stirrer? That's not what happened? That's not what happened according to you? Oh, but that is what happened, oh yes. You ball of sperm. Oh no, it's real. It's busted, it's really busted, look, look at my five fingers. Five fingers. Do you see them? One, two, three, four, five, and me, being a good man, the good man that I am, I gave you something to drink, I gave you my water. Water. My water. Nothing better than that. Nothing better under the sun. Without water, life doesn't exist. Who doesn't know that? Who doesn't know that these days? He shouted to passersby: Is there anything more precious than water, ladies and gentlemen? Did you know that water is necessary for life? That's a yes. You knew that. Because everybody knows that. Everybody. Even idiots, even children, even animals, even plants, everybody. The greatest gift you can give someone is water. Water. Just one drop and life takes shape. And I gave you my water, mine. Yes, I gave it to you like a saint tearing off a piece of his garment for a leper.

Does that sound familiar to you? My pocket water, my special water, and you, oh, you, yes, you, you're giving me cataracts. You gave me a broken arm. You're the source of scabies, chronic illnesses and harelips, scrofula, trichinosis, you busted my hand, my only hand, you fucked up my only hand. I don't give a shit about my other hand, I told you. My other arm, the one you broke a little while ago, I don't give a fuck about it, it's like it doesn't exist. I always ignored it, it's a vulgar heap of mucus.

Sara said the word: Disgusting. She said: You're disgusting.

What did you just say you little snot? Mucus, secretion, reject, loser, feces, piece of crap, are you defending him? You're defending your friend, is that it? Is he your friend? So you're capable of friendship? You little fuckwad. You're defending your brother's friend? You're defending that breaker of old men? The killer of old men, you're defending him? Little piece of crap. Little sludge, little muck. You should know that nothing is disgusting in this despicable world, because purity is born of putrefaction, remember that. Write it on your arm, as your brother would say, because I know your brother and I know his videos. I'm divine, I know everything.

And the man turned toward Jonathan, he said: You cracked my hand and now what do I have left? Poverty, the sky. Yes, the sky. Just a poor man, a poor old fart, look at me, no water, no hand, just the sky. He wagged his fingers in front of his face.

Sara said: You don't have anything at all.

Oh, you, do you want to see my peninsula?

No.

Then shut up.

The old man's eyes went from left to right, they jumped more and more quickly, more and more crazily. He said: Do you want to see my peninsula? Do you want to see my cave?

No!

Do you find me attractive? Do you want to see my peninsula? His voice became smarmy, he said: Do you want to see my alveolus? Do you want to see my cave? You want to see my pyramids, is that it?

Sara said: I don't want to see anything, leave us alone.

Very well. Very well, if that's how it is, very well. That's enough for me, this is too much. He rolled up his sleeve, and he said: Look! Look at this!

A wide, green, bulging boil that was about to explode covered his arm. The scab was soft, transparent. Something bubbled up inside, they saw it. Sara jumped back. The man pulled out a long needle from his jacket. He aimed, he lanced it, he said: I'm emptying it out, I empty it out every day, now's the time, oh, it's the best time of day, my liquid.

The thing dripped onto the man's clothing and he laughed. He didn't have many teeth. He said: I press it. I massage it. I jiggle it. Oh yes. I attack it. I ruin it. As if I were making love with God, yes. Sometimes, a hornet stings it for me, but it dies from the poison. The hornet. The hornet. And he started to drool. He closed his eyes and he muttered: Mmmmm. He remained in that bizarre state for a few seconds, then he opened his eyes. He said: You see, ugliness doesn't exclude grace. And he tore off the huge piece of skin the way you whip away a sheet during a magic trick. Then he threw the horrible thing into the middle of the square.

Jonathan felt the weight of his own face. He grabbed four pills from his damp socks and he swallowed them. The old man laughed. He laughed, he was crazy, sick, everything seemed sick, really, the square, the stairs, the city, the whole Earth. The old man said: I'm getting bored. I'm getting bored now. Look at me, I'm getting bored. I'm bored, I'm sweating from it. I'm sweating from boredom. Look at me.

Sara didn't respond, Salim didn't respond, and neither did Jonathan. The man pointed his old index finger like a piece of wood at the passersby, he said: Look at these people. It's like they don't live in their own clothing. They're absent, look at them. Sometimes, I feel like people are little walking suns and other times I feel like they're nothing. Don't you? He turned to the passersby: You're nothing! You hear me? You're nothing. Look at their bodies, they're woundable. Look closely. They're easily woundable. A piece of iron in the abdomen and they cease to exist. A simple piece of scrap metal. Oh, it breaks my heart. I can't. Go now. Leave, this is too much. I can't stand you anymore. You're bothering me. Go.

Sara said: We were here first.

Oh yes, that's true, you're right. In that case, my old, revolting body will take a walk, you'll see. My infernal machine will graze the earth. Then he looked at Salim and he said: Your mother is a thin woman. She wears black. She's hard, and her face has lost its color. She hides behind her hair, which gets greasy overnight. You'll find her always bent, turned toward a world that doesn't exist. The batrachian who accompanies you will be of no assistance, but you must help him. Your sister will dive into a dark thing. She will see more clearly there. That's it for me, farewell, my good fellows. He leaned on his cane and he got up. He found his balance, he took one step, but then he immediately turned around and waved his cane in the air. He yelled: Goodbye, my children! Goodbye, my good fellows! Then he walked, he walked, he disappeared into the city, but his shadow remained. It widened. It continued on. It crossed the square.

*

Sara typed the word SHADOW on her phone. She watched videos of shadows. She said: A shadow is often behind us, but the shadow should overtake us, it should go first. Every time it stopped, we'd just have to stop. Every time the shadow disappeared, we'd be erased, we wouldn't need to think. When babies discover shadows, they think they're animals. She showed a video of a little girl who saw her shadow for the first time and ran away crying. Salim asked them if they thought you could tear a shadow. Sara thought not. Jonathan didn't respond, and Salim said: You could probably do it in a laboratory if you had huge machines and deep pockets. He wrote the phrase:

I tie up my shadow in the yard

He posted the phrase on the network, and Jonathan liked the phrase. He sent Salim a message asking if they could talk. Salim looked at his phone and he said: I'm right next to you. Jonathan looked Salim in the eyes and they thought about each other for a short while.

Jonathan said: When you stay close to a person long enough, they disappear. He said: When I lived with my mother, she often ended up disappearing. We'd be sitting on the same couch, and I'd watch TV as if I were there without her.

Salim said: Yes. And Sara asked him if he remembered the woman who disappeared in their house. Salim didn't remember. She said: You were too little. Our parents had invited a woman over for dinner, it was one of our mother's colleagues, and she disappeared.

During dinner?

Yes. She came to our house in the evening with flowers, it was a woman in a blouse, she smoked long cigarettes. Every time she blew out smoke, she twisted her mouth to the side. She asked: Where is the bathroom? And our father showed her the door. She got up, she went into the bathroom, she closed the door, and she didn't want to come back out. They knocked, but she didn't want to come back out. They left her there all night. The next day, she didn't come out. The night after that, she didn't come out. The day after that, she didn't come out. She stayed in our bathroom for two months. She talked to us through the door, she said: I need time.

How did she eat?

We slid her crumbs under the door, that's what we did. It was just something we did every morning, like opening the shutters. We crushed the food, we slid it under the door. We showered at Grandma's house. After several weeks, it had become normal, as if nothing had changed. We ended the day, we took our showers at Grandma's house, we came home. In the end, we forgot about our bathroom. We put crumbs under the door as if the house had never had a bathroom, as if everyone in the world slid crumbs under a door. One day, she came out. Then we remembered she existed. Her hands were soft from living in the bathtub, it was like she had waves on her face and folds in her eyes. As if she were floating. She shook our hands, even yours, Salim, she shook your hand, you were just a baby, but she shook your hand, and then she left. I saw her one other time in our yard, she was tearing out our flowers.

Salim didn't remember a yard, he'd forgotten about the dinners, the flowers, and his young parents. He wondered if he'd be able to recognize his mother. He imagined a tall brunette all in black, but he could only see a faceless, pixelated form.

Sara said: I think she hated us, she tore out our flowers, she put them in her mouth, she shredded them.

What was her name?

We called her The Lady.

*

Dream #573

I open a door, I see my mother's ghost.

I say: She's not dead, I don't know who I'm talking to.

I say: Since she's not dead, she can't be a ghost. But I feel like my reasoning is very complicated. I feel like nobody will understand. I say: If she's not dead, she shouldn't be a ghost, I know it's hard, but please try to understand!

I'm talking in my mind and my words merge with deer in a room. Their antlers touch, and it's very beautiful. But my mother is an animal among the animals. She doesn't have any distinctive characteristics. In the dream, I'm afraid, as if I've suddenly understood that there is no difference between things and people. Everything looks enormous, everything looks like a ball.

I forget how to tell people apart from each other, the animals apart from each other, and the people apart from the animals. I've lost that ability. I cry because, to me, the world is the world. I tell my mother: I'll never find you, everyone looks like everyone else.

My mother's ghost laughs, but without a mouth.

Her laugh is a sound in a room.

The ghost's skull is broken.

The ghost is no longer my mother.

It's a neutral ghost.

It says: Hello, do you want to break my skull?

I respond: Your skull is already broken.

It says: I want more pieces.

It gives me a hammer. I take the hammer and I hit its skull. The skull breaks with a sound that doesn't match. It's the sound of footsteps in gravel. The ghost says: This is my punishment because, first, I killed my mother and then a fly. It says: I'm punishing myself because, first, I killed my mother and then a fly, what about you?

I ask: Am I dreaming?

It responds: In black and white.

I look at my hands, they're white and black, the ghost is light gray. It says: Nobody pours water in the sea. Nobody thinks of doing it. That's too bad. Nobody buys bottles of water to pour them into the sea. That's too bad, nobody thinks of doing it. That's too bad, because every time you pour water in the sea, something happens. It says: You can pour blood in the sea, it's like pouring water in the sea. Blood is made from water. People are made from water. If you want something to happen, you should spit water from your mouth.

I see the sea through the window and I go toward the sea. I open my mouth above the sea and water falls from it. I look up, I see the ghost swimming in the distance. It turns around laughing. It yells: You fucking asshole, I'm you.

999 SHATTERED BOWLS

1

Jonathan was removing the dead from his bed with the door closed. He was getting rid of them because of the nightmares, because of the nightmares he had from all the dead, because there are too many dead people. You look at your phone and you see a death. We're always seeing a death. All day and all night, we look at our phones, and they've announced a death. Newspapers and networks just announce deaths all day long and all night long, the ceiling spun. When he couldn't sleep, the ceiling spun, he could feel it, something was crawling toward him. What was it? Somewhere, it was coming. For him, for everyone, it was coming. With a distinct, calm, complete movement, death was coming. He sometimes wished he could pray like Salim, he knew it could work. Salim had said many times: It works, if you concentrate, it works, it works every time. But he couldn't, he didn't know how to pray, did you have to think in a prayer? Did you have to believe in God? Did you have to imagine the god, their face? If you're talking to someone, do you have to imagine them? He didn't imagine anything, but sometimes, he wished that one time, one day, at least once, his hands would come together and his whole body would pray, that it would even pray without him. Just once, one single time, he wished something would exist. Just once, for someone to look at him, someone in the dark, for someone to look at him one time, he whispered: Come on, please, come on.

But the wind whipped the buildings outside. It struck like continual slaps to the face. Claws, ambulance sirens screaming in the streets, but the streets weren't moving, they didn't change.

He imagined the air outside, black, the night surrounding the room, surrounding the apartment, all this black air like a mass surrounding the world. All this air, all this night. Dark, outside. Like a creature chewing. A creature, and small, weak people in the city, outside, or in their homes, in their cars, miniscule, insignificant, or in their beds, or in their sad clothes, people, and then, those images were replaced by other images in his mind. Images replaced images that he didn't understand, shapes, winkings. The images pecked at his skull, like a chick hatching from an egg, pecking, pecking, maybe that was praying, letting his mind wander through images, letting his mind make them, letting his mind think and watching his mind thinking, leaving his mind alone, so he prayed, he prayed, and he kept praying. Where did the dead go? All these dead people. What did they do? They left, they went back in time, in backwards time, against time. They went forward in reverse. On the network, Jonathan looked at children's pages, he looked at their faces, children of eight or nine, children who filmed themselves. They ate kebabs with fries, they dunked their bread in sauces, they bit into hamburgers while filming themselves. They played video games, they commented on their characters' movements, and in eight or nine years, other children would be eight or nine. He moved his lips upward and he contracted his nostrils. He contracted his eyes, he opened them as wide as they would go. He kept his face tense like a mask in order to feel, he whispered: Muscles, muscles.

He wished he had buttons for his own body to regulate it. A button for sleeping, a button for laughing, a button for speaking, a button on his stomach for sobering up.

He swallowed some pills, he tapped some images, he said to himself: I'm praying. He shared images on Salim's page, different butterflies, lizards, he sent a bit of everything, comets, illnesses under a microscope, Russian celebrities.

He took a picture of his room. He sent dark images of his room in the dark. He could send anything, miraculously, every image left. There was no limit, they left easily. They didn't change on the way, because our images don't change. If we save an image, we find it again ten years later and it hasn't moved. A long time ago, images moved, they lost their color. Images were put in books, in frames, they lived in the world like fruits and vegetables. We put them in wallets, in pockets, in drawers, and they changed, the way people do.

In real life, teeth fall out and hair goes white. Faces sag, but people don't change. We can't see people changing from second to second. We look at a person, but they aren't changing. When people look at themselves in the mirror, they don't see themselves changing. They aren't changing. They aren't progressing. This face. It would take years for it to advance. People could spend sixty hours in front of a mirror, they wouldn't see any changes. Everything is so slow. Everything goes so slowly. And hands? Do hands change? No. It takes months. It takes years for a change to appear. We can watch them, but they don't do anything, they do almost nothing. Every day, the same face. Every day, the same face as before. Every day, the same hands as before. Almost nothing happens. It's almost as if nothing happens, as if nothing changes. Jonathan let his mind invent a situation. He said to himself: I'm praying, and his mind invented a situation:

CHANGE COMPLETELY EVERY DAY

If we changed completely every day, we'd wake up with a new body every morning, a new smell. We'd bite into food with new teeth, we'd lick the floor, we'd lick the walls, we'd lick the roads and the cars, because everything would have a new taste. We'd want to discover it, experience the taste of street lamps, screens, the taste of mint or a madeleine, of the countryside, of beets. We'd walk in the streets, we'd walk slowly, because everyone would be a stranger to everyone else. We'd speak, we'd say:

I don't know you.

Me neither.

Did you try the rivers yesterday?

Yes, they tasted like grass.

I know. It's raining. Open your mouth. What's it taste like?

Endives.

It's snowing. Open your mouth. Well?

Oat flakes. Can I taste the back of your neck?

Yes.

Curry. Do you want to lick my back?

Watermelon.

I don't like your face.

That's okay, it'll change tomorrow.

The next day, we'd touch our new hair with our new hands. We'd cast our new eyes on new trees, and each branch and each lock of hair would be new. One day we'd have curly hair, one day straight, and we'd be bald the day after that. Our arms would be new, they'd move differently depending on the weather, backwards or twisted like curves, we'd film our arms, the movements of our arms, we'd film our legs, the videos would be new.

Every day, there would be a new sky above us, new colors, a new climate, cold gray, good hot, twenty hours of lightning, a two-second storm, green sand, dark mist. Sometimes, the sky would open up, we'd be able to see the galaxy. Sometimes, we wouldn't see anything, the sky would open up, but we wouldn't see anything. There would be ten openings that led nowhere. We'd take photos, we'd bite our nails, the next day, our nails would be long, they'd be painted, they'd be hard. We'd wake up next to a brand-new person, we'd say: Show me your face. We'd always be surprised by the faces, we'd measure time with faces. We'd say:

How old are you?

11,465 faces old.

You don't look it.

What about your baby?

365 faces old, it's his birthday.

What's his name?

Thomas.

What about yesterday?

Zaïa.

We'd taste different every day, we'd bite into our own arms every morning to get to know ourselves. At birth, mothers would taste their babies, they'd bite their thighs. There'd be photos of mothers with a piece of flesh in their mouths. That would be the birth photo. On the announcements, people would write: Abdallah, born June 5 at 12:00 PM, flavor: fern; Amida, born May 8 at 4:00 PM, flavor: chamomile; Huguette, born September 14 at 10:00 PM, flavor: tire. We wouldn't be able to choose the flavor of our children, but we'd accept them. We'd be sad sometimes, we'd be worried. A mother might say:

My son, when you were born, you tasted like dill. The next day, you tasted like pears, but the day after that, you tasted like a dead bird, my son. I tasted you and I got scared, I panicked. Your father let the nurses know, the doctors came into the room, they tasted you, my son. Your grandmother and your aunts, your grandfather and your uncles, we all tasted you, my son. Only your skeleton was left. There are dead birds in salads, in sandwiches, in dishes, so we sometimes also taste that way, my son. The doctors told me it was normal, my son. I've eaten dead birds, I've eaten the wings of dead birds and that's what you tasted like, you had that flavor, it was common and it was sad. Your grandfather cried. We perfumed you with vanilla, but, my son, you tasted like vanilla-flavored death.

In the street, we'd taste the passersby, it wouldn't be embarrassing, everyone's skin would be accessible. We'd walk around with a bitten hand, a missing nostril, a piece of eyelid, we'd walk around with split necks. We'd taste our friends' skin, strangers' skin, the skin of tourists, the skin of shopkeepers, but not the skin of poor people. The poor would never be bitten. They'd carry signs: Bite me. Just one bite, please. A little nibble. But who'd want that skin? Who'd want to bite poor people? We'd never see their bones. Bones would be glory, success, diamonds. The opposite of poor people.

Rich people would get bitten from the moment they woke up. They'd only go out as skeletons. Skin would make them laugh, and for costumes they'd grow cheeks. They'd touch their faces, they'd use the word: Sinister.

On the networks, people would post pictures of their bites. They'd write: Thirty-two bites today, a great day at work. Bitten by my boss. So happy, the jury decided to bite me. Every morning, students would bite their teachers and teachers would bite their students. Nurses would bite patients and patients would bite nurses. But we'd never bite the dead, never the dead. That would be punished. A long, hard punishment for dead-people biters. We'd put them in dark cells with other dead-people biters. They'd bite each other, they'd even bite each other's bones, it'd be horrifying, horrifying.

In real life, no one is surprised by their own face. Everyone recognizes themselves. Faces are fixed. When you look at children, they're not in the process of growing. When you look at children's mouths, their foreheads, their lips, they aren't progressing. Nothing is happening, they're not changing. We look at the world, and nothing is happening.

And two parents could say:

How old is your son?

Eight months old.

He still looks the same?

Yes.

I have twins, look at them. Look at their hands. They aren't advancing, they're not changing.

It's true, they're stagnant.

Every time I look at them, I recognize them.

Then Jonathan wondered if dinosaurs had had the same faces every day during the age of the dinosaurs. He typed the word DINOSAUR, he hit search, he read: The probability of drinking a glass of water containing a dinosaur molecule is 100 percent. The water drunk by dinosaurs is the water we drink. He whispered the word: Dinosaur.

He didn't feel like the person saying the word: Dinosaur. He couldn't feel this person's mouth. He couldn't feel it. He'd looked at himself last night in the bathroom at the bar. He'd fallen asleep last night in the bathroom at the bar. In truth, he'd fallen asleep from fear. He fell asleep from fear sometimes. He'd been thinking about things being replaced by things he didn't understand. Outside, the wind is tearing at the wind, it's tearing away layers of wind, the wind is tearing itself apart. Why is the wind tearing itself apart? That's what he'd thought. If the wind is tearing at the wind, which wind tears that wind apart? There are several winds in the wind, a boss wind, servant winds. If there weren't any eyes, there wouldn't be any images. If there weren't any ideas, there wouldn't be any eras. There are scenes because there are people. If there weren't any people, there wouldn't be any heads. Here's what he thought: It's like my head is like a horse's. It's heavy and it hangs like a horse's head. He prayed, finally, he prayed: There's a sick horse on a plain, this is the story of a horse, there's a sick horse on a plain, it's eating a cadaver on a plain, it's eating its mother's cadaver in a dream. A sleeping foal, a sleeping foal wakes up, it runs, it's a dead-foal race. Where are the dead? A door in a house that leads to another house. The door of the first leads to the second, the door of the second leads to the first. Has the world disappeared? I'd open the door, there wouldn't be a door, there wouldn't be a knob. I'd look at my hand, there wouldn't be a hand. Who are the people that draw on bathroom walls? People like my mother, my mother, like my mother, my own mother, my mother drew the singer in chalk on the street, on sidewalks, she told me: You look like him. She said: Look like him. I would fall asleep on her chest, I liked the smell of her breath from her nose, the smell of cigarettes mixed with pastis that came from her nose, I'd fall asleep, and I'd dream of locks of hair and roots, maybe I was praying, I don't know, they flow and my teeth fall into the toilet, a river and I'm drowning. Algae, and I surface, I've rescued something, I'm dirty. I was wearing heavy clothing and pink fleas. I come back to life, I dream, I'm cared for. I'm killed, the doorbell rings, I open the door, I die. I dream that I'm peeing, I'm standing, it won't stop. My mother is looking at me, she's drawing me. Moldy fields of wheat, I roll in sap, the dream of a spoon that holds nothing. I dunk, my mouth is empty, why my mother? I don't even have a tongue anymore, my mother laughs, she says: My big idiot. I'm lying in a burrow, there's a wasp on my forehead, I'm bleeding from my brow, I'm dreaming because I'm dreaming. My mother and her piece of shirt. My clone is talking to me, I don't know why, he's talking to me, we're fighting. A lamb is dying in the bathroom, my thighs, that's it.

*

Meanwhile, Salim was doing something simple and normal: he was looking at his phone. Images. Images of a woman, almost naked, sitting on the ground, she was holding up her baby, it was skinny, and it was upset with her. The baby opened its mouth, but it couldn't cry. The woman showed her breast, it was dry, it was empty, she said: Give us a drop, she was talking to the camera, she said: Give us a drop, please. She spoke in English with an accent, she said: At least. She said: At least one drop. She repeated: At least. She said: You're watching us die on your phones, you are watching us die from your couches. And that's what he was doing, he was watching people die on his phone, sitting on a couch. But that's how it was, there wasn't anything he could do, so he continued.

He touched the screen: in Florida, the principal of an elementary school had recommended that parents buy bulletproof shields for their children's backpacks. He made them himself in his free time. His own children wore shields. He showed three children lined up by height. The three children were cross-eyed. The principal said: I also make them wear a helmet three times per week, they're my children and you never know, that's not just an expression, it's the truth: you never know. He addressed the parents. He said: I recommend fear. A little fear. If your children explode and you say: I wasn't expecting it, nobody warned me, I won't accept that, because I've just warned you.

He touched the screen: a handcuffed surgeon, his white coat covered in blood, held by two police officers. The surgeon was yelling at the cameras: I did it for nothing. He was shouting: I didn't mean anything by it! I did it for free! Do you hear me? For free! A journalist said: This is Maurice Lonzzi. For the past several years, Maurice Lonzzi, head surgeon, has been carving his initials into the organs of his patients. Maurice Lonzzi has carved Ms and Ls into stomachs, pancreases, kidneys, spleens, bladders, intestines, hearts, and brains. Three patients are dead. One patient has lost their sight. One patient has lost the ability to speak. One patient can no longer move. One patient can no longer digest. The surgeon yelled: I did it for fun! Do you hear me? Fun!

Salim touched another image, then another, he lay down and he went through his mother's page, it was empty, his mother didn't post anything. He tried to figure out her password, he wrote his name and birthday, he tried his sister's name and birthday, he wrote his birthday and his sister's name, he tried his name, his sister's name, their birthdays, he wrote their birthdays and their initials. He wrote his mother's name, because he'd read somewhere that people use their own names for passwords. He tried his father's name and his sister's birthday, then he downloaded software that generates possible passwords. He saw thousands of letters and numbers scrolling. He typed a random name into the network and he found a woman who didn't look like his mother. He typed another random name and he found other women who didn't look like his mother. He wrote another random name and he found a brunette traveling in Japan. She posted videos of her trip in Japan. She didn't look like his mother, but it was almost interesting.

He typed the word JAPAN and he looked at maps of Japan. The shape of Japan corresponded with the word JAPAN, as if the map of Japan were saying the word JAPAN. He typed the word FRANCE and France had the shape of France, as if the map of France were pronouncing the word FRANCE. He looked at other maps of other countries, but the word FRANCE didn't correspond to the shape of the United States, to the shape of Senegal, or the shape of Iran. Did his brain create similarities between things, or were the things similar to the names that represented them? He said the word COLD. He said the word POTATO. He said the word SQUARE. He said different words out loud. He said the names of animals. The names of animals were similar to the animals, as if the animals were saying their own names. As if the names made the animals, as if they drew them. The word RHINOCEROS expressed a horn. In the word MARTEN, something raced by. The word FROG had long thighs. In GRASSHOPPER, a sense of delicate legs. The word PUMA seemed to pounce. The word OTTER slid. The word SUN illuminated. He could see the circle of a mane in the word LION. A current went through LIGHTNING, ELECTRIC, ELECTRICITY. He could see specks of light bursting in the word SPARK. As soon as he said them, the words disappeared. And when he wrote them down, the words disappeared, too.

Every time you write a word, it gets erased. Every time you say a word, it gets lost. We try to understand, we look for the definition, but other words define a word. We only use words to explain words. Words are introduced by other words. In the end, you find the breakdown of a definition that breaks down into definitions, like overlapping loops, as if words existed on their own, like independent organisms. Words don't need things to exist. They don't need reality. The word THREE doesn't need three objects to exist. He looked at his hands, and his hands said SALIM. They repeated SALIM. He looked at his shoes and his shoes said SALIM and his last name. The way they were worn out said SALIM and his last name. His pants said SALIM and his last name. He took off his pants, and his underwear said SALIM. His hairs said SALIM. Everything that belonged to him said his name. He took off his underwear and his private parts said SALIM. However, he hadn't chosen this first name. He hadn't given himself this first name, he hadn't given himself his last name. His first and last names were for other people. Other people say our names to point us out in space, they say the name SALIM and Salim appears in space. However, A CHAIR is not a chair in space. A CHAIR is the name that we say to point out an object in space. We recognize our things, we recognize our hands, we recognize our legs, we recognize ourselves thanks to our appearance. We say: It's me, and our body is separated from other bodies. If our body were inside other bodies, we wouldn't be able to recognize it. If our body were similar to other bodies, we'd be alone, but we wouldn't be alone, we'd be everyone else, but we'd be alone, but we wouldn't be alone. He looked at his hands, he wrote:

my hands are the shape of hands

He posted the phrase on the network. He looked up the definition of the word SHAPE, he posted the definition of the word SHAPE:

the contours of an object or creature
according to its parts

The roommate came in, and Salim covered his private parts. The roommate looked at him with suspicion. He asked if he'd heard from Jonathan. Salim replied: He's talking in his room. Then they both went silent to listen to him, but they could only hear the waterdrops falling on the floor and the furniture, and running down the walls.

The roommate took out his phone. He turned up the power on his microphone, and he recorded for a second, he said: This way, I can spy on people. Then he turned on the recording at max volume, and they heard Jonathan repeating words: Bite, New, Change, Bathroom, Dinosaur. The roommate turned toward Salim, he told him to forget about Jonathan and find his mother himself.

Salim said the city seemed to float next to him when he walked. The roommate said: Okay, but I don't like seeing you in my living room. Though, if you were invisible, I don't think you'd bother me. It sucks that people aren't invisible, shit, it sucks. And he hit the wall.

He smiled at Salim and he walked around the room in a circle. He walked as if he didn't want to walk, leave, or stay. Salim asked him what he usually did during the day. The roommate stared at Salim's forehead for a few seconds, and he said: I choose monotonous days, I hate distractions. For me, distractions are demons, like dentists, I hate dentists. I'm not going to tell you why. My daily life is difficult, I voluntarily put myself in tough situations, I force myself to do crappy things. For example, I read all the features of every item in the furniture section on Amazon. I start at the end so that I won't understand the sentences, I like not understanding. If you ever came into my room unexpectedly, I'd kill you, but if you came into my room unexpectedly, you'd also see I'm focused. I focus on things all day long. Often, I'm so focused I piss myself. If you notice I smell like piss, you'll know why. I don't need heat, I have my smell. Concentration provides warmth. I read every word in the catalogue. I pronounce each word and each number in my head and I read slowly. When I finish, I start over, I don't think about anything, that's all I do. Sometimes, I go on a bank website and I read all the terms and special conditions for every type of loan, investment, transfer, insurance, currency, and title. I stand on my tiptoes, I add suffering. I put my arms behind my head, I just remembered that, hey, I'd forgotten, I just remembered. I put my arms behind my back sometimes, I read without my arms, it's funny, I just remembered that. I just keep thinking about it, okay? That's it. I'm off.

Salim still didn't know how to find his mother, he didn't really remember her face, so he typed the word FACE into his phone. The faces were all faces. He typed the word SHAPE and he looked at the universe's shapes, the list of different shapes in the universe. Then he wrote the words JAPAN, FACE, and SHAPE. He found an announcement for a festival of facial expressions in Takayama, Japan. He visited the website. It was a traditional festival in Japan. Every year, the inhabitants of Takayama presented their faces in front of an audience. They showed their faces, they froze them like masks. They competed in 879 subcategories of feelings across ten categories of emotions:

calm
joy
anger
emotional detachment
sadness
surprise
fear
disgust
terror
rage

Every emotion was divided into sub-emotions. On the site, you could find photos of the faces. Zoom in on them. Rotate. Like. In the terror category, six participants competed in six subcategories:

traumatized
frozen in fear

frightened
horrified
panicked
full of terror

Salim compared the face of the frightened man to the face of the horrified man. The two men had large jaws and thick eyebrows. The frightened man seemed surprised and terrified. The horrified man seemed terrified and disgusted. He read their names and discovered they were brothers. He'd had a feeling. Sometimes, two people look like each other and, deep down, you can't say why. You can say: They have the same eyebrows, they have the same jaw, but that misses the main point. You can't state the resemblance. You can't name it. It's not just in one part of a person's face, it's beyond the face, it's in an impression of it. Farther down on the website, the feeling of joy was divided into seventeen subcategories:

cheerful
delighted
content
upbeat
glad
amazed
in great shape
glowing
thrilled
happy
radiant
beaming
pleased
satisfied
invigorated

enthusiastic

revitalized

As he looked at the faces, his own face changed. His face recognized itself in the other faces. The expressions of the Japanese contestants seemed to detach from their faces and land on his own. Salim thought that human expressions were just emotions placed in a circle. If we simplify our faces, they're like emojis. Emojis show an expression's feeling in its purest form, and the purest expressions reveal a face outside of time. They are like patterns emerging from matter. Emojis show our faces outside of time, and pure expressions place us in a lineage of human expression since the beginning of time. If we express joy purely, our faces enter into the lineage of the human expression of joy since the beginning of time.

On the website for the festival of facial expressions in Takayama, people were posing in front of a snowy mountain. They showed their faces by the snow. Salim imagined things in the snow, objects in the snow, computers, phones in the snow. He imagined liquids in the snow, coffee, tomato juice, boiling water, tea, wine, blood in the snow. He imagined inscriptions in the snow, on the snow, alphabets, symbols in the snow. Then butterflies, dead butterflies placed on the snow, he imagined monks, monks in the snow, on the snow, dead monks in the mountain, Japanese monks, monks in the sun, standing on the snow, living monks, monks in black, in winter, in fall, in summer, in spring. Monks and the seasons as they pass on the mountain.

He typed the words JAPAN, SEASONS, and MONKS. He found an Englishwoman's blog, she slept in monasteries in Japan, she was young, fat, and beautiful. She got her picture taken in different monasteries. Every time, she slept, she loved to sleep, she loved monasteries, she loved Japan. She collected photos of herself sleeping in monasteries in Japan in winter, in fall, in summer, in spring. In a video interview she said: I'm a poet.

Salim wrote the words JAPAN, YOUNG, and POET, and he found old pictures of a boy with a calm face. His face was hard from anger and calm, an anger like calm, but a calm like sadness, a distinct face. He was a high school student, his name was Takuboku Ishikawa, he died of tuberculosis in 1912 when he was twenty-six years old.

He wrote the words, POET, TAKUBOKU, and ANGER. He found three lines. He copied them, he pasted them on the network:

I smash one bowl whenever I am angry.
By all rights I should die
When I reach nine hundred and ninety-nine.

Salim liked his own post. He liked this poem. He imagined 999 shattered bowls on the floor, he imagined the shape of each part of each bowl. Every bowl piece became something other than a bowl. The bowl became a sum of little parts that were no longer the bowl. He also felt like the sum of parts that weren't him, like a functioning body, like a body assembled, but alive. He thought about the dead on Earth, the Earth's dead, there are a lot of dead people on Earth. How many dead had there been since the beginning of Earth? He thought of parades of ants on the side of the road and of the word ANT, and all the other words. Words were invented by the dead. All the words that travel through our throats have traveled through the throats of the dead. He would say this in a video, the words that have traveled through the throats of the dead came to them from other dead people. He lay down on the floor without his phone so he could look at nothing. The floor was damp and the drops fell.

*

When a tumor appears in the body, the blood changes course. The blood surrounds it, the tumor conforms, it becomes enveloped, the blood conforms, the whole body conforms, then the body dies quietly. A person is a piece somewhere. In bed, on a chair, in an office, at the mosque, in prison, on a beach. A person transports the piece and the piece is the person. They're a piece of the world. We transport a piece within the world. The piece conforms. One day, the piece dies. When you look at the sea, you can tell each wave is important. If you take out a wave, the sea disappears. You take out a single wave and the sea falls, it ends. There are other waves inside of a wave, thousands of waves, in every million waves, there are millions of tiny invisible waves. The grandmother could hear them. She heard the walls and all the furniture too, the boards in the closets, the folds, the nails, the boxes, a curtain, a lamp, a wardrobe, she knew them all.

We don't know objects well until we're sick, we don't know our rooms. We don't know anything about a house until we're sick in that house. We don't know the sounds. We don't know the times, the distances, the rhythms. We hear almost nothing until we're sick. We don't know the doors, the walls, the windows. We know almost nothing until we're sick, until we're lying down for months, stuck. We don't have time to get to know things. The grandmother heard the sheets, she heard her veins and the beating of her bones. We don't know bones beat because we hear almost nothing. But the grandmother heard everything. Threads had sprouted like lentil shoots between the grandmother and each thing. And each thing washed over her, because the weaker the body, the more the mind expands.

Every person should wear diapers and stop moving. Lie down for two days, ten days, ten years. Have food delivered to their mouths and stop moving. Something happens in your ears when you lie down, when you stop speaking, when you stop moving. In the beginning, sounds live outside you. Later on, they enter you, and distance no longer exists. You measure distance with objects, but you can't measure distance with distance. Objects contain no distance. Objects contain matter. They can't measure distance. Distances can't measure themselves, but sounds make faces in your brain when you watch with your eyes closed. Sometimes, the sounds are hard as if they were armed. They carry little pikes, sick people know this. Every person should lie down for years, stay silent, hear each step, first in the house, then outside, farther away, in the street, the town, the city, the cars, the birds, the dogs, the roads, the circle widens, the continent, the seas, under the seas, under the earth, the underground passages, the cellars, the field mice, the rockets. At night, she could hear children being brought into the world somewhere, the cord being cut. When you're sick for a long time, you hear the world's mosquitos. Tens of millions of mosquitos everywhere in the world. The mosquitos in every country. Billions of mosquitos. You hear the blinking eyes of each mosquito, and their breathing, their mosquito sighs, and the billions of mouth noises made by people chewing in the universe. The wind in empty seashells, the wind in the hills, in ducts, in attics. Ears become a monster, not even the sound of a single leaf falling escapes them. One day, the ear overflows and the present is no longer enough, you hear the past. The gestures of the past, the conversations, the movements of the crowd in a past century, fights in the future, wars, groans, an explosion. The ear is a beast on both sides of your head. One day, even your ears have ears, as if there were new ears growing inside your ears. They're transparent and heavy. Seven ears per ear. Fourteen ears on a head. Hands, legs, arms, become different forms of ears, different sizes, curved, in the shape of a sphere, in the shape of a ray of light.

She could hear the clouds floating over the house. To fall asleep, she listened to the little animals snoring in the forest. And she spoke, the grandmother spoke to herself, she said: Hey, what's that? She said: Hey, I can hear the snow turning into a puddle. I can hear the sound of light touching a roof. Oh, now I can hear marrow and my bones, I can hear the voice of a wounded serpent in the desert. Oh, now I can hear its wound swelling, I can hear its wound speaking. Wait, wait, I can hear the molten steel in a factory in Russia. Oh, now I can hear laughter from the Middle Ages, that's funny, they laughed differently back then. People in the Middle Ages laughed with their eyes. Their mouths were dirty, mouths were like the anuses of today, you didn't show them. When they laughed, they blinked their eyes, they blinked hard and fast, that was laughter, and I can hear it. I can hear animal skins, the way they wrinkle, the skin of a dolphin, the skin of a boar, the skin of a fox's paw. Hey, I can hear cat brains, I can hear cow tongues. Oh, now I can hear the sound of a knife. It's being plunged somewhere. Hey, I can hear smoke. The world is full, I can hear how full the world is. There aren't any empty places. Even in the empty parts, the world is full. I've never heard emptiness, even in the dark, especially in the dark. I can hear shadows, they overlap. Oh, now I can hear transparent things, they overlap. When you add transparent things to other transparent things, they form darkness. She could hear the sound of colors and the sound of waves, because nothing escaped her. She thought: If I could see the world, if I went out into the world, I would hate it. When you put them in a jar, scorpions hate glass. If

I went out into the world, I'd hate flowers, I'd hate lakes. If I could walk, I'd walk like a ghost in the streets and I'd hate the streets. The world would melt my retinas. I'd hate waves, the sea, shame, I'd hate leaves and all the hair on every person, on every cat, on every donkey, on every corpse, the hair that grows on corpses. On the radio, I heard the story of a woman in another country, condemned to thirty years in prison for a miscarriage. She said: I apologize before God, I didn't want to lose it, I'm sorry. It was on a news and comedy show. The hosts announced the news and they laughed. One host imitated the woman, he said: I'm sorry, I'm sorry. And the hosts laughed, then they asked each other to stop laughing, they said: We're joking, but it's serious.

The female nurse and the male nurse changed stations. They closed the curtains. They adjusted the light. They sat on the wood floor, they watched the grandmother. Her eyes were closed, the radio was playing songs.

All her life, the grandmother had heard love songs. When she was younger, she'd worked as a cashier in a supermarket, then as a secretary in an auto shop. Years at a cash register. The radio broadcast love songs. The songs told the same stories. Someone left, someone stayed, someone cried, someone begged, someone disappeared, someone cheated, someone returned, someone hoped. Someone kissed. Someone found someone. Someone and someone had a child. Someone and someone went on vacation in a car one summer. Someone and someone touched each other's skin. Someone and someone didn't understand each other. Someone refused. Someone killed. Someone kissed someone else's forehead, and one morning at the cash register, while scanning a box of cereal, the grandmother felt a shiver in her stomach. Something long, like a decision. It was the truth. The truth entered the grandmother. She understood the voices, she understood forever. The singers sang to counterparts in her, counterparts from her past, old feelings, seconds, things from her childhood, impressions, and her counterparts vibrated. A part of the grandmother entered the song, she walked through long tunnels. The grandmother would scan packs of gum, she greeted customers, she smiled, she chatted, but she understood everything, she understood the songs, the singers, all the feelings. The women singing spoke to all the grandmothers in the grandmother. The baby grandmother. The embryo grandmother. The very young grandmother, and the old grandmother, then the grandmother lying in bed like a log, and the dead grandmother. The singers touched the ridges in her brain.

One singer spoke to what she'd felt at the age of six, one summer evening, in her room. The existence of time. The feeling of existing in time. The singer begged, she made promises, but time said nothing. Time remained silent. The singer cried, her voice lost hope, and the grandmother understood. Time said nothing. The grandmother was typing the barcode for a pair of slippers, but she understood everything, she understood life. She understood all the creatures in the world, the tigers, the flies on windowpanes, she understood, and the song floated around her face. She was turning inward and outward all at once.

Another singer recalled an impression she'd had when she was eight years old while looking out her bedroom window. A man was repairing the sidewalk that day, and she'd become that man. He broke stones, she became the stones. A car drove by, she became the car, she became the driver, she became the rims, the tires, the sound of the car, and the sun, she became the road, the city, she lived for several seconds in this endless expansion. The singer begged, he sang, he said: Oh, no, no, don't leave, darling dear. Sweetheart,

sweetheart, stay longer. Darling. Oh. Oh, no. No. He said: I'm going to die without you, darling dear. No, no. Sweetheart. What will my life be without you, darling dear? My life, dear. My life, no. Darling dear. And the singer described the sky, he described the state of the sky, everything was good, he said: I'm eating bread, the bread is good. Thank you, darling dear. How good everything is, my darling dear, oh, oh. And the grandmother weighed three pears, and she scanned beers, she understood the songs. All the songs were linked. They lived with each other, they lived inside each other. A song couldn't exist on its own, as if all songs knew every other song from every era, every continent, like a group, a head, an organ. The grandmother imagined herself in a cave with ancient humans. They made music with wood, with leaves, with dirt. They sang and the grandmother understood, she didn't have to smile, she didn't have to speak, she didn't even have to move anymore. The music sank into her body without a purpose, without ambition, the music went through her. She made openings for it that didn't bleed, and they flowed, flowed.

Then the female nurse and the male nurse turned off the radio, and the grandmother thought: I can hear objects, but objects also hear me. Even the dead hear me, especially the dead from elsewhere. The dead speak through ghosts, they speak among themselves, they spy on us.

When we burp, ghosts listen to our burps, they hear our noises, they watch us. They know our breathing. They see our saliva, they know. The dead record us. I give them my sounds. Here you go. I give them my sounds, I hear them, they're talking. I know what they're saying to each other. Their voices move in oxygen, in steam, in gas, they say:

Do you know the story of this woman?

Which one?

The woman stuck in the bed.

The grandmother?

Yes. Do you remember the sound of her fetus's blood?

The lost fetus?

Yes.

She was young.

Yes, I was young. I was watching a cooking show. Women were chopping onions with a heavy machine. They put the onions in a slot, they turned the handle, and the onions came out in threads. The women took zucchini, they made three holes: two for the eyes, one for the mouth. They added onion slices to make hair. It made a head. They said: Look, it's a head. We call it the thread head. We just invented it. We're inventing this dish right now. Here is the thread head. And they laughed. It was a simple head, but ugly, a fake head, a fake person, made of zucchini, onion, full of threads. When I saw that image, my fetus slipped, it left my stomach, I felt it. I was in my bed, I lifted my sheets, I saw the blood. A meat smell washed over me. Then I called the doctor and he said: Don't move. Don't touch it with your hands. Don't use your hands. I'm coming.

I looked at my fetus. It was the size of a finger bone. It was red and mauve with black circles on the sides, the eyes hadn't grown in. I put my hands over my mouth and I caressed my fetus with my foot. It was warm, I thought: No one is older than a dead baby. No one is older. I rocked the head with my big toe. I leaned toward it and I kissed it without breathing in. I made a small sound with my lips, like the sound of seeds detaching from apples. I said: Don't worry, you'll come back in a fruit. You'll come back in a pebble. I don't know why I said that. I could see its heart through its body, its transparent skin, its black eyes with a yellow light in the middle. I remember one image: The doctor putting the fetus in a canvas bag, closing it, and taking it away.

I know they buried it. Then I didn't want to crush the earth anymore. I didn't want to make weight anymore. I bought stilettos to crush the smallest amount of earth, and I walked as little as possible. More than anything, I hated babies, all babies. Dirty babies, I thought they were dirty. It's true. Babies are dirty, they're sticky. When they're born, they're covered in ick, that's what I'd say. I would wake up, I'd say: Babies are covered in ick. All babies, all these babies, they're covered in ick. Ick surrounds them. I thought it, I said it: It surrounds babies. And when they're born, you wipe them, and the towel stinks. It stinks of meat. You pull them out of stomachs by their ankles, but they're born formless. Their heads are fat, they're sticky, but stones aren't. Stones aren't like that. Stones are the opposite. Stones don't have blood. They're dry or they're damp, but their color is light. Even when they're dark, they're light, they don't have liquids, they don't have a coccyx, they don't have peach fuzz, they don't have voices, they don't cry and they don't have any ick. Stones don't have ick.

I collected stones in vacant lots. It almost happened by itself. My hands collected stones. I chose the ugliest stones, the loneliest, the lamest stone, the one nobody wanted. I picked it up. I measured it. I sewed it a dress. I had beautiful fabrics, bright colors, I sewed for the stones. I had gilded threads, I paid a lot for all the materials. I picked up the stone, I put it in its dress, I put on its pants, its hat, its blanket. I put it back. I left it in the city. I said: You're fine, there you go. And I did that until my daughter was born.

2

Hello everyone, today we have a new video on the subject of thought, or death. You know what I mean, death, humans, animals, ants, on average, there are 50,000 ants in an ant nest. There are millions of anthills. Ants outnumber humans. There are 1,000 billion ants on Earth and seven billion humans on Earth. There are 993 billion times more ants than humans on Earth. And termites, termites and sardines, sardines outnumber humans on Earth. They roam the planet in groups that contains millions, in the water, in groups of billions. They outnumber women on Earth, they outnumber men on Earth, they outnumber children and babies on Earth. Even though there are billions of us, do you really understand what a billion is? The answer is no, you don't understand what a billion is. Nobody can know what a billion is. You can write it, you can talk about it, you can say the word BILLION. But we can't really know what a billion is. In the description of the video, he wrote: 1 million seconds = 11 days. 1 billion seconds = 31.5 years.

He brought his cup closer to the camera, it was in the shape of a gun. He pulled the trigger and the coffee swirled. He closed his eyes, he drank three sips, he got up. He took two small leaps that made several drops fall from the ceiling. He put his elbows on the table between the plates and the glasses, a drop slid down his hand, he whispered: In your opinion, how many people have died since life began? Think about it. When you think about it, the planet is covered in coffins. If you think about it logically, there's a problem, it's not possible, where are the dead? They should cover the Earth. He showed his phone and he typed: HOW MANY PEOPLE HAVE DIED SINCE THE BEGINNING OF HUMANITY? He hit search. He found 852,857 responses. He opened five articles based on their titles:

1. How Many People Have Lived on Earth?
2. There Are Fourteen Times More Dead People than Living People on Earth
3. How Many Human Beings Have Lived on Our Planet?
4. Are There More Dead People Than Living?
5. How Many Humans Have Lived Since the Beginning of Humanity?

He read: Since the dawn of humanity, 108.2 billion people have been born, ninety-three percent of whom are dead. This means there are fourteen times more dead people on Earth than living. Due to population growth, the living are catching up to the dead. In 2050, there will only be eleven times more dead than living people on Earth. He raised his eyebrows, he opened his mouth, but didn't say anything. He read: For most of humanity's history, life expectancy at birth was probably ten years. He pressed the trigger on his gun mug. He said: Time must have been slow back then. Time was drawn out, years were long. Maybe ten-year-old children had the faces of someone who was one hundred. They were born, then they thought: I'm almost at the end, it's almost over. Before, when children opened their eyes, they saw, that's all. They didn't ask for anything. For birthdays, you didn't do anything. For burials, you didn't bury anyone. Life was too short, there wasn't time. Children saw trees, rocks, they saw dead people, they lived in the world as it was. They stayed ten years, nine years, they stayed eight years. They died from anything. Before, people died from anything, without hesitation, questions didn't exist. People died from a fight or a walk, because they ate too little, because they walked too fast, because they didn't chew, because they bit down too hard. Advancing slowly meant dying. When people covered babies up, they killed them, babies suffocated, but when they didn't cover them up, the babies died of cold. People even died of warmth, appendicitis, all the time, from anything. From a sore throat, herpes, a migraine, an ear infection, a thorn, a sharp point, a speck of dust. Water was dirty, drinking meant dying, but not drinking also meant dying. A scratch, an infected hangnail, bitten nails, meant death. A drop fell against a glass object. He said: People used to live as if dying and living were the same idea.

He read: We think that, at the beginning of the human species' existence, infant mortality was very high. There were around 500 infant deaths per 1,000 births or even higher. Children were without a doubt an economic burden in hunter-gatherer societies. This fact probably drove people to the practice of infanticide. He stopped and he thought about the babies frozen by their mothers. The babies buried in gardens. Sometimes, a baby is found under a tile floor. In human interest stories, they talk about dead babies hidden in closets, in drawers, in forests, but how many babies have never been discovered? The babies that were frozen, cut, overheated, babies diluted in acid. He imagined statues of babies in big cities, in squares. Statues in honor of murdered babies, the statue of a frozen baby on a glass pedestal. Many statues in different parts of the city. Statues of mothers hiding their dead babies. Mothers hunched over, gray, lonely statues. He read: We think that the living population represents 6.5 percent of the human population ever born. He said: We have a higher chance of being dead. Statistically, we're mostly dead. He read: Behind every living man lies thirty ghosts. The journal *FiveThirtyEight* provides a sketch of the average dead person. This person would be young (life expectancy between 3500 and 2000 BCE was thirty-six years), rural (in 1950, only 29 percent of Earth's inhabitants lived in a city), and a man (if we presume that, as is the case today, more males are born than females).

He imagined thirty dead men dressed as farmers, they were thirty-six years old, they were smiling, a piece of straw between their teeth. They settled around him, some were floating, they lay down in the air, horizontally, vertically, they stood, along the walls, in a ball, or on the floor. Their bodies were supple, in need of nothing, the bodies of ghosts.

He said: Maybe the dead are floating above you, above your heads. I think they're aligned, they run into each other, and they make waves in your room. You're their guest, you see what I mean? We have all known someone old who's known someone old, and that old person has known an even older person. We can go back, and we can go back all the way to the first person in the world, to the first human. People are connected by people who are connected by people, from the last born to the first born. There are dead people around us, but they aren't bad, don't be afraid of the dark. When a face is in the dark, that face is gone. The ceiling continued dripping.

He said: The world is possessed. The thoughts of dead people enter our thoughts, people who lived once had thoughts. The thoughts of dead people can't die. A thought can't die. If thoughts died, there would be no object. We wouldn't know how to make fire anymore, we wouldn't know how to count, we wouldn't be able to speak, we'd have to learn everything, every day, from the beginning. There wouldn't be any cars, any machines, any shoes, there wouldn't be any paper. Dead people's thoughts live everywhere. All the objects that surround us contain the thoughts of a dead person. The cup is an ancient idea, the idea of a dead person. Thanks, dead people, houses are dead people ideas, thanks, dead people. Your clothes are dead people ideas. Thanks, dead people. So are sidewalks, cities. The world is possessed. We talk, but our mouths have dead people talking inside them. We talk through the ideas of dead people. With their words, thanks a lot, thanks to all of them. There was a random event and life arrived on this planet, dead people arrived with life, molecules, explosions, paws, mixtures, life arrived, things happen all by themselves, you see. There are a thousand ways to cry, but deep down, there's only one, you have to let your eyes do it. Why do we cry when we cry? We cry to exist. We cry to be someone who cries. We don't cry from sadness, we cry to say: I'm sad. For death, it's the same thing. We don't die from death, we die to be a mortal person. We die to make a dead person. He pulled the trigger, the cup was empty. He said: I'm copying my poem GHOST THOUGHTS down below. Don't forget to like and share, ciao, bye, see you next time.

*

> U in a squat? Did you move? Can you tell us about drugs? You think they're a good thing? Should a person do drugs? Should I do drugs?
>
> The light is ugly at your house. Like an ancient light. Historical light. As if you were in a failed parallel world
>
> Why did you stop posting videos? Where are you? Did you leave your house? What's with the water drops? Who do you think you are? You think it's okay to stop making videos when you have subscribers? You think it's okay to make videos with an ugly background? What's with the drops? Are you in a cave?
>
> Hello, my father killed my mother. My father killed my sister. My father killed my brother. My father killed our dogs. Two dogs. I loved them. Every day, I've wondered: Why didn't my father kill me? Did he think that I wasn't

part of the family? Did he think I deserved to live? I'm living. I'm living with a foster family. I feel like the father of the family doesn't like me. When I eat, I feel like he's looking at my teeth. He doesn't like my mouth. He doesn't like my teeth. He doesn't like my face. It's true, I make noises when I eat, it's true, I know that. He doesn't like me. He doesn't like my mouth noises, but I can't change my mouth. I'm trying to make it a different shape to change the sound, but I can't change the shape and I can't change the sound. When I walk in the hall, I feel like he can't stand the sound of my steps. I'm trying to make a different step sound. I'm trying to control myself, but I can't change the form of my steps. I feel like my steps will always be my steps. I feel like my steps are always going to correspond to me. Why? When I wake up at night, I see the father's face in the dark. When I turn on the light, it's the coat rack. But it was still the father's face. I want to become a locksmith because I love locks. Since I was little, I always looked at locks by putting my eye up to the locks. I've always loved locks. Maybe it's the sound of the key that I love in locks. Maybe it's the key going into the lock's hole. Locks are perfect. If a lock isn't perfect, it's no longer a lock. The middle part of a lock is in the shape of a human. Do you think we can tell if someone's a killer? Do you think there's something special in their appearance or do you think they're just like us physically? Can you do a video about killers? Thank you very much

Can you tell your sister that I love it when she tells memories in her room? Can she tell us about a new memory in her room? Sara, if you ever read this message, I'd like it if you told another memory in your room

Hello friends and dear friends, here's a generous 10,000

dollars for health reasons, Enter your contact info your cred card, no serious inquiries

The animals you're talking about are smaller than humans. Humans have the biggest population of any large animal. Get informed. Why aren't forests covered in dead ants? You think ants don't die? Ants die. So, why aren't forests covered in dead ants? Because flies, or even seagulls, eat their bodies in a few days and there aren't any more bodies? Ignorant. So ignorant! And what's with all the water drops? Are you at a pool or something?

Jesus paid the price so that whoever believes in him doesn't die. He paid the price with his blood so your sins would be forgiven. He paid the price to save you. He took your pain. No one goes to the Holy Father without passing through him. And the Holy Father is God himself. Jesus is the son of God. Believe in him and you will live. God is a God of love. God is the Spirit of love. God is Light. Believe and repent. You will live. I'm spreading this message to everyone. It's the truth. Jesus saved me. I tell people on the internet not to lose hope. Even if the world hates you, God loves you

Can you talk about life after death but from the perspective of dead people? We talk about living people all the time, but what do the dead think?

To the guy who writes the aggressive messages, how's your idiot brother?

My brother is doing very well. He gave me a knife to count your head. How many heads do you have? Do you want me to count your head? Do you want me to cut one off?

Where did you buy the gun mug?

Hi Salim, I'm writing to you because I have problems with my thoughts. I'm gentle. I have a good heart, but I don't leave the house anymore. I don't see anybody. I don't leave my room, I'm worse than you. I don't see my parents any more, I don't even want my cat to enter my room because of my thoughts. If I look at someone, I have bad thoughts. I see myself hitting them. I see the person crying. I see them begging. I see myself with a gun. I force the person to do horrible things and they cry. When I see my family, I imagine I'm robbing them with a revolver. I put the gun to my little brother's temple. I make my family do all sorts of things. I force them to dance naked, I say: IF YOU DON'T, I'LL KILL HIM, I'LL KILL MY LITTLE BROTHER! And my whole family dances naked while crying. Then I tell them to smile. And my whole family dances naked while crying and smiling to funfair music like animals in a circus. I tell them to act like circus animals. I saw a documentary about circus animals. I see my family like they're in a circus. I torture them. I tell them to fight each other. I tell them to insult each other. I'm crazy. I point an imaginary gun. I make them do ugly things. But I'm gentle. I adore my family. I love them. I love my mother, but I kill her in my mind. When I see her, I kill her. I make her do all sorts of things in my thoughts. So, I don't want to see them anymore. I don't see my mother anymore. I love her, but I don't want to see her anymore. I don't want to see my brother anymore. I don't want to see the cat anymore. I don't see anyone anymore and nobody can understand what I'm experiencing in my head. Do you understand?

*

The father left a heart on his son's video, and the father wrote a message to his son: Don't mix water and electricity, or clothing and electricity, or food and electricity, or objects and electricity. Electricity runs through objects and even through dust. Especially dust. Dust doesn't feel pain, it's not afraid of getting hurt. We don't notice dust, but it's busy. Every day of the week, when no one is looking, dust moves toward the light. Dust lands on lightbulbs, which become fragile because of the dust, they crack and explode, they wound our eyes. Every week is the same. It's always the same week. All the hours are the same. It's always the same hour of the day for dust. It doesn't do anything else. Before you wash lightbulbs, you have to cut the current. As a rule. You can die from a lightbulb. One woman died. She died from a lightbulb, from dust. I read about it online. A woman was looking at her hands near a lightbulb. The woman came closer to the light to look at the wrinkles on her hands, but the lightbulb exploded. A shard went into a vein in the woman's wrist. The shard traveled to the woman's brain. It circulated for sixteen years in the woman's brain. The woman became strange. One day, at mealtime, she poured oil into her glass and she drank it, she said: Some people like it hot, but I like it cold. The woman no longer looked her children in the eye. She looked at their arms. She spoke to their arms. She said: New York is in the Vosges. Trees are crimes, life is but a windy dream. I see you in a dimly dream. I see you dimly clear. Row, row dimly clear. I cross my tongue in the dark of my mouth, row, row, boat of deer. She was crazy. She put vegetable peels in dresser drawers. She lay on top of wardrobes and screamed: Call me nobody. Doctors examined her. They diagnosed her with Alzheimer's. She shook, she fell, they diagnosed her with Parkinson's. She started cawing, they said she was senile. After sixteen years, she died. The day of the autopsy, the doctors found the shard of lightbulb in her brain. They diagnosed her with a slow, degenerative deoxygenation of the brain due to the appearance of an unexplained phenomenon provoked by the intrusion of a real object into the organic matter of the occipital lobe. But the father knew lightbulbs, he knew them by heart, he could wash them with his eyes closed. He was thinking about how dangerous they could be for his children. He needed to discuss this with his children. He needed to tell them to cut the current. He needed to remember. He needed to tell them about the danger. He needed to say the word DANGER in an email. He couldn't forget. He made a cross with soap on the kitchen window. He wrote with his finger: DON'T DIE. That was all he asked of them: NOT TO DIE.

If we don't die, someone dies in our place, but either way, someone always ends up dead. The dead preserve the living. Every year, 275,000 pedestrians die in a car accident around the world, once 275,000 people are dead, nobody else can die, you have to wait until next year. You can throw yourself under a car, a bus, you can try, but you won't die. When you wash plates, you have to turn the sponge to the right, you have to use the soft side of the sponge so the plates don't die, but the father had broken many plates from cleaning them, he'd dissolved them. When you wash something for too long, it breaks. If you wash babies for hours, they melt. If you wash the floor for days, it disappears. If you wash your face for months, you erase it. The father loved dishwater. He loved it so much that he had to force himself not to drink it. But sometimes, he drank a few drops. No one dies from drinking dishwater. He said: Nobody has died from drinking this kind of water as far as I know. The father had drunk different waters. He'd drunk liters of it in his life, waters from different cities, from different countries. When he was very young, the father drank pond water. He'd lie down flat on his stomach, he'd drink from puddles. As a child, the child-father ate grasshoppers and roots.

That was back in the countryside, in the desert, things hadn't been going well. There were fights in the family. One day, when the father was an adolescent, his family kicked him out. His brothers hit him, they lifted him up, they threw him over the fence. The adolescent-father wished they'd take him back. He shouted: Take me back, I'll be good. What will I do now? Take me back. Don't leave me, Mama, Papa, my brothers, my brothers. But the oldest brother said: You are no longer part of this family. You can shout as much as you want, but we don't know you. And the other brother yelled: If you come any closer, I'll shoot. The adolescent-father knew he didn't have a gun, but he was afraid of being touched.

So, the adolescent-father walked in the dust and on the roads until he reached the desert. He was ashen, his face stuck in a sort of fright. He had only his shoes and he was so hungry that, some nights, he ate his own hair. He slept on the sand, a rock under his head. At night, the wind tortured his body, he had nothing. The adolescent-father felt his poverty like a toothache, it throbbed in his torso even when he slept. One day, the adolescent-father met a man in the desert. He had a white beard and black eyebrows. His face was covered in sand, nicked by small rocks. He was limping, his shoes were dirty, full of holes, he was grumbling, he was eating fat slices of eggplant dipped in oil he held in his hands. He was there, standing above the adolescent-father. He threw him a bit of eggplant. The adolescent-father stuffed it in his mouth like something you shelter from harm. But more than anything, before this man, the adolescent-father felt crushed by a horrible need, the need to be loved. He felt this horrible need, worse than hunger, thirst, pain, an enormous need, he moaned from it. He would have done anything to make this man love him, smile at him, make some kind of gesture. The adolescent-father would have liked to say something kind so this man would be unable to resist and love him, love him. The adolescent-father removed his shoes and he gave them to the man, who took them. The man said: They're ugly and they aren't my size. And the man left with the shoes under his arm and without a smile. Over the following days, the adolescent-father's feet got torn up. But sometimes, he was sure that the elements were protecting him. He looked at the sun, the sand, the air, he spent hours staring at the air. He left the country after that, but before leaving, the adolescent-father put sand in his eyes to ruin them, to remember the country by. And one day, his children were born, he became a father, he watched his children grow, their mouths, their legs. Sometimes, one of his children would fall asleep with their head in his hand, like a little animal. The father often thought: I, too, was a child once.

When he was a child, the child-father didn't know he was a child, he never thought about it. When he was a child, the father would lie down in the sand, he ran, he danced, he lifted tree trunks. He was strong and magnificent. But one day, his parents left him with his cousin. While his parents and brothers worked, the cousin took care of the child-father. She looked at him expressionlessly, the way you look at a penny on the ground. The real tragedy was that she hit him.

She hit him all day long. She hit him on the head with a hammer. She pulled out his eyelashes. She cut little pieces of his tongue with a needle. She slapped him in the neck and back. She tied his legs and arms together. She covered his face in honey, she left him in the sun, and insects ate at his cheeks. She observed him and she took notes. When the parents came home, they found their son covered in lumps. She said: Look at him. He never stops. He keeps hurting himself. She used the words unstable and disturbed. And when the parents looked at their son, they saw a problem.

The cousin tried heat, cold, odors, deprivation, making him hold his breath, she made him eat jars of mustard and jars of ashes, jars of spices and jars of salt. When the child-father threw up, she made him eat his vomit. When he cried, he had to start over again. He had to dig holes in the desert, his fingers split open. When the hole was dug, the child-father filled it back up. He could dig and refill up to sixty holes in the span of a week, deep holes, several meters deep. She timed him, she hit him with the tip of a belt, with iron, with her worst, and that soothed her heart. The cousin took her clothes off, she sat on the child-father's face, he couldn't do anything, she released her vile odors. She hung him by the feet from the ceiling until his face turned blue. The child-father could feel the veins in his brain. Sometimes, she tied him up, he had to sit, his feet didn't touch the floor, she gathered straw, kindling, and she lit a fire under his heels. If he cried out, she beamed. If he fainted, he woke up naked in the chicken coop. She'd scatter seeds all over his body, the chickens and the roosters would peck his skin, but a little red hen ran around him, screeching. She defended the child-father. She rushed around. She pushed away the other hens. Because the child-father loved the hen, the cousin cut off her head. She forced the child-father to swallow it. Raw. With the feet. With the beak. With the heart. With the eyeballs. With the feathers. The child-father had to stay standing, if he fell, she burned him under his fingernails with a hot pin. She dried his private areas with a hair dryer, and he peeled, he itched, she loved it. She told him to open his mouth. She dried his tongue, he couldn't speak. For days, he could no longer speak. His parents thought: He's retarded.

His parents looked alike. His father looked like his mother. His mother looked like his father. They had the same eyes. The same voice. The same hands. The same expressions. In his thoughts, the child-father saw his parents as one person. One decision. One distance. In the evening, when he went back to his parents, he moved around the house like a wounded tiger. He walked slowly and he closed his eyes. His parents looked at his face, they thought: Retard.

The cousin put electrodes on the child-father's ears. She administered electric shocks. She wondered: At what point does a person go crazy? At what point does the mind stop? At what point does the mind retreat? For the child-father, the fear of pain was worse than pain. The cousin waited a few minutes before torturing him. She watched his fear. When the pain came, it was a relief, a feeling almost of joy for the child-father. The feeling that it didn't hurt that much. It wasn't the most harm she could do. The most harm was death.

She made him drink twenty liters of coffee, so he couldn't sleep anymore. But that wasn't the worst thing. The most horrible thing was that, sometimes, she was sweet to him. When she was tired at the end of the day, she patted him on the head with her fingertips. She caressed his cheek. But there was no cheek under the cousin's hand, there was no child in that cheek, there was no life, she might as well have placed her hand on a vegetable. There was no child-father, and the cousin's hand jolted, like a motor starting. Then the caress became a small slap, then another slap, and she dug her nails into him, then a huge blow, a punch. He wouldn't have minded being dead. She hit him. By hitting him, she made him guilty. She made him strange. And she smoked. She smoked. She chose a place, she stuck in her cigarette. The child-father cried, she laughed sometimes, but often, she had no expression, she didn't have a yielding face.

Every morning, she arrived with liquids to boil, to put on his thighs, his arms, tea, mud, metals to heat, pliers, screwdrivers, knives. Sometimes, she convinced him his final day had come. She said: You die today. And the child-father yelled: Please. She pressed the knife against his throat and she said: It's time. She laughed. She pissed in a bucket, she had the cows and the dog and the sheep piss in the bucket, the child-father had to break records for holding his breath in piss. She timed him. She always had a stopwatch around her neck. She looked like a track coach. She said: You can do better. She didn't take breaks. She dunked his head in gasoline. She asked him to drink it, he drank it. But he wasn't allowed to die. He wasn't allowed to drink too much gasoline. Not too much bleach. Not too much detergent. Not too much acid. Being dead was forbidden.

One day, after tying the child-father to her bed, the cousin pulled a small feather out of the pillow. She tickled the bottom of the father's feet with it all day without saying a word. That day, the father lost the biggest piece of reality. He hallucinated. Then the cousin's cheeks turned pink and her eyes rolled back into her head. She said: Thanks.

Other times, the cousin put music on headphones, very loudly, the same song, 200,000 million times. The worst songs. The shortest. On loop. A slogan. She chose music from an advertisement:

> Rice tonight would be nice some rice my love some rice.
> Rice tonight would be nice some rice my love some rice.
> Rice tonight would be nice some rice my love some rice.

All day long.

> Rice tonight would be nice some rice my love some rice.
> Rice tonight would be nice some rice my love some rice.

The child-father clenched his jaw and unclenched it.

> Rice tonight would be nice some rice my love some rice.
> Rice tonight would be nice some rice my love some rice.
> Rice tonight would be nice some rice my love some rice.

The child-father could feel tears coming out of his ears, but the tears came and they went.

Rice tonight would be nice some rice my love some rice.
Rice tonight would be nice some rice my love some rice.
Rice tonight would be nice some rice my love some rice.
Rice tonight would be nice some rice my love some rice.

At night, the child-father heard the song in his head. He heard it in the shower. He heard it at mealtime, on loop. Sometimes he said it out loud, he repeated: Rice tonight would be nice some rice my love some rice. His parents looked at him. They thought: He's slow.

When you're a child, you don't know things have an end. You can't know. You can't leave. You can't turn your back. Children go along with anything. You hit a child and the child goes along with it. The child-father no longer moved. He knew she would hit him. He didn't exist, she just hit him. She could have hit another child. Any child. However, when she hit him, the child-father existed at the highest level, the greatest level of existence, he multiplied. He became life the way you do in accidents. Accidents free your thoughts. Your heart rises above your head. That's why everyone loves stories about catastrophes. Everyone loves stories about sicknesses and kidnappings, killers, stories about cellars, earthquakes, airplane accidents. Everyone listens to the stories of calamities, epidemics, tragedies, even animals do. If they could, animals would watch news stories about their species. They would listen to a story about an animal killing an animal, chopping it up or shutting it away, holding it prisoner or robbing it. One day, the cousin died. Young. She was burned alive. At home. Because of a candle.

The father said to his children: You shouldn't leave a candle lit. Salim, if you light any candles, you have to keep an eye on them.

Got it? If you light a candle, you need to stay close to the candle. You need to watch it. Your eyes should never leave the candle, Sara. If your eyes leave the candle, that's a mistake. There are a lot of mistakes in the world, and mistakes lead to death.

The father looked up. The neighbor was watching him through her binoculars. She was gesturing. She was pointing at something. The entrance to the house. The father walked to the door, he opened it. He found a blue flower with mold on its petals. He went back to the kitchen and he placed the flower, gently, into the trash.

*

Do dead people have erections? Someone dead for an hour? Someone dead for a day? Someone dead for a minute? Someone freshly dead? If a dead person has just died, can you make them ejaculate? She thought about it and then she stopped thinking about it, then she imagined the size of her coffin. Sara imagined it was black, no, she imagined it was red, then she thought about people who are very tall or very fat. Are coffins for people who are very tall or very fat more expensive? At what weight does the price go up? At what width? What size? How many euros per centimeter? The world is paranormal. Life isn't natural. Life is in nature, but life isn't nature. You don't find life in nature. If you look for life in nature, you find nature. You never find life. You find a rock, but you don't find life. You can't say: Look, here's life. You can't point at the planet and say: That's life, that's it. We don't have pieces of life. We can't point at the universe and say: That's life, that's it. We can't point at life, point at a baby and say: That's life. We don't know where life is located. We can perceive it deep in a person's eyes, in their pupils, but you can't say: This is life, by pointing at a living person, pointing at their pupils. It'd be easier to see life outside of life. Sara thought: I'm experiencing life at the same time as other people in the world. People in the world are detailed. Everyone goes through life with their millions of details. There's meaning in people's bodies. On a person's back, on their neck, on their hands, everything is expressed on people. A shoulder is expressive. The back of the head is expressive. There are expressions in hair, in each lock. Every part of the body on every person expresses something. It's too much.

Every time someone came up to talk to her, she thought they were too close. She saw people according to their details, because there is always a detail that surpasses the person. There's always an enlarged pore, a hair, or excretions, tears, odors, fat, zits, lumps, an eye that sparkles.

The eye of an older person, for example. That eye is so old. That eye seems so sticky. Your eye is so sticky. It's hard to look at it. Did you just put oil in your eye? Are you going to die in a second? Everything is so close, it's sickening.

Why is reality so close? Why are people so close? Why does reality always stay too close by? Why can't it move farther away? Can't we put it aside for a few seconds? Can we get some room to breathe?

She wished she could change their faces with her phone, change the faces of passersby with software. To make them blurry, farther away, less real.

Other people are other people, it's weird. People exist. Their movements exist, they move around and they breathe. There's nothing stranger than that. You look at a head, you look at the heads of other people, and it's so weird. Then you look at your own head, but it's even weirder, it's weird up close, it's weird and personal. It's weird from the inside. We have heads. They belong to us. They're our heads. But there's nothing weirder than that.

You look at your head in a mirror. You don't know what's inside. It's not something you can understand. You move your eyes, but you don't know how they work, it's not something you can understand. Even if you study science, you can't understand how a person is made.

There's this hole full of teeth in our faces, we fill it every day with liquid things and solid things, but we don't understand why. When you think about it, it's just weird, everything we are, there's nothing weirder than us. We feel pain, we walk, and we breathe. We take in air, it enters us, then we spit it back out. We talk, we talk, and you can't imagine anything weirder, because there isn't anything weirder.

Nothing is weirder than a person in the world, there's no equivalent. People are weirder than everything else. There's nothing weirder than going to sleep and waking up every night and every day. Nothing is weirder than growing, being born tiny, measuring a few centimeters and stretching out, becoming long, becoming taller than children.

There's nothing weirder than forgetting. Seeing a thing and forgetting it. Living through a scene and forgetting it. Forgetting parts of your own life. Forgetting your birth, your own birth, a part of your life, forgetting years. Living through several years, forgetting those years, there's nothing weirder. Is there something weirder? There's nothing weirder than being 100 percent sure of ending up dust. Looking at dust and thinking: I'm going to become that dust. We act as if everything were logical, but there's nothing less normal. We say: I'm here, I'm alive, as if it were simple, but when you think about it, there's nothing weirder than having skin that goes soft. There's nothing weirder than having hair that goes white and falls out. Living for years by calculating time according to the light of a star on fire that shines on us, isn't that weird? There's nothing weirder than this system, than this life, this day-to-day, these habits, there's nothing weirder. And animals? All these animals. All these creatures that move around us and near us. All these creatures with different shapes, different bodies, but they all have a face, there's nothing weirder or more complicated or more beautiful.

There's nothing stranger than coming from other people, being born from each other, being born from another person's body. Living in someone else's stomach, being conceived by other people, nothing is stranger, and nothing is more normal. It's normal, because it's all we have. It's our life, it's normal, we can't say: No.

No one can say: No, I'm not okay with this. No one says: I'm not okay with breathing. I don't want to digest things anymore. Trees don't make sense. There's something wrong with the sky. I don't understand the sun, storms shouldn't be possible, they're too weird. Why am I not other people? Why am I just one person? We would have accepted anything, we'd have accepted floating, for example. We'd have accepted light not existing. We'd have accepted any face, any head, we'd have accepted any appearance, anything could have seemed normal to us.

We understand things around us with the knowledge inside us. We look at the sky, and we remember the sky, we look at the ground, and we remember the ground. We look at a person, and we remember people. There are organs inside passersby in the streets. The passersby produce substances with their organs. If people didn't have bodies, they'd feel calm. If there were no bodies, everyone's parts would be close together. Their eyes in their feet. Their heads in their tongues, in their hair, on their backs, like a circle, a ball. People would be balls.

And Ball, Sara, thought, was the name of her cat when she was eight years old. When he shed, she collected his fur, she put it in a jar she filled with warm water, and the water became special, thick, soft, gray. At night, to fall asleep, Sara touched the fur in the water. She put her hand in the jar and her hand fell asleep.

At the age of eight, Sara decided to burn down the Earth. She started with a field near the town, but then she wondered why the world hadn't burned down before. Firefighters didn't exist in prehistoric times, in the Middle Ages, during the Renaissance. Fires could have grown, they could have spread, they were free, but the fires stopped. They gave up.

She burned branches in the field and newspapers under a bridge at the edge of the town, the fire rose, but it also died. She burned water. She put water in flasks and the waters burned in the fire, they burned because water burns. We don't know why fire stops, there's no explanation. Oceans could burn. Fire burns puddles, it could burn the sea. But fire gives up. It doesn't have any confidence. It can't keep moving, but people keep moving and they have no shame. People go inside somewhere and, wherever they go, they have no shame. People pick a place to be as if it were their place. A person gets on a train and they look for their place. That's all they look for, that's all they want, that's their only thought. That way of lifting their nose, lifting their eyes, partially opening their mouth, the person murmurs their number, it's their number, their place, their seat, they repeat it: Seat sixty-eight, nose up: Seat sixty-eight, I've got seat sixty-eight, as if that seat belonged to them, as if life were just waiting for them. And their body says: It's me. It's mine. Here's my train car. This is my seat. This is my car. I'm in this car. This is my train. I'm taking this train. I'm going somewhere. I'm here.

When you look at a person, you can hear them saying: I'm here. They don't even have to open their mouth. Humans walk on the ground, and the ground belongs to them. Someone enters a room and it's as if they were saying: This room is mine. A man appears in the street and it's as if he were saying: I'm here. Everything is mine. I'm existing right now. Someone goes into the sea and pushes the sea aside. They push the water, they go in, they go into the sea. The sea is their place.

Because she couldn't look at people, Sara looked at pieces of people. People weren't finished. They didn't have enough time to have a finished face, not enough time to learn to speak, not enough time to learn to move, they were real, and so they were poorly made. Wherever you go, there are people, even in small cities, you only run into people, even in forests, in the mountains, you always end up running into someone. There are always humans who are always people, who are always too close and too real.

But there were gestures Sara wished she could save in her phone to remember people by. A gesture from her father, a gesture from her brother, her grandmother's last gesture before becoming paralyzed. Do people who are paralyzed remember their last gesture? Before becoming paralyzed, I was brushing my teeth. Before becoming paralyzed, I was waving to a friend. This is my last gesture: I was pointing at the sky. Before becoming paralyzed, I was turning the steering wheel.

People say mummies don't have any gestures left, but one day, in a catacomb, when she was visiting the city's underground, Sara saw the mummy of a duchess. Everything was dark in the crypt, the attendant had said: No touching. Sara went up to the mummy, she heard wind in the mummy's throat, she saw the chest go up and down. She said: I think she's alive. And the attendant said: No. She's been dead for 1,200 years.

There are things we see that don't exist.

Later on, one night in high school, everyone was sitting on

chairs against the walls in a garage where there was music playing. No one was speaking. Pink and blue lights swept across their faces. No one was saying anything. Everyone was taking photos of their own faces in the lights. Everyone was posting those pictures on the networks. Everyone was liking everyone else's pictures on the network. Everyone was leaving hearts and comments. Everyone was drinking, everyone was drunk, but no one was moving, no one was speaking. Videos played on the phones. And there was this one girl who always posed as if she were in a profile picture, every moment of her life, she stuck her lips out, she opened her eyes wide. It had become natural for her. She looked like a profile picture. One day, her parents punished her because she'd stopped speaking, she was acting like a picture. When her parents took her phone, the girl's hands continued to gesture in the air, as if she were scrolling in the air, her hands moved, her eyes stared at nothing, like the father in the kitchen sometimes. Sara would go into the kitchen and she'd see her father looking at nothing, his eyes straight ahead.

*

GHOST THOUGHTS

hi
soon I'll be among ghosts
oh
you walk
and
your feet don't agree with you
you should try to deform life
with a hammer
try to caress people's eyelashes

with a screwdriver
yeah

you can deform
the ears of god
with a screwdriver

oh
I see
a chair in the air and I sit on it

I'll pick up an animal
to show it pity

in my brain
a little ball tells the truth

give ice to your fridge
pour orange juice on your oranges
find another eye between your eyes

use a screwdriver
to uplift your wound

THE SHINING HILL

1

The female nurse says the word: Night. The male nurse bends over, they look at the sky. The female nurse speaks. The male nurse responds. They say sentences relating to the grandmother. Quietly. They say she's dying. She's heading for the fabric of the Earth. They examine drops of blood through a tube. The male nurse says: Rotten blood is the color of kings. The color of portraits of kings. Of a past age, red sheets, and heavy fabrics. Canvas tapestries. Pink gloves and black puddles. Red holes on the right side. Dissections of cadavers in an amphitheater. Bloodletting nobles and jus de boeuf. Horrible things are often beautiful. Horrifying things. The color of rotten blood. The explosion of a bomb. A tsunami that drowns a city. Bodies reduced to ash. A volcanic eruption. A pile-up on the highway. An avalanche. An apartment building collapsing. A cyclone. A storm. Landslides. Illnesses under a microscope. Whirlpools. Floating clothing. A bad sign. Frozen bodies. Ultrasounds of malformed fetuses. The female nurse taps the glass tube and the blood vibrates. She says: Blood is only one liquid among many liquids. Not so long ago, peace agreements were sealed by rubbing your mouth with blood from an animal or human. Animals and humans don't share the same blood. Some animals survive without eating, without drinking, and without sleeping. She says: Some animals can remain motionless for months or years without dying from hunger or thirst. She talks about cockroaches, certain frogs, the kangaroo rat, and the Himalayan jumping spider. She compares herself to these animals, she says: I'm comparing myself to them right now. I'm comparing myself. I feel the hunger, the fatigue, and the thirst almost every hour. She giggles behind her hand. She says: I feel these needs all the time. She laughs as if someone were tickling her. She says: I have these needs. And her laughter stops. The male nurse says: People who are sick and people who aren't sick can't understand each other. If people who aren't sick understood sick people, they would die. If sick people had the vitality of people who aren't sick, their sickness would spread throughout their bodies in the span of a second. The female nurse sits on the bed. She takes the grandmother's hand. The male nurse spreads cream on the grandmother's cheeks and all over the rest of her face. She puckers her lips. The male nurse says: This does you good. This does us good. This is good for everyone in this room and maybe outside of it. When you feel good in a room, maybe you're sending that good out into the world. I don't know. We're doing good.

The female nurse combs the grandmother's hair. She puts oil on the ends and they shine, she doesn't even have any white hairs. The male nurse presses a switch and the bed lowers. He takes out the grandmother's dentures and her face caves in. The male nurse says: False teeth don't imitate real teeth. False teeth imitate false teeth from the past throughout the history of false teeth. False teeth carry on the history of false teeth since their invention. Everything made imitates that which has been made before. All objects carry on the history of the object's construction. He says: I'd like to remove my brain the way you remove dentures. I'd like to soak it. I'd like to take out my brain before I go to sleep. I'd like to leave it to soak in a glass of clear water. The female nurse kisses the grandmother's right eyebrow. She says the word: Brow. The male nurse says: The words brow and brain are similar, but different. The female nurse nods, but she's stopped listening. They look at each other and they wait. They start talking again. The female nurse loses an eyelash. The male nurse catches it. They say that baby skin regenerates. They say: To grow, babies have to shed bits of their skin. They lose pieces of themselves. That's the only way to have a shape. The grandmother blinks twice. The male nurse leans his head against the grandmother's cheek. The female nurse leans her head against the other cheek. The male nurse reaches out his arm, he presses the side of his phone. He shows the photo. They say: We're good. They post the photo on the network.

*

Everything seemed to be waiting for something. Jonathan said: Your brother is searching random names on the internet. He's saying your grandmother is molding. He's researching mold and blood. He's contacted a mold specialist. Your brother writes him long messages, but the mold specialist responds: K, Ok, Yes. I feel like your brother doesn't want to talk to me anymore.

Sara lies down on the steps. They fall silent. Two dogs appear. They run toward each other. They run into each other. They form a moving ball. They disappear.

Jonathan says: I watched a documentary about people in Japan who don't want to leave their houses, hikikomoris. I noticed their skin turns green, some of them are white, but others turn green. In the documentary, a guy was wearing a red sweater, and I don't know how to explain it, but the sweater was green. Others are transparent, it's like their bodies are being erased. I saw a wall through a guy in the documentary. When he talked, his bedroom wall appeared behind his face. He hadn't left the house for thirteen years. His father said: My son has disappeared. He's speaking to you from the world of the disappeared.

Jonathan says: If you put the AC and heat on at the same time, will it get hot or cold? What do you think? Sara doesn't respond.

Her eyes reflect the screen. He says: Just imagine the man who was on the brink of inventing the word brink. He couldn't even say he was on the brink of inventing the word brink. Sara doesn't respond. Jonathan puts three pills in his mouth. He looks at his phone, he looks up, he looks at the square, he looks at Sara, he moves his legs. He says: Did you know there's a type of tree that leans toward New Caledonia? You can plant one anywhere, it always leans toward New Caledonia.

Sara stays silent. Jonathan speaks. He says: Sometimes, when I see the sky, it makes me want to kill a random person. They fall silent. A woman comes and sits by them. She's wearing an apron that's too short and her knees, swollen with arthritis, look like the heads of two children. She pulls out an apple, some thread, and a needle. Sara says: She sews fruit every morning.

The woman puts her glasses on. She ties a white thread around her finger. She pulls the needle and sticks it in the apple. Jonathan films it. He asks: Why are you sewing fruit? The old woman doesn't respond. He asks the question more loudly. The old woman doesn't respond. He walks up to her, he yells the question in her ear. The woman lifts her needle, she pokes Jonathan's hand. He bleeds a drop. He films it. The old woman has black eyes. She says: Why do bees make honey? She turns around. You can see her elbows moving.

*

The grandmother's body is here, but you could put it on a boat and the wind would carry it away. You could put it on a stone, in quicksand, she would disappear or sink. Does that change anything? If dust fell on this grandmother, that dust would remain. You could wrap her in clothing or wrap her in branches, she wouldn't say anything because she can't say anything. You could throw her in a river or in a parking lot. Would that change anything? You could leave her alone at home, leave the house forever and leave the grandmother behind. The nurses could stop coming, the father could disappear, the children could leave, the grandmother could stay alone, a tube in her mouth, soup in her stomach, everything would enter and exit in a natural rhythm. No one would change her bedding. It would rot like everything else, to the rhythm of nature, to the rhythm of the Earth, the animals, the stones.

Yesterday, the pain left. It crawled around the room. It kneeled. It was quiet. Its shape turned against its skin. It turned onto itself like a spiral. It was looking for pain, because pain loves pain.

We often think one pain cancels out another pain. We often think a big pain cancels out a small pain. We bite our arms to lessen our leg pain. But pain swallows pain. A big pain swallows little pains. Little pains don't disappear, they participate. I told the pain: You, you just look like a spider with two legs.

Pain makes fast and slow movements inside a person. I could see it in the shadows, I felt sorry for it. I said: I know you. Its eyes were light, maybe it didn't have eyes at all, but it looked at me. The pain didn't stop shaking. When pain attaches itself to someone, it surrounds them. I said: You are the loneliest thing in the world. I wished I could throw it a coin, give it a euro, but pain doesn't understand anything. It doesn't understand facial expressions. I said: Are you hungry? I would have given it a coin so it could rest or eat, but pain only settles inside of people.

The person suffering thinks about pain, but pain only thinks about itself. It always reminisces about pain. It's obsessed. Pain is empty. When it settles in, pain detaches the person from the person. When it comes close, it wounds. It has no friends, it has no family. But it's pain that gives things their shape. Plants bow with pain. Pain makes the world. Inside a uterus, faces are formed from pain. When you try to pull an arm, when you try to pull out a limb, pain appears. When you try to stick your tongue all the way outside your body, pain prevents you. It knows the measurements. The pain was long, it hid its face. I said: I'm not going to insult you, I feel sorry for you. Doctors look for pain's starting point, but pain is a wheel and its beginning is everywhere. Pain is serious. I said: You always act the same way, whether it's with a child or an old woman. You're always yourself. But you don't have anything that's only for you. You don't have anyone. Suffering doesn't belong to the people suffering, suffering belongs to suffering. And my pain sighed. My pain made a noise like a scratching insect. Its eyes moved. And my pain disappeared.

2

Little creatures live on our faces. Because they're so tiny, we can't see them. Every day, tragedies take place on our faces, wars take place, catastrophes. Creatures murder each other on our faces, they betray each other, they beg. Creatures unite in a circle around a nose, they execute another creature. We don't know what's going on. Creatures have trials on our faces, they sentence each other, they kill each other. When they've lost all hope, these creatures jump from our faces, they commit suicide. Sometimes, it's a normal day on whoever's face. The creatures go to work, they walk, they cook, they take care of their children. They have lives, histories, but we don't feel it, we don't feel anything on our faces. We don't know what's going on. We don't understand the creatures that live on our lives, we don't know them. We don't talk to germs, to mites. We don't know what they think. We don't feel them living. Jonathan could feel something like a film of blood over his eyes. When you close your eyes, you think you're seeing nothing or night, but you're seeing yourself. We close our eyes, we cover them with a film of blood, a film of skin, a muscle. That's our skin, that's our blood, our eyelids. We don't close our eyes, we cover them with a part of ourselves. Jonathan had woken up because a dog placed its paws on his eyelids. The dog had lain down on Jonathan in the park and it had warmed his stomach.

When he opened his eyes, the dog got up. Jonathan whistled. He threw grass at the dog, but the dog had disappeared. Jonathan threw grass toward the sky, but the grass fell back on his face. He didn't feel it. He had eyes and a mouth, but he didn't have a face. He had eyelids and eyebrows, but not a face. The light in the sky shined on the grass, it surrounded the trees and the flowers, it penetrated the earth and flies went by, their wings shining in the air. Jonathan put his hand in his pocket, his phone was gone. He couldn't look at his phone anymore, he couldn't write to Salim, he couldn't write to anyone, because God doesn't exist. God takes phones, he gets revenge by making them disappear. He punishes people because they don't let him exist. God collects phones. He shouts on the phones, he says: And why wouldn't I exist? Explain it to me, why wouldn't I exist? God keeps phones lost at parties, on trips, or in the street. God's the one who loses them. God is surrounded by phones in a black room. All the screens light up his divine face. God has long fingers, he touches the screens. The light bathes his person, it's as if he exists in the contours of the light. He doesn't respond to messages. On the phones, he puts things in order, he erases old pictures, old photos, he erases the past, he erases videos. God makes nothingness.

They'd pulled him by his jacket and his jacket was gone. Jonathan had left his jacket behind, but he wished he'd left himself. He didn't have a jacket and he didn't have a phone, but he had the smell of strawberry. He'd doused himself in strawberry syrup. He'd dashed behind the bar after a bottle, and he'd dumped it over his own head, over his own hair, on his own pants. He'd covered himself in strawberry syrup. They'd kicked him out. They'd treated him like a drunkard and a druggie, he was sticky. He remembered the daylight when he'd left the bar. He walked in the streets and the streets sped up. The sky slowed down. Because the streets were empty, he could tell they were beautiful. But he didn't know his own name. It didn't last long. He thought: What's my name? and he didn't know the answer.

Then he might have fallen asleep against a chain-link fence. Maybe in the park. Maybe with the dog. Maybe when we mix up our intentions, they cancel out. He was taking a piss. He was taking a piss against a tree. The cold reminded him of his childhood when he ran in the forest while his mother slept. The Earth was so big, so long, and so little liquid left his body, so little piss, so little height, so little self for an Earth, so long, huge, you can't stretch yourself that wide. Even if you spread out your body, it wouldn't cover the Earth. If we crushed our bodies with a rolling pin, they would only make a little rug. If we dumped all our blood in the sea, it wouldn't change color. Jonathan wished he could flood the Earth and water the plants so they would unfold, rise up from his liquid.

He looked up and saw a lasso in the sky. A lasso in the sky in space. He felt his heart behind his tongue. The lasso turned in the sky, it was hitting the sky, as if the sky were getting beaten, as if it were being punished.

A hand touched his shoulder. It was a man with a scar on his forehead, he said: I don't like the sound of piss. You've been pissing for five minutes, asshole. Jonathan zipped his fly, then he said: Did you see? And he pointed at the sky.

What?

The lasso in the sky, did you see it?

The man's eyelids hung, he said: Can't you see I'm drinking? That's all I do. Do you want to wake up in a coma with your eyes taped shut? That's my life. My mouth feels like I just went to the dentist. My mouth is always like that. The veins on the man's forehead bulged. He pressed his two hands against the tree. They became white, red, he pulled off a piece of bark. He put it in his mouth and he chewed. Jonathan felt liquids coming out of his ears, like liters of liquids that weren't liquid but pieces of liquid thoughts. Wordless thoughts that ran from his ears. The man said: Did you know that alcoholics can burn? He was opening and closing his mouth, his face like a beast. He said: Spontaneous combustion, pal, didn't you know? Now you won't be able to say you didn't know. If someone asks, you can say: I knew it. And thanks to who? Jonathan rubbed his hand over the upper part of his face and he said: Did you see the lasso in the sky?

What did you say?

In the sky, there, did you see it?

Listen carefully, there are people you can't talk to because their brains are like pudding. You know what I mean? A vanilla pudding. Have you seen those? Vanilla or caramel, asshole, do you need me to draw you a picture? Cafeteria pudding. From what I've seen, you're just a guy who pisses too long and too hard. And that bothers me, you bother me. Drunks speak for themselves. I get to speak, and you get the hell out of here.

*

The water went down his esophagus. He was trying to go down with it, but he couldn't follow. The water went into his body, but he didn't know the way it went. It sank down, but he couldn't disappear with it. He couldn't go down. He wished the Earth's crust would open so he could land in a texture close to velvet at the bottom of a hole with no edges, at the heart of the world, in a black substance capable of snuffing anything out, of absorbing people. He wished he could write a message to Salim, but he didn't have a phone. He said: Where is he? The roommate responded: In your room. He's sleeping. He's growing. You sleep when you're growing. At his age, I was growing, it made me sleep. I slept a lot. One time, I slept for several days, my parents prayed, they were worried. They kneeled next to my bed. When I opened my eyes, my father would wink at me. Every time I opened my eyes, I looked at my father, he winked at me.

Jonathan asked: Did he find his mother?

The roommate responded: I don't know, but we should measure him.

The drops fell. The ceiling curved. Jonathan's pills were becoming diluted in a bowl on the table. They formed a sort of white and gray paste. Jonathan said: We should repair this leak.

It's stuck.

What do you mean?

The roommate said: It's settled in.

We should call a plumber.

I just told you, it's settled in. I called the plumber, he came, believe it or not. He sorted everything out, the dripping stopped. I gave him five stars. But an hour later, the water started falling, huge drops, worse than before. I called him again, he came back. He was a serious guy, we talked a lot. He has problems with his son who's disabled. He showed me photos of his son who's disabled. The roommate mimed something like hooks with his hands in front of his face. He let his head fall to the right while twisting his mouth and he burst out laughing. He folded his hands in front of his face, he stuck out his tongue to the side, he made sounds like a dog panting. He said: Did I do it right? It's a problem with his brain. The plumber told me everything. His son has problems in his brain. He needs to have doubles of everything. It's a rare disease. When you give him just one thing, he has an attack, and it's serious, he's epileptic, he could die. The plumber needs to give him two of everything. He can't forget. He has to give him two glasses of water. Because the kid's in a wheelchair, he has to have two wheelchairs. Two pairs of pants. Two jackets. Two pairs of underwear. Two pairs of shoes. One for him and one for nobody. Two beds. Two plates. Two bibs. He eats every meal two times. That's six times per day. That's a lot of work. Sometimes, the plumber shows him his hands to calm him down. It soothes him. He shows him his two legs, nature is well designed, right? Nostrils, arms, testicles, it's soothing for him. The plumber touched our ceiling with a monkey wrench. The plumber looked at his monkey wrench and he said: There's nothing I can do. As if the monkey wrench were speaking to him, as if it were giving him instructions. He looked at the monkey wrench and he said: I did what I could. He said: Plumbing is like everything else, it has its limits. You're at one of the limits. Got it? We're at one of the limits. All water in the world is connected, that's what the plumber told me. That's why it punctures, it weighs things down, so it can reunite, it can meet. Our water is meeting with neighboring waters. It meets up with the other water in the neighborhood. The city water. Our water has met the sea, sludge, soup, he told me, water flows, it evaporates. If you hit water, it absorbs the blows. There's nothing we can do against it. We're at a limit and I'm getting used to it, we need to get used to it. When you think about it, there are advantages. To get hydrated, all you have to do is open your mouth. If you imagine people dying of thirst, you won't want to complain anymore. And you don't have to bother showering, it's as if you were living in a shower. And in terms of decor, it's really pretty. In people's houses, the decor doesn't move. In general, you'll notice, there are picture frames on the wall that don't move. But at our house, everything moves, everything changes like landscapes or something. We're lucky.

The waterdrops struck their heads. Jonathan said: This morning, I met a man who got angry at me in the park. He insulted me.

The roommate stuck out his hands. He collected several drops.

He rubbed them on his forearms. He said: I'm going to ask you one question and you're going to answer it: Did you break his teeth? Jonathan shook his head no. The roommate rubbed the inside of his ears with his pinky fingers. He said: I knew it. In your shoes, I'd have broken his teeth. When I say break his teeth, I don't mean that I'd have made his teeth fall out of his mouth with my fist. No. Not at all. What I mean is, I'd have made his teeth fall out of his mouth one by one, and then I'd have broken them one by one. Maybe with a rock. There are lots of rocks on the mountain. So, on the mountain, I think I'd have broken his teeth with a gray rock, you know which rocks I mean? Those rocks that are a little sparkly, you know? With a big gray rock or maybe with my foot. Yes. If there aren't any rocks, I can do it with my foot, but I'd have broken his teeth. That's for sure. And there's thirty-two of them. Did you know that? Thirty-two. You want to know how I know?

How you know what?

The number of teeth. I know because I broke my father's teeth, and I counted them. My father loved rocks and teeth are rocks. A tooth is made of minerals, which means rock. My father's name was Simon, and that means rock. He wouldn't have liked to see people wasting rocks. He wouldn't have wanted them to go to waste. So, when he died, I crushed everything. I collected my father's teeth, I went into the morgue, I took them, I put them on top of other rocks on the mountain, and I crushed them. Into powder, you know? Powdered teeth. A white powder, you know? My whole family committed suicide. We lived in a castle, I told you that, right? I think I did. I think I told you that story. On the mountain, you couldn't waste rocks. What do you think a mountain is made of? If you take away the rocks, what happens? It's bad. My tooth hurts, you see? This one. The roommate pointed at his canine. His fingers were dirty and bitten bloody. He said: It hurts. It really hurts. It's just one tooth, but it really hurts. How long do you think a tooth is? Not that long, maybe two centimeters? One centimeter? A tooth is tiny. You have to get close to see a tooth. If I put a tooth five meters away from you, you wouldn't be able to see it, that's for sure. That's why dentists wear glasses. I hate dentists, by the way. Have I told you that? They use products to stop pain. Isn't it normal to be in pain? Don't even mention dentists in front of me. Don't give me the address of a dentist, or I'll find him and I'll bust his teeth. One by one. With a rock.

Jonathan stuck his fingers in the bowl of pills and licked his hand. The roommate said: Every time my teeth hurt, I suffer like anyone else. Everyone has problems with their teeth. Even babies. Pain connects me to babies, but dentists take away pain, they put pain to sleep. That's a problem. That's their vision of things. They don't like pain. But pain is neither good nor bad. It has the right to live. That's the science of life. We have the opportunity to be in pain. When we suffer, we're doing something. But dentists want to undo everything with their shots, with their syringes. Most dentists are addicted to anesthesia. Every day, they have anesthesia in their hands, that's not normal. They're breathing in anesthesia, don't you think that makes them crazy? They eat anesthesia, I'm positive they do, they put it in their sandwiches, they put it in cakes. They like to keep their kids anesthetized. They anesthetize their children. They put it in their candy. At the dentist, there are always photos of drugged children in posters. Have you ever noticed that? It's as if they were turning a faucet the wrong way. Stopping pain. Destroying pain. Putting pain to sleep. Demolishing pain, controlling pain. But what happens when pain is over? When pain is over, you rest. To be happy, you have to suffer, be hungry, be cold, experience tooth decay, you can't make fun of pain, let's not make fun of pain. Let's respect it. There's almost nothing worth respecting. I want people to respect pain. I want to accept suffering. There's nothing more beautiful than accepting suffering. Name one thing more beautiful. Name one thing. Just one. No. It doesn't have a name. Something greater than pain doesn't exist. There's nothing higher. Nothing greater than suffering. Accept suffering. Accept it.

Jonathan wiped drops from his cheeks. He took two shallow bowls and put them on the floor. The roommate said: Teeth are made for that. He pointed at his mouth. He said: It's that one, do you see it? It hurts. I'm suffering, I'm suffering right now, I'm in the process of suffering. I suffer and suffer. The drops fell rhythmically into the shallow bowls. The roommate drummed his fingers, he superimposed his rhythm over the rhythm of the drops. He said: One, two, I'm suffering, one, two, I suffer. Since I've been here, I've suffered, one, two. My tooth is making me suffer, one, two. Suffer and Suffer. One, two. There are two brothers. Suffer and Suffer, one, two. The first brother is named Suffer, and the second one is named Suffer, one, two. Suffer and Suffer, one two. Do the brothers Suffer serve any purpose? One, two. If I didn't suffer, I wouldn't be able to speak, one, two, I wouldn't need to speak, one, two. The day of our birth is the day of the birth of suffering, one, two. What is the point of suffering? Do you know? Do I know? One, two, endlessly, endlessly, one, two. There are two brothers. One, two. The first is named Endlessly and the second is named Endlessly, one, two. Even the little finger, and even the iris, and even the earlobe, even the parts we don't know, one, two. Suffer and Suffer. One, two. Even a tooth one centimeter long, one, two. Suffer and Suffer, one, two. You can suffer from an amputated limb, one, two. Suffer in your sleep, one, two. Suffer and Suffer, one, two. Then the roommate took a breath and he said: I knew a guy who pronounced the word hurts like hurts-uh. He added an uh to the end of it, like the word alone wasn't enough. I get that, he's right, we should say: Hurts-uh. We should say: Hurts-uuuh. The guy said: That hurts-uh, that really hurts-uh. I was twisting his arm and he drew out the uh. The guy cried while drawing out the uh. Hey, I'd forgotten, I'd forgotten that story. It's funny, I just remembered that. And the roommate gripped his tooth with his dirty nails. He pulled it out. He said: It's over. He was bleeding. He swallowed his own blood as if he were swallowing soup, with a noise in his throat. He licked his lips and he threw his tooth on the table. It bounced twice, a drop fell. Jonathan said: I don't feel good. The roommate responded: It's true, you look rough. And he wiped his red tongue on his palm. He said: What's going on with you?

It's something with my heart. I feel like my face is hard. Do you want to touch it?

The roommate touched Jonathan's cheek. He grimaced with pity. He said: It will give you peace.

What will?

Death.

He got up. He collected the bowls. He drank water from the first bowl, then water from the second bowl. He said: No, I'm kidding. I meant going to the hospital. If you go to the hospital, it will give you peace. A nurse will put you in a bed and she'll take care of you, that's what they do. I know them. When my family committed suicide, supposedly because we were part of a cult, supposedly because they thought it was the end of the world, supposedly because my uncle had told us to die, I was put in a hospital. Going to the hospital gave me peace.

Jonathan's lips were blue. He said: Do you think I should call the fire department?

That's up to you. If you think you're dying, maybe you should.

I feel like my heart stopped.

It's possible. People sometimes die very young. Call your cousin, the one that cut his stomach open with a window, the one that plays darts.

No, I'm going to call the fire department.

Why? Didn't you tell me your cousin was a firefighter? Did you lie to me? And the roommate opened his mouth in the air. He said: The water's good. It's really good. It's really, really good. Since he'd pulled out his tooth, he'd started lisping, he was drooling into the S sound. He said: It's super special and super safe. The drops. It's super special and super simple.

Jonathan was pacing in a circle. Drops were falling on his shoulders. He said: I think something's wrong. He was going faster and faster. He said: I don't even have my phone. Can you lend me yours?

The roommate slid his tongue along the edges of his lips. He stuck it out until it touched the tip of his nose. He smiled. His gums were red with blood. He said: No, but you can ask the neighbor to lend you his. The neighbor that lines his children up against the wall. The upstairs neighbor. I never lend my phone to anyone, personally. I do research on my phone. I've configured it, I don't want you damaging it with your shaky hands. If you feel faint, I don't want you dropping it. I work on my phone. Right now, I'm reading Google's confidentiality guidelines backwards. I start with the last word and I go up. I take a break every three hours to watch videos of obese people being humiliated by a muscular trainer. They promise to lose weight and they cry. They say: I promise. A doctor touches their stomachs and says offensive things. Are you crying? If you want, I can slap you to get rid of the tears. My uncle did that, it's good, it works, it got rid of all my tears.

*

The neighbor opened the door before Jonathan could ring the bell. He took him by the arm. He sat him down on the only chair in the apartment in front of the only table. Small, square, ugly. He served him a coffee that he sprinkled with bits of almond and vanilla powder with paprika extract milled by deaf women in Nepal. He said: It's decaf, for your heart. The room was dark, it still would have been dark with 2,000 lightbulbs. With a fire. With a house fire. It would have still been gray. It would have stayed dark even in the sun. The neighbor was wearing an apron and a little badge that read: At your service, with a smiley. He had a kind of necklace with a little sign that said: Our mission: to inspire and nurture the human spirit—one person, one cup, and one neighborhood at a time.

Five other signs were hanging on the front door:

> 1. Creating a culture of warmth and belonging where everyone is welcome.
> 2. Acting with courage, challenging the status quo, and finding new ways to grow our company and each other.
> 3. Being present, connecting with transparency, dignity, and respect.
> 4. Delivering our very best in all we do and holding ourselves accountable for results.
> 5. We are performance driven through a lens of humanity.

The neighbor said: I alternate. I choose depending on my mood, depending on the climate. The climate affects my mood, it affects me. Had you come on a different day, you might not have recognized me. My features shift according to the wind, temperatures, atmospheric pressure, humidity, the time the sun rises and sets, precipitation, hydrometeors, natural reseeding, and my children. They're like me. Their appearances change. They're growing. Look at them. Look at my children. I like it when people look at my children. Look at the bodies of my children. I have numerous children. They have numerous bodies. My children were produced by my own body and by the body of my wife, present here. The wife didn't react. The neighbor said: We've produced these beings that are alive and our children. We call them simply Our Children or sometimes The Children. When I say The Children, my wife knows right away that I'm referring to these people here. Look at them. We conceived them.

The seven children stood still against the four walls. They stared at the reflection of their faces and the reflection of the back of their brothers' or sisters' heads in the mirror. They stared at these reflections, which formed an entire body out of the front of their faces and the back of another child. Some of the children had the front of a five-year-old boy and the back of a fourteen-year-old girl. They'd looked at these reflections forever in these mirrors.

Jonathan was looking for his pulse. He looked for it in his temples, he looked for it on his forehead. He put his fingers in his ears, then around his arm, on his knees and on his stomach. Everything was cold. His heartbeat was gone. The doorbell rang. It was Salim. The neighbor opened the door and stared at him shamelessly. The neighbor contemplated Salim while rubbing his index finger and thumb against his chin, he tilted his head like someone who knows about painting. Salim lowered his eyes, but he came in. He said to Jonathan: I'm sorry to bother you, but your roommate asked me to come up because you're having problems. What's going on? Why are these children being punished?

The neighbor's eyebrows and lips expressed vexation. He placed Salim by Jonathan the way you would an object, very close together, on the same chair. The only chair, in fact. Jonathan turned toward Salim and Salim turned toward Jonathan, their noses touched. Jonathan told him about waking up in the park. The lasso in the sky, the waterdrops in the living room. His heart. The lost phone. His mouth had a terrifying odor. Salim tried to stop breathing. He put two fingers on Jonathan's neck, then he put two fingers on the inside of his wrist, then he put two fingers on his forehead, then two fingers on the back of his neck, then on the back of his knees, and Jonathan said: You see? It's been like this since this morning. It's like there's no more heartbeat. The neighbor held out his phone. It was a phone from the old days, it didn't have a screen. He said: You'll see. One day, all this will seem like a distant memory. Believe me, our memories erase obstacles. On the other hand, there are things you don't forget. There are things you can't forget, like the number for the fire department. Everybody knows the number for the fire department. You see, I have an uncle that lost his memory. My uncle walks around downtown wearing a T-shirt that says: I have Alzheimer's, my address is 8 Berger Street, leave me in front of the door. Every day, he walks around the city, and every day, someone leaves him at this front door. You know, people have their hearts in the right place, all you have to do is make them pity you. People pity my uncle. But he never forgot the number for the fire department. That's all that's left. When you ask him how he's doing, he responds: Eighteen. When his wife asks him if he loves her, he responds: Eighteen. When you ask him what his name is, he responds: Eighteen. Sometimes, his wife tries to make herself believe he hasn't changed, that he's a man like any other, that his disease is gone. She asks him: Robert, what's nine plus nine? And my uncle's never wrong. The neighbor looked directly at Salim, he said: Please know that I take care of my children. Here, we're in my house and my children don't have a lot of space, it's true, but they get a lot of attention. Attention is the supreme proof of parental love, of love, period. It's better to have painful attention than an absence of love. I love my children. I wouldn't know how to tell them apart from each other, but I love them as a group. My children form a group that I call The Children. They don't have individual names, but when they're tired, I put ointment on their eyes. Maybe I get things wrong, maybe I make mistakes, but I put ointment on their eyes and they fall asleep. They dream. I've raised them perfectly. Please know that I adore them. Maybe I get things wrong, but I adore them. Period. We'll see when they're grown. We'll see if they hate me. It's hard to know. Maybe I'm wrong. Okay, go ahead, call the fire department now.

You say you'll call the fire department, but really you just call one firefighter. You get one person on the phone, and Jonathan got a fireman, he said: My cousin is a firefighter, please do something. Please, I've tried every part of my body, I don't have any heartbeats. I swear, I tried everywhere. I asked my friend to check, I don't have any palpitations. I don't know what to do. I'm calling to tell you I'm dying. You can't say no to me.

Sir, that's impossible, you aren't dying. Go the emergency room, you'll be taken care of by a team that will tell you what to do.

A team of how many? Please, come quickly. Come yourself. I don't want to see a team, I need your help, please. I'll give you anything you want, come, I'll give you everything. You'll be compensated.

Sir, you're going to go to the emergency room and a doctor will take care of you.

It's a question of seconds. I'm having an attack. I'm having one. Please. I'm having one right now. Please, it's happening right now.

The attack. It's happening, please. I can feel it. I swear. I swear on my own grave. I promise. I beg you, I'm crossing over from life to death. I can get on my knees. I can do whatever you want. Come. I'll do anything, please, it's an emergency. The seconds are ticking. There's nothing more urgent, it's horrible. The seconds are ticking. I beg you. I swear I'm dying. I swear I can feel it. I'm dying right now. I swear I'm not wrong. I'm young and I'm dying. I can't be wrong. It's too much, I can feel it's too much. I'm sure of it. My friend checked. Everyone around me is worried. Everyone can tell I'm dying. Everyone feels sorry. Everyone is waiting for you. I beg you. You can't leave me like this, I'm at death's door. I'm at death's door. This can't be happening. Please!

I don't think so, sir.

You don't think so?

No, I don't think so. You aren't dying.

But what if I die?

That would surprise me.

Yes, but what if I die?

His mouth was dry and felt like it was too big for one head. He said: But what if I'm dying? I have bad saliva in me. I can feel it. It feels like dying, I'm dying, I swear. What if I die?

That would surprise me, sir.

Yes, but I'd be dead. Do you understand? If I die, I'll be dead. Would you rather be surprised or dead? Which one?

Surprised.

So try to understand what I'm telling you.

Sir, you aren't describing the symptoms of an attack. I've been a firefighter for twenty years. I can recognize an attack by a person's voice. During an attack, whether of the heart or the brain, the trachea decreases its volume, which makes the voice high-pitched. But every four seconds, due to a muscular reflex, the trachea returns to its initial shape and the voice reassumes its natural tone. Then, once again, the trachea decreases in volume and makes the voice high-pitched. And so on. When you first start out, it seems like people are making prank calls. You think it's two idiots, but it's just one person and they're having an attack. Of the heart or brain. Your voice is stable. It's very stable, sir. You've been talking long enough for me to notice.

Listen carefully, who has the heart here?

What do you mean?

In a high-pitched voice, Jonathan repeated: Who has the heart here?

Both of us.

Yes, but you don't have heart problems. Right now, you don't have any problems with your heart. Whose heart has stopped here?

The fireman said: No one.

In a serious voice, Jonathan said: It's serious. This is as serious as it gets. I can't think of anything more serious. Out of all the calls you're going to get today, this is the most serious. The most urgent. Do something.

No.

It's an attack in my stomach.

That doesn't exist.

You've never heard of an intestinal infarction? I read about it. I'm having an intestinal infarction. It's serious. People die. I'm dying of it. I'm dying. I'm dead.

Do you have any stomach pain?

No.

Well then, I'm going to hang up.

No! Please. My heart stopped over an hour ago. It's horrible. Please. It's horrible, please. Please. I woke up in a park. It's horrible. My heart stopped. I beg you. I don't know what to do. Please. Please. Have pity. Why would you be so hard on someone who's dying? You're going to die one day too. Please understand, have pity. The neighbor tapped Jonathan's shoulder. The firefighter said: You don't have the symptoms, sir.

But you know there are isolated cases. You know it.

No.

There aren't isolated cases?

No.

No exceptions?

No.

Just come, that's all I want. Come, please. I'm begging you, that's all I want. I'm begging you. My cousin is a firefighter, I'll put in a good word for you. I'll put in a really good word. What's your name? Let's say your name is Bruno. I'll tell him: Bruno is the best firefighter, the best man, he saved my life, Bruno saved my life. Bruno saves lives. Every day, Bruno helps others. I beg you, Bruno, come. Take your truck, the smallest one, even the smallest one. You can come in a car. Come however you can. I don't care. Come on a bicycle. I'm trying to hold on. I can hold on until you get here. It's not easy. My heart stopped. It's not responding. I've put my fingers everywhere. Please.

Jonathan threw himself on the floor. He kneeled near the chair. The neighbor put two hands on his head. The children closed their eyes against the walls. He said: I'm begging you, I'm begging you, I'm on my knees. I just got on my knees at my neighbor's house. My neighbor put his hands on my head. I'm begging you. I'll give you anything, I'm dead.

No, sir.

You don't believe me? You think I'm lying? I'm warning you, if you don't come right now, I'm going to set my apartment building on fire. The neighbor withdrew his hands. Jonathan looked at the seven children in panic. He said: I live in a building full of children. Too many to count. I'll blow the whole thing up. I'll blow everything to pieces. I'll blow these kids to pieces. I'm going to set the building on fire. Everyone will be outraged. You'll get notifications every second for days. For years. Imagine the headlines. Deadly fires because of a firefighter who refuses to move for a serious attack. Dozens of children dead because of a firefighter. Because of his cruelty. Because of his cold heart.

Okay, sir, I'm going to call the police.

No, stop. Please. Don't make it worse.

Are you going to start a fire?

No.

That's good. Now, you're going to go to the emergency room and you'll be taken care of by a team of professionals who will calm you down. You'll get to sleep, sir. You'll see. They'll give you a shot and you will sleep.

For a long time?

The firefighter said: As long as necessary. And he hung up.

Jonathan put his head in his hands. Salim took a picture of him. The neighbor said: All my children were born sick. They were dying. They lost their hair and their incisors. None of it grew back. I thought my children were going to die young, but one day, I met a doctor who took care of them. He healed them in a few minutes. He changed them. Today, my children are the picture of good health. I barely have to feed them. When I beat them, they scar over in three minutes.

The voice of the youngest child rose above their heads. She was singing in a language that didn't exist. Then, one by one, all the children started singing in a round, a profound song that went higher and higher then lower and lower. The neighbor took Jonathan's hand and he wrote with a black marker: DOCTORSOSSO. He shouted over the voices of the children: You'll find him at the end of the street. A few meters away. At number five. The neighbor kissed the seven children on the backs of their heads. Their voices mingled. They multiplied. They vibrated in their skin. The neighbor opened the door. He pushed Jonathan and Salim outside.

*

Salim kept asking: Are you okay? And Jonathan kept responding: No. They kept going, and the atmosphere changed as they moved, the street became drab, pale, a street in any city, any country, or a film, a dream, until they reached the office of Dr. Sosso.

The building didn't have a plaque or a doorbell, a door, not even a wall, just a passage, a sort of hole in cement. Everything was dark. They lowered their heads. Salim said: It's like the tunnels in video games. And Jonathan hit himself on the forehead, he put his hand to his face and pulled it away quickly, as if from disgust.

They came across a woman in a long black dress. She said: It's jam-packed. You'll have to wait a long time. It's packed to the rafters, up to here. And she gestured above her head. She said: Up to there, do you understand? Up to there. Salim rubbed his eyes.

When they entered, nobody greeted them. The walls of the waiting room were covered in posters. Mostly pictures of children, blond children, brunette children, black, white, wounded, a cut cheek, smiling, syringes in their hands. Sad women on a roundabout, on grass, laughing, in a circle, naked. Pictures of German women holding birds in their hands, thermometers, a stethoscope, a glove, medical chairs, portable urinals, restraints for madmen, stags, partridges, moose, bear teeth. A picture of a wolf in the snow, of a doe surrounded by leaves in autumn, a pine tree, and plants. A print of a Gaugin painting, a Botticelli painting, water, rivers, newlyweds, medical diagrams of the human body, medical diagrams of a dog's body, medical diagrams of a donkey's body, hand stencils from the Chauvet Cave, everything connected by a birthday or Christmas garland. Each picture was attached to the wall with a very large, crooked nail, five centimeters in diameter, ten centimeters long, that tore the posters, fractured the images.

In this waiting room, eyes regularly turned toward a very large screen broadcasting the latest news on mute. Nobody said anything, they looked at the big screen or their little screens. A man was breathing heavily. A little girl was coughing and sneezing, but poorly, as if she were pretending.

Old wooden chairs surrounded a little black table where several magazines were molding. They were actually rotting. A revolting froth was spreading, spongy and white, like wet powder, melty and soft. A complete softness. Salim's heart broke. He looked at the mold and his heart broke, he felt pity. Softness provokes weakness in people, as if their bodies were turning into jelly. Softness is close to pity. Elderly people provoke a pity that makes the body melt like mold. When an elderly person holds an object in their hands, when they turn it between their fingers, it's as if they were holding nothing. You could put the most beautiful object in the world in their hands, a beautiful rock, you could put the most expensive object in the world in the hands of an old man, you could put a gold bar in his hands, a luxury watch, a wad of cash, a diamond in his hands, there would still be poverty, there would still be misery. Very old people don't hold anything in their hands, their hands are empty. Even if they're holding something in their hands, their hands are all they have.

Salim imagined a filthy old woman. She had stains from tomato sauce around her mouth. She didn't have any teeth. Long black hairs, covered in snot, poked out of her nostrils. Her ear hairs were covered in wax and the corners of her eyes were crusty. A crust that was dry on the edge and moist in the middle. And a slobbery tongue like a slice of roast beef that moved and made a noise like pasta. Then he imagined a softness on this face. A goodness. A softness and pity. Shame. Softness is so close to pity, it's so close to shame. Softness is close to pain, it's close to pain and shame and sadness. It's close to disgust, anger, rage. Softness is a danger. For people who have suffered too much, softness is the greatest danger. A moment of softness can lead to death or madness. For people who have suffered too much, softness is worse than a bomb. A single caress and these people fall. They come undone, they give in. They crack, then they explode, and everything comes out. They overflow, they're done.

How many people have died from softness? It's impossible to count. After living through the worst kinds of suffering, people have died from one moment of softness. A gesture from their child, from their family, or worse, a gesture from a stranger. A word, a pat on the shoulder, they've died from it. In truth, the brain isn't vast. Its regions overlap. The area for spite is close to the area for indifference. The area for cruelty is close to the area for attention. The area for anger is close to the area for fatigue. The area for fatigue is close to tenderness, the feeling of goodness is close to pride. The area for pride is close to the area containing the feeling of emptiness. The feeling of emptiness is close to the feeling of god. The feeling of god is close to solitude and company. The area for solitude is close to involuntary laughter. Involuntary laughter is close to feeling sexual. The sexual area is close to the feeling of death, because there are no boundaries in the brain. The feelings touch. And softness tears people apart.

Salim imagined his finger on that mold, on the rotten magazines in the waiting room, and then, he felt that softness in his upper body. When a tear came, he treated it like a drop of water.

He imagined a list of special training programs for the military and police. Trainings on the dangers of softness. He imagined four titles for training programs and made a note in his phone:

1. The benefits of the harshness of night at police headquarters when dealing with victims of violent rape.
2. Aiding victims via sharp language, gestures, and intonation.
3. Adding a tinge of coldness, detachment, and severity to responses in all circumstances, in particular when greeting persons older than seventy-five who are crying and/or moaning.
4. Keeping your face emotionless (eyes + eye outline + nose + mouth + mouth outline) when dealing with children tortured by their parents for a period of three to ten years.

Jonathan said: What are you writing? And Salim didn't say anything, but he moved his hand in a way that meant: Nothing. The news flashed across the screen, murders, fires, viruses, a tornado, attacks, an abused dog, its mouth sewn shut, and Jonathan wondered if he'd done it all himself. It was possible, he could have. The poor dog, the poor people, it was a feeling he'd had since the park, since waking up, he felt it, poor kids, poor people, poor parents, a feeling of acid in his throat since the morning, the poor old people, but above all the poor dog, the poor dog, its face, its cries, the pain of that dog. He was almost sure of it, how was it possible? How could he have done all of that? He felt all the murders in his hands, and he whispered: It was me . . . It was me . . . As if all the crimes were his, as if the word crime and the word Jonathan were two words up against each other, as if they were just one word, as if they contained crime and all crimes, yes, all crimes from the beginning, from the beginning of crimes, all the crimes from before the world began and all the crimes after, encouraged by his own crimes like an infernal ball hurtling through the universe and time, starting with his sleeping body in the park that morning. Wasted, alone, with the lasso.

And his thoughts laughed with their tiny yellow mouths in his brain. They burst out laughing and they bounced. They guffawed in one big, annoying breath. He looked at the phone of a woman seated near him who was reading an article about fake news. He read two sentences:

1. Lying is fast.
2. You can find proof of anything.

He read them without understanding them, without reading them. It didn't make sense, it wasn't important. He put his fingers on his wrist, no heartbeat. He put his fingers on his stomach, was he breathing? He didn't know. He looked at his fingernails, his own fingernails, it was as if they were smiling, his own fingernails, they were mocking him with their dirty white mouths, his own fingernails, his own breath, his own heart. Everything was mocking him. Salim elbowed him and he showed him his phone screen. He'd written: Your legs are shaking, stop. Jonathan froze his legs and he looked at the woman sitting across from him. She had tics, a lot of tics. She raised her eyebrows and she shrugged her shoulders constantly, as if she were repeating: That's obvious, of course, that's obvious. Every two seconds. Her face didn't stop, she put up with it. She was expressing both: That's obvious, of course, and: I'm tired, I can't do this anymore.

The doctor tapped Jonathan's ankle with his toe. He said: You coming? So, he got up.

The doctor shook one of his hands, then the other. He shook them for a long time, as if he were weighing them. Then he brought Jonathan into a large white room. The doctor was wearing metal glasses without lenses, sheets of gray metal in front of his eyes. He was blind. He said: Please lie down. Jonathan lay down on a kind of stretcher.

What can I do for you? Be specific.

My heart stopped.

Very well, I see. And, with a small gesture, the doctor closed Jonathan's eyes. He put his fingers on his eyelids. He made circles. He pressed harder and harder on Jonathan's eyeballs and tears welled up. The doctor said: That's normal, that's the goal of the procedure. The doctor collected the tears in a little vial. He said: Now, get completely undressed.

Jonathan took off his clothes, it was like the fabrics slid off his calm limbs, he felt guided. The doctor poured the tears from the vial onto Jonathan's stomach and rubbed. He rubbed harder and harder, deeper and deeper into his torso, he penetrated the skin, the flesh, the stomach, the intestines. He relaxed everything, and everything went soft. The doctor touched the sides of Jonathan's organs, he held Jonathan's organs, he massaged Jonathan's organs. He grabbed his organs through his skin the way you grab a glass from a cabinet. He understood. He kneaded. He worked. He introduced. He said: Allow me to introduce you to your spleen. He moved it around. He surrounded it. He coated it. Perfectly. It sizzled. He said: Feel your spleen, it's responding. Then: Feel your intestines, these are your intestines. Do you feel them? I'm traveling along your intestines. I'm sliding. Yes, I'm sliding thanks to your tears. Do you feel it? I'm sliding, I'm hurtling down them, I'm visiting them. Feel your colon, that's your colon. I'm traversing it. I'm taking a stroll. Organs produce needs, and needs produce organs. It's an exchange. Don't say anything, your organs are speaking to me, they're responding. I'm not talking to you, I'm talking to your organs. Try to remain silent. This is your stomach. Feel your stomach. I know what you're thinking, I know you. I know people, the world is full of people. The world is full of tears. The world is full of warmth, you know that. You're burning. The world is full of powders. Full of tears and people. A human being. What are you? A human being. What are you? A human being. What are you? A human being. What are you? A human being. Yes. We think a person without legs can't run. That's true. Some people will never be able to run, walk, read, see, speak, live. Some people will never be able to sleep, swim, understand, climb, build, sing on key. There will always be something missing. There will always be someone missing something. That's nature. Don't think about it. Do you feel it? Don't think about it. Feel. You feel it. Don't think about it. Don't think, okay, this way. Don't look at yourself that way. Okay, this way. Don't look at yourself through that lens. That's it. You understand. You're starting to understand. Your body is starting to understand. The doctor poured some tears onto Jonathan's chest. He said: Now the heart. First, he rubbed around his nipples with his fingertips, then he rubbed the pectorals with the whole hand. Harder and harder, faster and faster, like trying to start a carousel. He breathed in more and more deeply. His hands sank deeper and deeper. He exhaled. Jonathan's skin became tender like warm dough. It was supple and pliable. The doctor's hands were absorbed, they sank into the ribcage, his arms were immersed up to his elbows. He grabbed the heart with both hands. He said: There it is. Oh, there you are! And he clenched the heart, then he unclenched, and he clenched it, then he unclenched it in his big blind-man's hands. Twenty-eight times. Twenty-nine times. Thirty times. Thirty-one times. Thirty-two times. Thirty-three times. Thirty-four times. Thirty-five times. Thirty-six times. Thirty-seven times. Thirty-eight times: Feel it! He lifted the heart up. He raised it up. He held it. He pulled it. He brought it to Jonathan's face. He said: Look. In a nearly crazed voice, he said: Have a look at this for me. Look at it. This is one of your main organs. Quick! Lick. Lick it! Lick this organ for me! Hurry! And Jonathan licked. He licked his own heart through the skin of his torso. The whole surface of his heart. The doctor turned the organ up, down, right, left, and Jonathan licked it. He licked every millimeter and the doctor opened his superb hands, he let the heart go. The organ sank back into the body, you could hear the sound of a thing coming back to its rightful place, and the doctor raised his arms up. He cleared his throat. He turned around. And, while washing his hands, he said: I get patients like you every Sunday. All the people you saw in the waiting room have the same problem.

Jonathan said: The little girl . . . The little one . . .

The doctor wiped each of his fingers with a rag. He said: Don't speak. Rest. Yes, yes, especially her. Especially the little girl. Of course. Especially the children. All children. There are mostly children in hospitals. Parents don't know what to do with their children. They make mistakes. Many children die every hour, it's very common. It's a miracle when children survive. Just this morning, a woman told me she took her son's temperature by turning on the oven. She put one hand in the oven and her other hand on her son. She would compare the two temperatures. She thought her son was cold, so she wanted to put him in the oven. This is common. Very common. Heat. Cold. Hunger. Thirst. Parents don't know what to do. I massaged her heart. The mother's. Everything went back to normal. The other day, a father told me he was taking his daughter's temperature by collecting damp leaves in the forest. He'd place a leaf on the child's forehead, if the leaf dried, the father got worried. If it didn't dry out, he didn't get worried. I haven't heard from that family since.

Jonathan got up. He said: Doctor, I saw something that wasn't real. The doctor didn't respond, he didn't have any particular expression on his face, but he was standing straight. Jonathan said: I saw a lasso in the sky. I swear, it's true. The doctor nodded his head calmly for several seconds, at least thirty seconds. He finally stopped. He said: Why do you think the lasso wasn't real?

I was with a man who didn't see it.

Do you trust this man?

No.

Then it's fine. Don't ask yourself any more of these questions. So many questions. Endless questions. Honestly, do you understand anything? The answer is no, you don't understand anything. You will never understand anything, none of us will ever understand anything. Not a single crumb. And that's fine. Take a crumb, for example. Do you understand a crumb? No. So it's fine. Can you possibly understand the crumb? The answer is no. Always no. Nothing else. Not a single phenomenon. Not the smallest thought. Not the smallest person. Especially not people. And not a single word. Not one word. Honestly, do you understand the word tree? The answer is no. Deep down, the answer is no. You don't understand anything. Not one sound. Not one image. Nothing. You know, it's fine, it's fine when you think about it. When I was starting out in my career, I worked in the emergency room. One night, I heard meowing, but there weren't any cats on my unit. I thought: I'm imagining things. I said to myself: Gustave, you're imagining things, my friend, you're imagining things, you're tired, you're imagining things. But I wasn't. There was a woman and she was meowing. She'd just had an accident involving her head. She wanted to talk, but she meowed instead. She wanted to scream, but she meowed. Even now, I can hear her meowing in my head, especially at night, and even now, right here, I can hear her. I can hear her meowing right now in my office. Every day, I hear her, she meows. A lot of people have to die. A lot of people want to talk. They want to make a gesture. Sometimes, when we want to scream, we start meowing. We want to say a sentence and we meow. That's the truth. We find many things disgusting. I'm happy to be blind, but I don't see nothing. I can see a blue surface. I see emptiness and points of light. Yes. Blue. If I were given the chance to recover my sight, I would say: No. Simply: No, or: No, thank you, to be polite. That's what I would say. I never complain, but, I pity people who do, that's how I feel. I'll live my life and I'll practice my art in innocence and purity. Right now, you have to go, but before you do, touch the top of my head.

And Jonathan did.

*

My children, Here are eight things you need to know. Read to the end.

1. If all the leaves on all the trees had tongues and these tongues talked about you, if they described you day and

night for centuries, they wouldn't be able to say who you are.

2. If you find a fat maggot in a bowl of cherries, the bowl of cherries becomes disgusting, but if you find a cherry in a bowl of maggots, the bowl of maggots does not become delicious.

3. Fruit falls on its own, but it doesn't fall into your mouth.

4. There are three kinds of people. First, those who don't touch your innermost self, they stay far away from you. Ignore them. Then there are those who touch your innermost self, but at the wrong time, they hurt you. Push them away. Finally, there are those who touch your innermost self the right way and at the right time. Keep them close.

5. Death will deliver you from all the people who annoy you.

6. Every century seems horrible. That's normal, don't worry about it.

7. Luck only has one boat. Don't miss it.

8. There's danger everywhere. Be careful.

3

The subscribers were sending hearts, they were sending emojis of wilted roses. They sent sad smileys, smileys with glasses, swords. They sent popcorn, animals, knives. They sent her bouquets, tulips, arrows. Sara added a filter and her eyes became wider. She made a halo appear above her head, tattoos on her cheeks. She lay down, lay down and told a story: This is a memory, I was twelve years old. My mother left around that time. I was spending a lot of time outside, I looked directly at the sun, so I had patterns in my eyes, I saw shapes, like consequences without a cause, like answers, but I didn't know the questions, as if I'd told you: The answer is 318, but you don't know the question, as if I'd shown you an object and said: This is the answer, but you don't have the question. That's how I saw the world, I was surrounded by answers. So, I don't know if my memories are true, or if my mind created them to please me, or to please itself. I don't know, but one day, I got to my middle school and the hall monitors were handing out white jumpsuits. We had to wear them, we were all in white, all the students. The jumpsuits sounded like pigeon wings when you moved your legs, and even when you weren't moving, you could hear the sound all over the school. The sound wouldn't have existed if it had been on its own. If there were no silences between sounds, you wouldn't be able to hear the sounds. If a single sound invaded the world, we wouldn't be able to hear it, even a big sound, a single heavy sound, if it happened without silence, you wouldn't hear it, it would cover up everything, it would even cover itself. But if there were only silence, silence couldn't exist, we wouldn't be able to notice it, that's when I understood. When things stop, they exist. Things need to pause in order to exist. It's the same with people, they need to be alone.

When we're with another person, we can't exist normally. The other person draws us outside of ourselves, they take us outside of ourselves. We become responsible for this moment with the other person. We can't see ourselves anymore. You have to take a break to keep from losing yourself. But when we're alone for too long, we don't feel like ourselves. We can't see ourselves anymore. We can't feel like ourselves with other people, but we can't feel like ourselves without other people.

She lowered her phone toward her mouth and the halo descended, it was floating now above her lips. She said: Everyone wore white jumpsuits in middle school, the hall monitors, the teachers, the principal, hundreds of students in white jumpsuits. One morning, some old women arrived, they repainted the building, the chairs, the tables, the windows, these very old women with white hair, thick like a pony's mane, these thin old women, smiling in blue overalls. They painted the floor, they painted the walls, they painted in white. They had dogs, you know, those little white dogs with curly fur, they had these dogs that followed them everywhere, old dogs that limped, these old, old-lady dogs. They had white eyes. The old women painted the light switches, the cables, the blackboards. They carried around jars, rollers, paintbrushes. They would arrive at the middle school with their ladders, and I would look at their shadows through the window. I would see their shadows in the courtyard, I would try to see their shadows as people, I told myself the shadow was the person and the person was the shadow. I told myself the person came from the shadow. I imagined there was a shadow under the shadow, several shadows under one shadow. And the women painted, the paint ran down the walls.

She waved her arm in the air, she filmed the sheets, a lamp, then by accident she brought the camera too close to her face, she filmed her nose, it filled the screen. It was as if the nose were speaking. It said: So we asked the teachers what was going on, but they answered us in strange phrases. We collected them like action figures, we exchanged them, some had more value than others. When we asked: Why is the school white? They responded: The world moves forward, but as it moves, it turns. When we asked them: Why are these old women coming here every morning? They responded: The smallest gesture is uncertain, the smallest note, the universe floats in the void, a void with no color, why should we fear it? When we asked them: Why do we have to wear white jumpsuits? They responded: In existence, there is one true mystery and it is the only mystery. When we asked them: Why are you talking like this? they responded: I keep this mystery in my pocket, so the mystery always keeps me in its pocket. When we asked them: Why white and not green or blue? They responded: Why does a man with no bow search for arrows? When we asked them: Will the school go back to normal? They responded: The sky is only a reflection of the eye, and yet, the eye has no sky.

We didn't know what to do, so we did nothing. We stopped speaking, we stopped eating, we stopped working, we stopped laughing, we stopped fighting. The principal got worried, she gave a speech in the cafeteria. She smiled a lot, she said: Listen, I'm following a directive, like your teachers, like everyone on staff, we're following a directive from the highest levels. We have to wear white and repaint the entire establishment white, that's it. We don't often understand these directives, but we must trust and respect them.

Sara moved the phone away from her face, and the halo returned to its place above her head. She said: After several days, the surfaces turned gray, the paint ate up the dust, everything was dirty. The walls, the floor, the chairs, and even us. The paint was sticky. It collected hair, gobs of spit, it sucked things up, it accumulated them. I remember feeling disgusted. We often threw up in the hallways, but our vomit mixed in with the paint and we walked on it, it was horrible, it turned black. One morning, they asked us to give back the white jumpsuits.

She yawned without opening her mouth. Her eyelashes cast a shadow under her eyes. The subscribers sent emojis of paintbrushes, emojis of palettes, laughing emojis, emojis of white roses, black roses, blue roses, emojis of pillows, emojis of old women, emojis of white dogs. She pressed stop and she searched for pictures. She found pictures of white ponies, blond ponies, snow, flour, ghosts, paint, shadows, faces painted white, and she posted them on her wall.

Her room was huge. A little red lamp illuminated the bedside table, her bed, and her face. The other part of the room didn't get any light, it was dark, it was the dark zone. Sara called it The Hole. Back when they moved into the old school, the mayor had asked them not to touch it. He'd said: I know there is some kind of shadow in one room, just ignore it, it's never caused any problems. It's just a shadow, a big shadow. Don't go near it.

Yes, it was a big shadow. A heavy, abnormal shadow like an empty shape. They couldn't get rid of it, they couldn't light it up. Sara and Salim had thrown lamps, candles, firecrackers, and flares into the zone, but nothing took, everything went out. The shadow was hard. It was like the end of the world. When she looked at it long enough, Sara could see a person, like a crouching man, neckless, with orange eyes, with dark circles that hung to his mouth, and shining lips. Maybe he was drooling, maybe he was bleeding. His nose formed a loop in front of his face. When the man in the dark zone moved his body, his gestures were like one single gesture, the darkness linked them all together.

Sometimes, Sara wondered if it was real. When we look at the dark, when we look at darkness, what are we looking at? We're looking at the spots in our pupils, we're looking at the inside of our eyes. Our brains create an image, our brains create what we don't see, but we can't imagine things that don't exist, we imagine what we've seen before. We mix what we know, we don't imagine a color. If red didn't exist, we wouldn't be able to imagine it. We can't imagine a sensation. If heat didn't exist, we couldn't imagine it. We wouldn't be able to imagine fear, embarrassment, or surprise. We see almost nothing, you could say we see nothing, that we see what we've seen before. Sometimes we think we recognize someone, but we're wrong, we think we recognize someone, but it's a stranger. We see something, we don't know we're imagining it, we think we're seeing reality. From far away, we think we see a man, but it's a tree. We think we see a fox, but it's a pile of leaves. We think we're reading a name, but it's a different word, it's a different image, it's a memory, it's a mistake.

Once when she was little, Sara grabbed onto her mother's thigh at a supermarket checkout. When she looked up, she saw the face of an unknown woman. The woman was laughing, the mother was laughing near the woman. The two women were laughing. Sara let go of the strange thigh and she cried. She'd felt a sadness in her body. She was crying, and she wasn't confused or ashamed, she was inconsolable. Reality wasn't fair, it wasn't normal.

When we're reminded of an object, we can find that object. Our memories see it, and our memories find that object in reality. Our memory has touched the world, and our memory never stops touching the world. We touch the world with our memory. We recognize words because of our memory. We recognize ourselves because of our memory. When we forget a person, we can't find them again. If something isn't in its place, then we can't see it, we can't understand it. If our street became longer, narrower, or darker, we wouldn't realize it. We don't notice much. The world is huge, and we only see what exists in our minds. We see what's normal. We see what we've seen before. We see very slowly. We've seen what we see. We look at the past, the sky is blue, the sky is gray, the sky is black, the sky was blue, the sky was gray, the sky was black. If the sky disappeared, we wouldn't see it. If a finger vanished from our hand, we wouldn't notice it. It would take us days, it would take us weeks. We wouldn't be able to see it. If things don't last, they don't exist. Nobody remembers a raindrop. Nobody remembers an eyelash. Nobody says: I remember this drop of rain that fell on my arm in 1996. I remember an eyelash I had when I was ten, it fell on my table. Everything happens at the same time, millions of colors and substances, gestures and sounds, but our heads are brief, we see almost nothing.

We see things inside ourselves. When there's a mountain in front of us, we see it in our brain. We have a mountain in our heads. We look at the sky, but we don't see the sky in the sky, we see it in our eyes. Later on, when we're all robots, we will be able to place our eyes outside ourselves. We'll put our mind outside ourselves. We'll put our intelligence at a distance, outside, farther away from ourselves. We'll remember everything, we'll name every hair, every scab, every phase of our fingernail growth, every millimeter. We'll have words for every gesture, for every odor, we'll recognize everyone in the universe, every animal.

Sara thought she could become blind. She remembered one night with her mother in the living room, they were watching a historical reenactment on TV. Her mother had fallen asleep, her mother often fell asleep in the living room, and Sara stayed up alone next to her. It was a show about a very old village, the presenter said: This village no longer exists, but thousands of years ago, all the inhabitants of this village became blind because of an illness in their blood. And all the inhabitants were given black tunics, sent by the king, as a form of consolation. It was a long time ago, thousands of years ago. The blind inhabitants would meet, they would assemble in the mornings and the evenings around a table. They told each other stories. They said what they saw, because they saw things behind their eyelids, they saw objects that cried, crystal snowflakes, mouths in the form of a staircase. They described these things to each other. They mostly talked about a woman, they called her Cream. She was a redhead, she gave advice. Cream walked through the streets, she blessed the inhabitants. Cream walked on walls, she kissed animals, and she stuck out her tongue. Cream didn't sleep, she stirred soups with a ladle. And when Sara fell asleep next to her mother that night, she saw Cream in her dreams, sitting on the roof of a church. Cream was making signs. She lifted the posters up. She lifted four posters that said the words:

I

AM

NOT

HERE.

*

When they moved into the old school, the father had decided to stay in the kitchen like the spoons, like the knives, but the kitchen was too long. It was hollow. It was empty.

Sometimes, the house felt like a large animal around the family, an elephant that loved them, that warmed them. Sometimes, the house surrounded them like a ring.

Sometimes, the father caressed the walls or the floor, and other times he caressed the objects. Every person in the world felt mysterious to him, especially his children. Mysterious. As if they were floating away from him in one endless movement.

Sometimes, the father thought about one particular day. He'd cut his leg on a nail at the worksite. His colleagues had dropped him off at the hospital to get stitches. In the waiting room, the father had started to feel uncomfortable because of a child. The child was looking at him and smiling, but to the father, there was nothing funny to smile about. The father didn't like irony. The father worked hard. He'd cut his leg while working, that wasn't funny. But the child wouldn't stop looking at him with this huge smile. The father coughed. He scowled. He stared the child down, but the child continued to smile. Within a few seconds, the father hated the child. The father became wild with anger at this child. The father stuck his tongue out at this horrible child, this animal. He stuck his tongue out as far as it would go at this devil child. He hated this monster like a rash. His eyes, his head, his stupid face. The father hated the fine hair on the devil child's head. The father flipped off this stupid child. He lifted his middle fingers as high as they'd go at this laughing child, but the child's smile didn't budge. His perfect smile. Cute. Childlike. Even his nose smiled. His cheeks smiled. Every ringlet on the child's head seemed to smile. The father felt strained. Horribly strained. Dominated. Almost unhinged. So much so that he was baring his teeth. His mouth was smiling despite him. It was smiling with hatred. This was a long time ago. And in the end, the child had gotten up with a white cane, he ran into two chairs, he ran into the father's chair. A nurse had come to help him. She'd held his arm.

Sometimes the father thought: If they wanted to put me in a box, I'd say yes.

Sometimes, the father sent emails to his children. Even when his children were next to him in the kitchen, he would write them emails, even when his children were talking to him, he would say: Be quiet, I'm writing you an email.

Sometimes, the father screamed over water. He filled the sink, he leaned over, and he screamed. The sounds made waves. The father screamed what he saw: I SEE WAVES ON THE WATER WAVES ON THE SURFACE I'M LOOKING AT MY OWN VOICE. The children had grown used to his screams in the night. The grandmother had grown used to this man who screamed. The female nurse and the male nurse didn't notice it anymore. The father was hurting himself, he was ruining his throat, he had the voice of an old man.

Sometimes, the father watched his children's videos and he tried to find his face in their faces.

Sometimes, the father imagined his own head on the kitchen wall. He imagined his head so hard it appeared on the wall in front of him.

Sometimes, the father repeated: Bad, bad, bad, bad, while flicking little drops of dish soap on his forehead. One night, the male nurse had taken him in his arms, he'd said: You have children. Another night, the male nurse had said: What's going on? And the father had responded: I feel far away from everything. I even feel far away from vegetables. When I peel them, I don't feel anything. How can I be so far away? I look at my hand, I think I could cut it. It wouldn't hurt if I cut it. And the male nurse said: Don't worry, a vegetable is composed of millions of moving atoms. He said: We're never holding the same vegetable in our hand. The vegetable we're holding is already dead when we hold it. The male nurse had sat down with the father in the kitchen, he said: What is a person made of? A person is made of one thought after another. It would be easier to count every hair in the world than the thoughts of a single person. Everyone is replaced every second by a different person. And the father had cleaned the male nurse's hands with his hand sponge. The male nurse said: You're in the kitchen, you're in the house, but before arriving here, you were elsewhere. Before you were elsewhere, you were somewhere. You can go all the way back to birth, back to nothing, don't worry.

Sometimes, the father was silent. That was all.

Sometimes, the father would try to turn himself off like a lightbulb. He turned off the bulb. He tried to turn himself off along with the bulb. Sometimes, the father could understand what it meant to be a corpse. Sometimes, the father looked for pictures of crowds on the internet. He tried to look every person in the eye. Sometimes, the father sent messages to the social worker, he said: Trust me. Sometimes, the father cleaned the lightbulbs while saying: These bulbs aren't going to wash themselves, that's for sure.

Sometimes, the father listened to the radio. He'd listened to the story of a man who was locked in a hole with no light for years, his hands placed on the bars of his cell. When he got out, he didn't know how to walk anymore because his hands had become too heavy. He fell forward from their weight.

Sometimes, the father thought about the day when his cousin had hit him with an iron bar. The day she'd burned the bottoms of his feet. The day she'd put detergent in his eyes. And the day when he'd stopped crying. He'd stopped. He'd said: I've stopped. And when the cousin beat him, he thought: Okay. She made him swallow coal and he thought: Okay. She whipped him with cables and he thought: Okay.

*

Dream #574

I'm not wearing any clothes, I no longer have a face, I don't have a name, I'm scared, I'm trembling, I remember my childhood like a squishy ball.

My mother says that I need to get a screwdriver to fix my problem. She says: Shitty Sun, that's the screwdriver brand.

I'm afraid because I recognize my mother's face, but it is not her face. It's the face of a stranger, but it's my mother inside of the face. I startle, I wake up, but into another dream.

I'm shopping in a home improvement store, I'm looking for the Shitty Sun brand of screwdriver. I ask a salesperson to help me, he's deaf, he points to the apparatus in his ear, he says: I'm deaf, he says: When you say Shitty Sun, I don't hear you. I don't hear the word screwdriver. I can't hear what you're saying. I don't understand the words, got it? I can't hear the words coming out of your mouth.

I walk through the store, but it's a loop, there's no exit. In one aisle, Michael Jackson is there alone, he asks me where the hammers are.

He's speaking to me in Arabic, and he's crying. He says: I was unlucky, honestly, I was unlucky. He says: I'm still alive, but I was unlucky. He says: I'm hiding in the sewers, but it's leaky, I can't even move my face anymore. Look at my face, look at it please, look closely.

I say: It's true, your face isn't moving.

Michael Jackson says: What's your name?

I say: I don't know.

He says: We move toward the future, because that's where we'll find out what happens next.

4

When we're having a bad day, when we're having the worst day, we say: It's a rotten day or: It's a bad day, but the day hasn't done anything, it hasn't done anything to us, it hasn't done anything wrong. The day doesn't have anything to do with us, it's not concerned with us. The day has no relationship to us, it doesn't have any relationship to our impressions. It doesn't have any contact with our lives. The day is just a day. If we remove ourselves from the day, if we remove our person from the day, the day is a day. It remains a day. A normal day, like every day. All days are good. They're all perfect. When we watch the day end and the sun disappears, there's only one thing we can say: The day was a day. It doesn't matter what we think about it, it doesn't matter what we feel, it was a perfect day. It didn't need us. A day doesn't need anyone. The worst days of our lives are as good as our good ones. There's no difference between a good and a bad day, there's no division. There's no fracture between days. They're honest, days are days. If the planet explodes, if the world collapses, if the planet bursts, does that change anything for a day? No, the day takes place. It's the beginning of the day. It's the middle of the day. And it's the end of the day. It ends. It was a day. No commentary on reality could ever touch reality. No impression of reality could ever touch reality. No explanation of this reality could ever touch reality. For nature, time is nothing. Salim showed a photo of Jonathan to Jonathan, crouched on the ground at the neighbor's, his head in his hands. Jonathan said: I've changed, I don't recognize myself anymore.

They walked and they walked. Salim lit the way with his phone. Under the bus shelter, they looked at each other's faces in the night. Salim's eyelid was twitching. When our eyelids twitch, other people know we're wondering if they notice it. Our eyelid twitches, nobody mentions it, but a thought about the eyelid crosses our minds at the same time. Two people become linked by this thought. Two minds become pointed toward each other. The two minds bump into each other like cars, but a mind doesn't enter another mind, the way two clanking teacups don't enter each other. The person with the twitching eyelid directs their thoughts toward the mind of the person watching, they think: Has he noticed my eyelid is twitching? The other person thinks: He's wondering right now if I've noticed his eyelid is twitching. The two people observe their minds and their minds touch, but neither mind enters the other. Jonathan put his index finger on Salim's eyelid. He felt the pulsing under his fingertip.

The fields were damp, the grass was bowed. They were walking on a dirt path, the air was calm and icy. Steam escaped their nostrils, the wind whistled in the trees, in the leaves, in the emptiness. Salim said: Everything is flat, when you think about it, even mountains are flat, if you look. Mountains are made up of flat lines, it's the direction that changes. Mountains are flat going upward. The sea is also flat. Even waves. All shapes are flat. Everything is made up of lines and lines are flat. If you look at trees, you can tell they're flat, it's the direction that changes, they're flat vertically. And us, if you look, we're flat, you and me, when we lie down, we're a line. When we get up, we're a line. If you look carefully, we're a line. Their steps crushed the grass through the orchards, Salim said: I wish everything we touched lit up. We'd know what we've touched. Imagine everything we've touched around us lit up. It's over there, behind the trees. Do you hear that?

Is that a cow?

It's crying.

They saw a barn in the light of the moon. A dog approached them without barking. She was black, she licked their hands in the shadows and her lips trembled, her teeth were chattering. Jonathan put his coat on her back. She licked his right cheek. She was wearing a collar that was dark pink like the inside of a baby's mouth. Her name was Daphné, it was on the tag. The door was heavy, they opened it. Inside, dozens of sad, dirty, white stalls with metal gates stood in rows. A deep, dry odor entered their nostrils. It went down their throats all the way to their hearts.

Jonathan said: Breathe through your mouth.

And Salim said: That's worse. I feel like I'm eating the smell.

Jonathan said: Breathe every third breath.

In each little stall, there were four or five silent calves. Lying in the mud, crowded against each other, they'd just been born. Dozens of babies almost asleep in boxes. Between each animal body, the space wasn't empty, the space held a warmth.

A calf was crying in the aisle, he'd escaped. He couldn't stand on his feet, he would get up, then he would fall. He cried, he was white, his mouth opened and his tongue was black. He had long eyelashes and his eyes were watering. The calf's voice rose and fell. Notes left his mouth like a wave, they spread in the dark. No human in the world could understand this language. No human in the world could understand this cry. But no human in the world could ignore this language. No human in the world could ignore this cry. It would have been a lie to say: I don't understand what he's saying. It would have been a lie to say: I don't understand his language. Anybody in the world could understand, and nobody could understand. All the human bodies in the world understood this calf's cry without needing to understand it. Every time he tried to get up, he fell again, he cried, he shook. Jonathan and Salim sat close to him, they touched his nose, his back, his ears pierced by a tag that read 1717. The calf looked at their faces. He suckled at Salim's fingers, the pointer and the middle ones. He left a little puddle of saliva in the night, in Salim's hand. The black dog placed her paws on their laps, she tugged at their pant legs with her mouth. She led them to a hallway to another building: an even narrower hothouse full of cows. Two long rows of cows attached to tubes that pumped their udders. Their eyes were black. They looked at nothing. They seemed to know everything and surrender. Their bodies functioned without them. Occasionally, their tongues poked out, they sighed. A cow mooed, but nobody heard the cry that left its throat, not even Jonathan, not even Salim.

He said: Do you think they've ever seen the light of day? And Jonathan didn't respond. They stood for a moment by the cows. Salim said: They'd be better off dead. Jonathan said: Yes. Salim said: It makes you want to kill them, Jonathan said: Yes. Salim said: Luckily, they're going to die, Jonathan responded: Yes. Salim said: Look, the date of their death is marked on their ears. This one's going to die in a week. Stay strong, friend, stay strong, it's almost over.

They pet the tops of their heads. Their brown eyelashes lowered. The calf's cry echoed in the night, and Salim said: We've invented so many things. We've built big warehouses far from the city, we've built walls around slaughterhouses and farms to keep from knowing the animals were alive, as if they were already dead from the beginning, as if they'd never lived at all. He said: Every time we look an animal in the eyes, we should feel ashamed. Any animal, even an insect. We should feel shame, even if it's a cat, even a horse. It hurts to see their eyes.

The dog put her paws on Salim's thighs, then she nibbled on Jonathan's leg, so they got up. In the first barn, the calf was still crying. Salim took it in his arms. He said: I wish you'd been born dead. The calf stopped crying and Salim said: It would be better off dead. The calf's eyelids lowered and Salim said: It would be better if it had never been born. The calf's long legs pushed against his neck and Salim said: It would be better if animals didn't exist, if we were alone on Earth.

His warmth and the calf's warmth created a new warmth, and Salim said: He's beautiful, it makes me feel sorry for everything. I feel sorry for everything. Look, it's my mother.

She was standing with her arms crossed in the doorway at the end of the hall. Her body was hard to make out. She said loudly: You don't have the right to be here. She was tall and her voice matched the sad sounds of the room. Her shadow stretched all the way to her son. She said: Come here, Salim. His face changed, it sank, he could feel it. From close up, he saw the mother's face, she had a lot of cream around her eyes. Her skin was glowing. She smiled, but by the end, the smile was no longer smiling. Her face was in a hurry not to smile anymore. Salim felt like the back of his neck was breaking. She said: Did you come because of your grandmother? The nurses called me, your father . . . I'm not going to give you anything, you knew that. I'm not giving any of you anything. Everyone has to die. We have to. We die. No one needs to stay sick. We die. It's the same for everyone. Have you seen your grandmother's mouth? Have you seen the shape of it? Its outline? Have you? Her lips are almost gone, her teeth are gone, there's only her tongue, just a piece of skin. Every mouth becomes like the grandmother's one day. If you grow old, your mouth will become like hers. Mine will become like hers. You can't stop it. We can't save everything. Sometimes it's better not to help, Salim.

He was silent. She said: On a farm in the village, there was a man who drank a lot. One evening, the man got home late at night, and when his wife got up, he hit her. He woke up their child, he hit him, he killed him. He killed his child. He killed his only son and forced his wife to eat the pieces of their son. The woman had to eat her dead son's finger.

Why are you telling me this horrible story?

Some people shouldn't be saved, Salim. Someone saved that man. People in the village helped him. But sometimes, we shouldn't help anymore. It's too late, it's not the right time anymore. You have to let people die. You have to look inward, live your own life, have a strong heart.

She kept moving her thumb and forefinger like a tic, something ugly. She said: I won't give you anything.

Salim said: Let us take the calf.

Fine, take it. You and your friend can take it. Leave. Take the animal. I'm sick of hearing it, I don't want to see you anymore. Go.

Salim said: What do you do here?

I've lived, that's all. You can't really know your parents, Salim. When you arrive, they've already lived, they've already changed. You get here too late, you can't meet them where they are. She stepped back and gestured with her head. The dog ran toward her, you could hear the little bell on its collar. The dog licked the mother's hand, then the dog turned around and placed her body close to Salim's. The mother smiled, but then she stopped smiling, and said: Go, leave now. The story ends here.

*

After, Salim and Jonathan walked around the farm, the sky was black, the dog followed them. Chickens were sleeping in a cage, their heads under their wings. A little farther on, in an iron enclosure, pigs were piled on top of each other. The piglets of a dead, gray sow were still trying to suckle. Maggots were coming out of the sow's mouth. A piglet jumped with joy next to the cadaver. Everything was dirty. Salim wished he could kiss that mouth, kiss the sow's hairs, her nostrils, and her dead lips, ask for her forgiveness for everything.

Something dark was covering the world. They walked for a long time. They walked through brambles and a fine snow started to fall, slowly. It fell on their backpacks. The wind blew through the linden trees. Hunting dogs howled somewhere in the distance. They came upon a hill covered in moss, they went up and up. At the top, day was breaking, the grass was covered in drops of water, snow, white insects. Inside every blade of grass, inside every insect, life was saying something. Everywhere there were seeds and weeds, invisible eggs, tiny things capable of growing, of containing muscles, nerves, vessels, a mind, a shape, brains. Salim's eyes were hard. He was looking straight ahead. He was shaking. He said: If someone hits the back of your neck, will you die without suffering? Jonathan responded: I don't know. He said: If someone puts your head underwater, do you die without suffering? And Jonathan responded: I don't know. He said: If someone puts your head underground, do you die without suffering? And Jonathan responded: You might not die. He said: If someone holds your nose and eyes, do you die without suffering? And Jonathan didn't respond. He said: If someone smashes a rock on your head, do you die without suffering? And Jonathan didn't respond. He said: If someone hammers a little nail into your brain, do you die without suffering? And Jonathan said: Maybe. He said: If someone strangles you with a charger cord, do you die without suffering? And Jonathan said: I don't know. He said: Is it possible to die painlessly? And Jonathan said: I don't know. I don't know. Salim typed KILL A CALF into his phone. The sky was turning white. The calf huddled against his stomach. His heart beat. Salim could feel his organs. A snowflake landed on the calf's muzzle. Jonathan said: It's like fog is moving in and falling, it's falling on us. The green and white grasses leaned in the wind. Jonathan took out his box of pills. He put them in his hand and, one by one, he handed them to Salim, in time, like a clock. Salim put the pills, also in time, into the calf's mouth, who swallowed them in its sleep. Its mouth was sweet and burning hot. Salim said: Look, it's like he's swallowing all the suffering. It's like he's swallowing all the suffering in the world.

*

My children, I don't know if there's anything you need to know.

YEAH YEAH YEAH YEAH YEAH YEAH

1

Hello, everyone, today I have a new video for you on the subject of time, meaning murderers. Imagine a murderer, one that kills children. He cuts them up and he eats them. You say: That's horrible. You say: His hands are horrible. You say: I don't understand the look in his eyes. You say: He's a mistake. You say: I can't imagine myself in his shoes. You say: He's sick. However, the beginning of evil is inside you. The beginning of evil is in every person. The beginning of evil is in each part of your person. On your faces and your hands, in your spinal columns, inside your cells and in your nails, look closely at your reflection. Take an honest look, just once. Honestly, your reflection wants to leave when you look at it, right? Don't you think? If you're honest, if you look your reflection in the eyes, you can tell it wants to leave. Don't you think it wants to leave? Look at yourself, we all look like ourselves, I look like myself, you look like yourselves. We look like our images, but we don't look one hundred percent like ourselves. Do you see what I mean or not? Your reflection looks like you, but it doesn't look like you. It doesn't talk. It will never talk to you. You can talk to it. It will never respond. It's calm, and even when you're angry, it's calm. When you're beside yourself, when you're furious, look in your mirror. Your reflection stays quiet. It's always quiet. It lives in calm. And murderers are murderers, but it's not because of murder, it's because of what surrounds it. Do you know what I mean? Murder is always surrounded. It has its inner circle. You can kill to defend yourself, you can kill without meaning to and that's not a crime, but it's a murder. Sometimes a lie, a detail, a drop becomes a crime. You eat a starving person's piece of bread, you raise your hand to denounce someone who didn't do anything. The crime is on the outside. The crime is outside the criminals. But when we see it, when we hear it, when we smell it, crime enters us like an odor. It touches our evil. In some countries, you can be condemned to death. In Cambodia, for example, you take twelve policemen, you give them rifles, eleven of them contain blanks. At the moment of an execution, the policemen shoot the man, who dies. No one knows who killed him. There's no guilty party. There's no murderer. But there is a dead man. The murderer who feels innocent is innocent. The murderer who feels like a murderer is a murderer. In general, there isn't a murderer. In general, there's no difference between a murderer and a non-murderer. One day, a murderer is born, but one day, a murdered man is also born. The two men were made in the same way, from a clump, a clump of blood. From a seed, a ball. You were all balls. They were balls. I was a ball. We've all been balls. A ball. A clump. Like a piece of blood gravel. If we wanted to show the beginning of a person, it would be half a centimeter on the tip of a single finger. That's the beginning of a person. Later on, the ball would make a head and legs, arms, eyes, a look, a voice, fingerprints. When you're walking in the street, look at the faces, imagine clumps of blood. Look at your parents, your grandparents, look at your ancestors, imagine clumps of blood. You can see the past, if you concentrate, you can see other people's pasts. You can see the world's past.

He took two sips of coffee. The room was dark, very neat, he turned toward the camera, he said: I've lived inside a woman. But where was I before that? And you, where were you? Did you exist? My father and my mother made me, I'm a part of my mother and a part of my father. I'm fifty percent my father and fifty percent my mother. I am a piece of two people but there's nothing new in this piece. It's a mix of former people, former things. There's nothing new. You are a mix of former people. We are a mix of former people. If we were in a video game and someone removed the information YOU ARE IN A VIDEO GAME from our brains, we'd have no reason to believe we were in a video game. We wouldn't have any way to imagine it. It would be reality. Maybe thoughts appear in our brains because of chemistry, and nobody is responsible. We're not responsible. When we're proud of ourselves, we're proud of chance. When we think we're strong, we really think chance is strong. When we think we're beautiful, it's chance we find beautiful. But we transform. Look around you, look at your life, people change you. When you talk to someone, you transform. You transform them. If the person whispers, you whisper. If the person says stupid things, you say dumb things. If a person doesn't respect you, you don't have respect for that person. We can't control it. Do you wonder how much an airplane weighs? Maybe you don't care, but an airplane weighs seventy-seven tons, or the weight of one person multiplied by 140,000. And why am I talking about airplanes? It's because they fly.

When I was six, I was at an airport with my father and we were sitting in the dark because of an electrical outage. It went on for hours. We couldn't see anything. I closed my eyes. I was hungry. My father put bread in my mouth. I recognized the taste of bread. I thought: Why does bread taste like bread? Bread tastes like bread to me, but bread tastes like bread to other people too. Why do foods taste like anything? Why can I recognize the taste of a food? Even me. Even a child. I was a child then, I thought: Even me. Am I the same as everyone else? Am I a copy of everyone else? I thought about trees. You see long rows of trees on the road, they look alike, they run alongside each other, they're twins, triplets, they're linked. They grow for the same reasons. They grow because of things in the earth. Things that die and go into the earth, animals, plants, food, and even trees when they die. They go into the earth. When we die, our bodies rot in the earth and trees grow. When a tree dies, its body rots in the earth, but we don't grow. Humans don't grow the way trees do. Trees grow, they grow from the bodies of dead trees. They grow from the bodies of dead animals, from the bodies of dead humans, but humans don't grow that way. We can spray water on our dead, we spray water on cadavers, but humans don't grow. Maybe flowers or mushrooms, but humans don't come up. Humans don't come from dead trees, they don't come from dead animals, humans don't come from dead humans, they don't come from the earth. So, what do humans come from? A human comes out of a human that came out of a human, but we don't know where humans come from. Maybe the same people have been coming back forever. You're watching my video now, but you've watched it in other lives. You've lived 1,000 times in your house, in your apartment. I've made this video 1,000 times. I've been born a thousand billion times. I've died a thousand billion times. Always the same death. Always the same life. Always the same. People from ages past live again in ages past. People from the Middle Ages live again in the Middle Ages. People today live again in the world of today. When we think about past ages, we might wonder: Where was I? Where was I in the Middle Ages? Was I already in the present? We were already in our age living and dying. Do you see what I mean or not? I did research. One part of our brain is for seeing, it's in the back of our heads. Memories are in the lower part of the brain and the part that understands is above it. Movements and willpower are in the front, behind the forehead. But there's no place for reality in the brain. I looked, but there's no place for it. They're looking for it, but it doesn't have a place. Because we can't find it, we believe. If you believe you exist, you have to believe in everything. If you exist, if the Earth exists, if trees exist, then all things exist. You can believe in God. Maybe it's a man, maybe it's a woman. Maybe she doesn't think. Maybe she thinks: I'm god. All day long, she tells herself: I'm god. I'm god. She doesn't think. All night, she tells herself: I'm god. I'm god. She doesn't think. That's her life. That's God's life. She doesn't feel anything. She doesn't hate anyone. She doesn't love anyone. She is God, and that's all. Meanwhile, we age like cars. If you buy a car, it doesn't get any younger. It will get older and older, it will be harder and harder to drive. If you buy bread, it becomes hard a few days later, it won't become fresh, it won't become softer. If a flower is beautiful, it will die. Everything will get worse, that's the only way it goes. We only go in one direction. You can kill someone, but you can't make them come back to life. When you cut up an animal, you can't stick it back together again. Everyone gets old the way a car does. Have you ever seen an old man sob? Type OLD MAN SOBBING into your phone. Watch the video. There are videos of old men sobbing. There are thousands of videos of old men sobbing. Watch. Watch the person. They hold their heads in their hands. Watch the shoulders. They tremble. Watch them like clumps. They're clumps of blood. Matter. It's just matter. Do you see what I mean or not? I'm going to post my new poem YEAH YEAH YEAH YEAH YEAH YEAH for you. Don't forget to like and share, ciao.

He turned off the comment section.

*

The oily steam softened the father's lips. He waved his arms in the air, and he said: We're going to have a good meal! At the same time, seated in a chair, her torso tied upright, the grandmother was drooling all over her bib. There she was with her brown face, almost black, her light sunken eyes, her body overflowing, obese, heavy. But her body emitted a sense of thinness. Cold. Around her face, around her hands, around her body, a veil, a sense that the chair held only an empty skin.

The father yelled: Wash her, wash her hands. Wash her fingers. Her fingernails. Under her fingernails. Sara. Salim. Scrub under her nails and on her nails. Take the sponge. Wash her mouth. No. Not like that. No, Salim. Harder. Not like that! You're not helping. I'm asking you to help me but your help isn't helping. That's enough. Yes. Sit down, I'll do it, I do everything in this house, I have to do everything.

The grandmother blinked twice. The father wiped the sponge over her face, he wiped the sponge over her hair and the back of her head and on her forehead, on the edges of her ears, around her neck and on her arms. He mumbled things they couldn't understand. Suddenly, he turned to the gas stove, he took the pan and he put it under his children's noses. He said: Look at these sausages, they're grilling. They're grilling, and what am I doing? What am I doing, Salim? I'm turning them. He said: I turn them and turn them, why? Why do I turn them? I turn them for you, so they don't burn. Okay? So they get hot but they don't burn, okay? So it tastes better. Okay? Does burnt food sound good to you? Do people like burnt food? Are there burnt food restaurants? Are there chefs that specialize in burnt food? No. Who wants something burned? Nobody. You hear that Salim? Nobody. So, you have to work. Yes. Work on the sausages. You have to work at everything in life, even sausages, are you listening to me? Listen to me!

Sara said: I went into the dark zone. The dark part of my room. I went inside it.

The father bit his lip, he caught a piece of dry skin with his teeth, he pulled, he bled. He said: The mayor said not to touch anything, you're always making up stories. No matter where you go, you find a story. If I put you in a box, you'd find a story in the box. That's for sure. A story anywhere. Part of your room doesn't have any light. It's not a dark zone. It's not a hole. It just doesn't have any light. Stop talking about it.

Salim asked: What was it like?

Sara said: It was dark. I was surrounded by darkness. I looked around me and there was only darkness. I couldn't see myself anymore. I couldn't tell where I ended and the darkness began. I let it take me, you know. I became the dark part, I became the place. I became the dark zone. I could have become a green part or a red part or a wall. I could have become anything. I felt like I could have become anything.

The father started yelling: Enough with these stories! And he dropped the pan on the fire. He moved the sausages several times, he sighed, a drop of blood dripped down his chin in a straight line. His face was burning. His cheeks were yellow and soft. He said: Now, we're going to have a good meal. Are we here to enjoy a good meal or not? Is the family all together or not? We're finally all together. We're going to enjoy a good meal, that's it. I don't want to hear any more stories, Sara. I don't want to hear anything else I don't understand. I don't want you to talk anymore. Let's have a toast. That's it, we're going to have a toast, you hear me? Salim, get out the stemware, the fancy glasses, the ones up there in the back of the cupboard. I washed them eight times this morning. Eight times. Nine times. Get them out. Ten times. Twenty times. No. Don't touch the cupboard with your fingers, don't touch the door with your fingers. No fingers!

The father leaned his hands on the big table, then he lifted his legs. He tipped his body forward. But he didn't have any strength, he slipped. He spread out his hands, he pressed down again, he lifted his legs and his pelvis. Finally, he got on the table and he held his glass in front of his face. He said: I'm raising a toast to this family in this house. His glass was empty. The grandmother burped. He said: I'm raising a toast to people who disappear and reappear and cause problems. His face sank into his shoulders. He pointed at his son, then he hit his own chest and he said: I raise a toast to the social worker and the problems I have to deal with. I raise a toast to all the problems in the world. I raise a toast to problems. I raise a toast to my daughter who leaves at night. Every night, I don't even know where she goes, and when she comes back, she looks like a ghost. I raise a toast to the ghosts. Yes. To all the ghosts while I'm at it, all the family ghosts. To everyone who isn't here. Sara said: Stop, Dad. But he was yelling: I raise a toast to people who can't move and have to lie down 24/7. He winked at the grandmother, then he froze. He said: You're going to make me burn my sausages! He got down, he tripped, he fell on his hands, on all fours. He was pretending to laugh, but his face contorted into a series of quick grimaces. He got up. He furrowed his eyebrows while smiling. He took the pan and he turned the sausages, then he tossed them in the air like pancakes: Hey, look at that. Hey. Did you see? He tossed them higher and higher. Three centimeters above the pan. Ten centimeters above the pan. One meter above the pan. Above his head. Two meters. Two and a half meters, then they touched the ceiling. He said: They're ready. He salted them. He peppered them. He got on his stepladder. He started to clean the ceiling with a cotton swab. He cleaned up the edges of the stains, and then he erased them micromillimeter by micromillimeter with his tongue sticking out.

Salim touched the grandmother's forehead, it was hard, like wax. Sick. She'd become sicker than every sick person. She was sicker than an animal on the side of the road. She'd gone so far into sickness that, today, she was sicker than sickness. Every part of her body harbored sickness to the highest degree. Sickness lived everywhere on her and her clothing. If you put a cardigan on her, the cardigan would start to look sick. If you put a blanket on her lap, the blanket would start to look sick. The grandmother was sick in every detail of her body and every noise in her body, and all the smells of her body said: I'm sick. Her sickness was profound, thick, and vast like a long, flat, gray moon, sprawling, treeless, mountainless, and empty. And when Salim focused, he could hear it. The liquid sickness, heavy in her body. Was she proud of it at least? Like a child showing off and counting their scars at recess. Like a child drawing scars with a black marker or wearing bandages without a wound to decorate their legs. They wear wounds like medals. They wear sicknesses like crowns, like a brooch, like a scarf. You can wear sickness like a rare piece of clothing. Salim asked: Are you proud? And the grandmother blinked twice.

Time to eat! The father set the plate of sausages down. Salim said: You have blood on your chin. The father wiped a sponge over his lips. Salim said: It's dry, you have to scrub. The father used the rough part of the sponge. He made his lips red: Is it okay now? Salim said: It's better.

Please eat! Enjoy. Dig in!

And they ate. But all of a sudden, Salim got bored. He thought about babies, babies in strollers, in cradles. We put babies on their stomachs, on their sides, but they don't do anything. Babies symbolize boredom. We put babies in chairs, but they have nothing to do. They can't talk, they can't read, they don't even have phones.

They wait and they suffer. We hear them crying, but they don't have a choice. They have to wait. When he was little, Salim got bored. He got bored in the morning first, then he got bored in the afternoon. The sky was really long, he looked at it, he didn't have anything to do. He often resorted to fear. When the grandmother was cleaning, when she was going from one spot to another, he'd hide behind a curtain, under a table, in a closet, and when she walked by, he would scream. The grandmother would jump, she'd clutch her chest, she'd lower her head, she'd breathe, then she'd say: Stop doing that, Salim. Stop doing that. You're going to be the death of me, Salim. And sometimes she cried, then she smiled. She loved him, she'd say: You got me, Salim. You got me. And he thought: To get a person, you have to scare them.

He received images. Jonathan was sending photos of flowers, different kinds of flowers and monuments. Long flowers and monuments. He looked up images of flowers in the shape of things, in the shape of a silhouette, in the shape of a strand of hair, flowers in the shape of a pendulum. He read things about frost flowers, he didn't know about them. Frost flowers form in the polar seas above the waves. He looked at pictures. He thought about stalactites and he looked up stalactites. He read that ice stalactites grow under the ocean. He looked at pictures. When the air's temperature goes below –18°C and the water stays temperate, stalactites appear. He shared pictures of stalactites on his page. He looked at pictures of waves, different kinds of waves, all these waves, all the waves washed over stones, people. The same waves of course, the same since the beginning. All waves have lived several times, all waves have seen the world several times, maybe millions, maybe billions of times, he looked at the waves, they didn't fall. Waves don't fall, they stretch out. Waves don't rise, it's their natural height, their size. They don't ascend. There are luminous waves, waves of light. He looked at pictures of luminous waves and he sent pictures of luminous waves to Jonathan. He sent pictures of frost flowers to Sara who looked at her phone and wrote: Thanks. The father yelled: I'm going to make you eat your phones! I'm going to put them on your plates, and you're going to eat them. Eat your phones! I'm going to grill them, you hear me? I'm going to grill your phones, I'm going to put mustard on the screens and I'm going to stick them in the oven. Do you hear me? I'm going to boil all the phones in this family! All of them! Even mine! I'm going to boil them all together and they're going to melt. Yes. And when they've melted, I'll make one single phone! One! I'm going to mold it, I'm going to sculpt it, I'm going to create one single phone, one huge phone. We'll look at it together, all of us together, all day long, the whole family. We'll look at that phone. Okay? Now enjoy your meal! Enjoy yourselves, you hear me? And make sure your grandmother enjoys herself. Put some sausage in her mouth. Go on. Give her some sausage.

Sara put a piece of sausage between the grandmother's teeth. She patted her mouth with a napkin, but her lips hung. Suddenly, her face lit up, and then she lifted her right hand. She gestured toward Sara's head, she made a kind of circle. Then she lifted her other hand, and she made the same gesture at Salim's head. Then she blinked, she blinked, she blinked. You could hear a clacking sound.

*

A moth enters the room. The moth is banging against the walls. It bangs against the ceiling, against the windows, against the lamps and the lightbulbs. The moth falls, its wings quiver on the ground. It turns back on itself. In a circle, around its center.

*

When there's a dead person you call the fire department. No. When there's a dead person you call the police. No. When there's a dead person, you call the morgue. No. When there's a dead person you don't call anyone. Dead people have nothing to say, they are dead in a room. They can't help. Dead people don't have an opinion. You can't keep the dead person in the room. You can't leave the dead person in the house. You have to take care of them, you can't worry about it later. Tomorrow. Next year. Dead people don't move. Their faces have stopped. Dead people don't have any ideas. You think: The dead are calm, they're at peace now. All dead people are at peace. But dead people don't know they're dead. We think the dead no longer suffer, but the end of suffering is a feeling. A dead person doesn't have any feelings. They don't know the end of suffering.

The father said: We have to make sure.

Sara said: How?

Salim said: I'm going to look online.

The father said: Wait, let's listen to her heart, if it's not beating, that means she's dead.

Salim said: I don't want to hear a heart that isn't beating anymore.

The father said: What does it say online? Be quick, Salim.

He wrote: howautw know. Then: how toauowkno if somb. Then: howwww. Then: how to knaowk if soemotn is dea. Then: ow to know f. Then: How to know if someone is de. Then: How to know if someone is dea.

Well?

All the answers are long.

Okay, listen. We're going to sit and we're going to read. We're going to sit on the ground, then we're going to focus. We're going to do things in the right order. Be quiet. We're going to sit on the ground. Sit down. We're going to sit in a circle. We're going to think without looking at her. Don't look at her! Pretend she's not there. We can't think if we look at her. Don't look at her. We're pretending she's not there. Focus. Now, Salim, read.

He read: Traditionally, to know if someone is dead, we observe the disappearance of different traits. We know that, when someone is alive, they speak and move. Their body is warm, they breathe, and their heart beats.

Okay, yes, I get it. Continue.

Over the centuries, medical knowledge has improved, and today we know that the brain is the central hub of a human being. It controls the organism's vital functions, such as temperature, respiration, physical movement, and speech. If the brain stops working, the person dies.

Ah, yes, I see, okay, okay.

Therefore, death is the irreversible and complete cessation of the brain's functions. The doctor responsible for determining if the brain has ceased to function will check for basic reflexes controlled by the brain. They will ask themselves the following questions: Do the patient's pupils still react to light? Does the patient react to pain? Are coughing and swallowing reflexes still present? If the patient is on a respirator, you must prove that the patient can no longer breathe on their own. It's called the apnea test. If no reflexes are detected after testing, sufficient evidence has been provided to diagnose brain death. That's the official time of . . .

What's that?

It sounds like a doorbell.

We have a doorbell?

The father said: Yes.

Nobody's ever rung the doorbell.

The father said: Yes, the female nurse and the male nurse rang it their first day.

Why isn't it stopping?

The father said: I don't know, but we won't be able to hear her heart if it's ringing. This is infuriating! Infuriating! Well, don't worry, children, we'll take care of it. We have to do something. We're going to open the door. We have to. We need silence, we'll take care of this. One thing after another. One thing after another, okay. Answer the door, Salim. Quick, get up.

Salim ran down the stairs and he opened the door. It was the neighbor, she was wearing her binoculars around her neck, her finger placed on the doorbell, she looked at Salim. She lifted her finger, she pushed past him with her shoulder and she came inside. In the kitchen, she kept pointing at the grandmother with her finger and she said: I'm certified in first aid, I can help you. I'll proceed. I must place my ear against her head.

Salim said: Yes, go ahead.

Direct contact disgusts me.

The father said: Yes, I understand. We understand. We'll put a plastic bag over her head. He brought a plastic supermarket bag that said: Our Mission Is To Make You Happy.

The neighbor had all of her lower teeth but none of her upper teeth, she said: That's too much, just cut a piece that's the diameter of her head.

Salim asked what the diameter of a head usually is and the neighbor said: Between nine and thirteen centimeters. Sara went to cut the bag. The father didn't know what else to do. It was all taking too long, too long, so to keep things moving, he started the dishes.

Salim read things about the diameter of the head and the cranial modifications practiced by certain cultures for social and aesthetic reasons. He discovered the phenomenon of infant cranial modification. He looked at several pictures of babies with flat heads. Out of habit, he sent the pictures to Jonathan.

The neighbor said: Place the plastic on the crown of the deceased's head, at the top, like the Israelites.

Without looking up from his phone, Salim said: Maybe she's not dead. We don't know if she's dead. Sara put the piece of plastic on the hanging head.

The neighbor said: Now, look at me. The father turned off the faucet. Salim locked his phone. The neighbor leaned over slowly, very slowly, almost not moving at all, her eyelids quivered. She leaned over for more than thirty seconds. Everyone was silent. Everyone was watching her. Nobody moved. It was as if the air in the room were suspended over the face of this old woman. When her ear touched the piece of plastic, she straightened back up and said: It pains me.

What?

I share in your great sadness.

What do you mean?

Nothing escapes.

Escapes what?

She has passed on.

Then the neighbor went into the hallway, she went down the stairs. Slowly. Slowly. She left the door open behind her. The rain stopped. In the kitchen, the curtains swayed.

2

Dream #575

I'm wearing a jacket of black feathers. The feathers are bad. They're haunted, I can tell. I'm contaminated, I clench my jaw, I break a tooth, I spit it out in pieces.

I want to get rid of this terrible jacket. The problem is I don't have a jacket. In fact, I am the jacket, it's part of my body. I can't take it off.

I lie down, I think about it, I get up, I open the door, I say: Too bad.

What do I find behind the door? A waterfall. And what do I find by the waterfall? A nail. I pick it up, I pierce the waterfall, it crumbles, I see Jonathan. He says: What's on your head?

I touch my head, I feel it, I say: It's a sword.

I look at myself in the mirror and I'm handsome. I lean over, I pull the sword out of my skull. There isn't any blood, there isn't any pain, no mark, no liquid, no hole.

I place the sword in my bed like a small child, and I cover it with a sheet. But Jonathan is fidgety, he sticks out his tongue, he moves around, he lifts the sheet, the sword is gone.

I'm not upset. I think I have an idea. The idea: it's normal not to find anything.

I lie down, I'm calm, my eyes close, I see the inside of my body, I see x-rays in my body. Inside the x-rays of my body, there are other x-rays of my body, I go inside them like a tunnel, I move through the images for a long time.

*

First, you must remove any medical equipment. I'm referring to the following: IVs, drainage tubes, blades, catheters, capsules, tracheostomy cannulas, as well as any other type of invasive medical device. I'm referring to the following: hearing aids, glasses, casts.

She didn't have a cast.

All the better. Jewelry, bandages, clothing, pacemaker.

She didn't have a pacemaker.

Very well.

The funeral director was an ordinary man. The only things you could say about his face were: eyes, lips, and a chin. He said: We will obstruct all orifices with cotton and do the cadaver's hair in her customary style. What was her customary style?

Salim said: Normal. We brushed her.

Very good, thank you, young man. Please know that we will close her eyes with adhesive lenses under the eyelids. We will also suture the mouth closed, which is customary. It's invisible. We will expel all substances from her stomach by exerting light pressure on the abdomen.

The father said: Yes, that doesn't just happen on its own.

The funeral director responded: For now, mortuary care is not automated. Even if, in certain regions, most notably in Japan, robots prepare cadavers who have undergone minimal damage. I had the opportunity to see a few pictures and, I must admit, they do impressive work. It wouldn't bother me. Working with a robot, I mean. It wouldn't bother me. On the contrary. Well. So, the substances . . . In the stomach . . . Yes . . . As you were saying: It doesn't just happen on its own, and in a way you're right. However, to be entirely honest, I think that if we left the deceased in a forest, the gas and substances would exit the body on their own. Of their own accord. But we would have to wait hours. Hours standing with our arms crossed. It would be difficult for everyone. Then we dry the deceased three times in a row with white linens, brand-new, clean linens.

The father said: That's good.

The body will be perfumed with musk in the armpits, between the thighs, the forehead, the hands, the knees, the feet. Three sheets will be slid under the corpse. The corners of the sheets will be sprinkled with musk. They will be folded one after the other. The left panel first, then the right, and so forth, layer by layer.

Do you need help?

No, sir, this is my job. However, have you cried yet?

The father said: No.

Oh . . . Listen, I have experience with these things. If you could say one thing about me, it'd be: He has experience with these things. We don't know this man, but he definitely has experience. You might say: A priori, we have no reason to believe this man, but we do know, however, that he has experience. There's no doubt about it. You know how many dead bodies I've prepared? You don't know, so I'll tell you: 34,518 and I'm not counting the grandmother. So, listen carefully. There's something that happens with death, for the living, I mean. Nothing happens for the dead, but for the living, something happens: death overflows. Yes, that's it, it overflows. As a mortuary specialist, I must caution you: death shouldn't alter the image we have of the dead person. Do you understand? Don't let death transform the person. Don't let death transform the person according to your tastes. I'm familiar with this. I understand the compulsion. I assure you: Just because a person is dead, it doesn't mean you need to make them better or more beautiful, because that's how you kill them. You kill them each day. With a lie, a simple lie, a banal lie, just one more lie, but this time, it's serious. You shouldn't multiply your love by two or by five, nor your sympathy, not even your tenderness or whatever else. You loved the person a certain way. Your love was what it was. If you change your love, you're lying. You're killing. You're killing a dead person. Do you realize that? By adding qualities to the dead person, by attributing qualities to them that they didn't have, by exaggerating their qualities and sweeping away their faults, you end up forgetting them. You forget that person. They turn into a story, a myth. You replace their image with another image. You choose an image that works for you. You paste this image over the dead person. If the dead person was someone close to you, you invent your own story through them. Unfortunately, you believe it, that's the worst part, this conviction. Using a dead person to tell your own life story is a serious problem. It's a serious problem because, once a person is dead, they are simply dead. It doesn't matter what their pains, sicknesses, trials, goodness, misery, heart, or biography were like. Once you're dead, you're just a dead person. But the living make up stories, they can't help themselves.

The funeral director pointed at Salim, he said: Listen to this analogy. A passenger gets on a boat. The boat goes to the middle of the ocean. The passenger hangs himself. He dies at sea. Should the people closest to him imagine the dead person at sea? That's the question. Should the sea constantly remind them of the dead person? Has this man become the sea? And most of all, has the sea become this man? Do you understand what I mean? I know cadavers better than the back of my hand. I could clean a cadaver with my eyes closed. I could clean one without using my hands. I could close my eyes. No eyes. No thinking. You know, most of the time, cadavers are in a terrible state. You can't imagine. Some have been lying in water for months. They bring me cadavers from the streets, cadavers of people who were starved, frozen, drugged. A lot of cadavers are full of drugs. They're like sacks of drugs, actual sacks of drugs. I lock them in a vault because those cadavers are coveted. Coveted by addicts. Obviously. They collect the blood and they drink it. It gets them high. Blood forms a pool inside of dead people and, in this case, the pool of blood gets you high. Some cadavers are estimated to be worth millions. And they also bring me cadavers that have been murdered, run over, suicides, the list goes on. I've got rows of dead people in the freezer room back there. This is my everyday life. When I look at a living person, I see the dead person they'll become. Occupational hazard. The second I look at you, I see your cadaver. It's my job, what I've been trained to do. I'll tell you one thing: This is the most demanding job there is.

The father asked: And what do you call it?

What?

Your job.

I'm the director of a father-son funeral home like my father and my grandfather, my younger brother, and then my son when he's born, or my daughter. I'm an embalmer like my father before me as well as the opposite, like a daughter before her father. I take care of the dead. I would gladly have shown you the embalming lab, but I have too much work, so let's resume. We will slip a bag with a bit of dirt in it under the deceased's neck and . . .

A man entered the room. The funeral director got up. He followed him into a corner and whispered: What's going on, Patrick?

We have a rotten wound on our hands, sir.

Very well, just as I suspected.

The funeral director turned around. He looked at Salim right in the eyes. He said: Because you are directly related to the deceased,

I'm going to ask you to follow me. Right now, the body is transforming, and that's a gift. We can't miss this opportunity. Let's go. Hurry.

The funeral director pressed a huge red button. A door slid open with the sound of a breath. They entered a room that was large and brightly lit. It had a cold smell. The funeral director said: Even if you've never smelled a dead person before, you recognize the smell of a dead person, don't you? It's instinct. It's a smell that lives inside our spirits, or our bodies, or both, or a combination of the two. It smells like dog kibble, don't you think? Nobody can stand the smell of dog kibble in this business. Outside of work, we can't stand dog kibble. I can't stand the smell of dog kibble.

The funeral director gestured toward a table at the back of the room. His assistant lifted a sheet. She was naked, her eyes open. Her face was the color of duck feet. In the middle of her body, a long cut, oval like a saucer, stretched out calmly, full of pink and white worms the size of a finger. They were squirming.

The young assistant said: She's rotten.

The funeral director responded: Indeed.

Then he gathered spit with his tongue. He sucked his cheeks into his mouth and he spit into the wound. He said: Now you do the same, it's one of the most beautiful things you can do. It's not disgusting. She doesn't have any blood. The wound is empty. She's a quasi-empty dead person. It's like spitting into a well, it brings good luck.

The young assistant gathered spit with his tongue and he drooled into the grandmother. He drooled with all his might, with his whole face. It looked like the lines on his face wanted to slide off and run into the wound. When it was his turn, Salim very carefully spit a little thread of drool.

The funeral director said: That's good. Congratulations. Now, Patrick, clean all this for me. Take the worms and put them in a plastic bag. Leave them in the forest. Make sure not to kill them, Patrick, or it will bring us bad luck. It will bring the business bad luck. It will bring the family bad luck. It will bring bad luck to everyone, without exception. Take care of those worms, Patrick, they are the beginning of life, the continuity of death. Ideally, you'd remove them with your tongue to keep from hurting them, but it's fine, do the best you can. And let the young man sew the wound shut. That will bring good luck to everyone. Focus. Be precise. And the funeral director took Salim's right hand and the assistant's left hand. He said: Let's form a circle. We're going to sing the house song. Listen carefully, young man, this is an excellent tune. I sing it to every dead person. This song was invented by my great-great-great-great-great-great-grandfather. Listen to the words carefully and, above all, repeat after me: What do flowers do on the mountain?

Salim repeated: What do flowers do on the mountain?

The flowers will sew with our bodies.

Salim repeated: The flowers will sew with our bodies.

A mountain is filled with the dead, yodel lay hee hoo, yodel lay, yodel lay.

Salim repeated: A mountain is filled with the dead, yodel lay hee hoo, yodel lay, yodel lay.

A mountain isn't empty, yodel lay, cuckoo, yodel lay, hoo.

Salim repeated: A mountain isn't empty, yodel lay, cuckoo, yodel lay, hoo.

A mountain is full of snow and ghosts, yodel lay, hee.

Salim repeated: A mountain is full of snow and ghosts, yodel lay, hee.

I'm harmless.

Salim repeated: I'm harmless.

I'm so harmless.

Salim repeated: I'm so harmless.

But then who isn't?

Salim repeated: But then who isn't?

The funeral director sighed with pleasure. He said: Now, let's repeat it in unison. We'll sing it twice in a row. Patrick will do the high parts. I will do the low parts. You will do the middle parts.

They sang twice:

What do flowers do on the mountain?

The flowers will sew with our bodies.

A mountain is filled with the dead, yodel lay hee hoo, yodel lay, yodel lay.

A mountain isn't empty, yodel lay, cuckoo, yodel lay, hoo.

A mountain is full of snow and ghosts, yodel lay, hee.

I'm harmless.

I'm so harmless.

But then who isn't?

The funeral director said: Now, I must leave you. I'm going to take care of a few administrative questions with your father.

*

The funeral director stuck his finger in his cup. He said: Coffee gets cold fast, but not dead people. They conserve heat like a thermos. Do you know the story about the soldier from Siberia? No. You don't know it. Well, it's the story of a soldier from Siberia, poor man, obviously, there's a war going on. This man is alone. Lost. All his companions are dead. All he has is his horse, but the horse dies of cold and exhaustion. Our soldier feels like he's about to freeze to death on the plain, when suddenly he has an idea, so what does he do? You don't know. He cuts the horse open. The dead horse. He takes out its entrails and he slides inside. Inside the horse. He falls asleep like a baby. A spoiled little baby in the stomach of a dead creature. A little sleeping baby. And that's how our Siberian soldier survived until he was rescued. The end. I should tell you that death often arrives for sick people before they actually die. Do you understand what I mean? Death begins somewhere. It has to start somewhere. For sick people in particular, a part of their body dies several days before their death. It's already dead. They die first in their stomach or their elbow, it depends on the person. Death can start anywhere. Sometimes, the body splits in two and one side devours the other. But other times, the dead part is miniscule. I've had cases with dead lips. You can start dying in your finger. In a limb. You have to start somewhere. The bone rots, evil prevails. The funeral director started laughing. He said: I love this silent wit. Do you see how quick-witted it is? Death, I mean. I love it. But death disgusts me, I'm like anyone else. Like you. I'm normal. And dead people stink, it's revolting, that's obvious. But back to what I was saying . . . So . . . Once death takes hold of the entire body, the dead part opens. It explodes in a way, it's quite beautiful. Once we notice the decay, the animals come, they appear. Invertebrates, most of the time. I'm referring to the following creatures: maggots, larvae, caterpillars, roundworms. Have you heard of roundworms? They're very soft, very delicate. This was the case with your grandmother. She had been dead in her stomach for weeks at least, maybe even years, it's common. Your son is taking care of it.

Suddenly, the father could no longer remember the grandmother's face. He could only recall the general shape of it. He remembered a circle, but the circle was empty. The funeral director asked the father to sign twelve papers, but the father was holding the pen backwards. He couldn't remember his signature. He made an x. He signed the twelve papers with an x, a circle, a triangle, he turned all red. The funeral director said: When we blush, our stomach also blushes, did you know that? The father responded: No. Often, the family blushes at the moment of death. Everyone feels uncomfortable. But I'm going to offer you a calming thought. Take it like a Xanax. If pressure is exerted on your pupil, you will see a red image, but pressure exerted on a dead person's pupil no longer produces an image. Take electroshocks for example. If you administer electroshocks to a dead person, you don't shock them. The electricity travels through the soft areas, but nothing happens. Try to imagine a pain, imagine this pain growing. Imagine torture. Make the pain grow and grow and grow, then stop it, stop it cold. Then say to yourself: It's over.

*

The young assistant hosed down the inside of the stomach with a little rubber tube. He collected the liquid and the worms, he put them in a little bag. An odor of wax and tissue floated in the air. He gave the needle and thread to Salim. The grandmother's eyes seemed deeper-set than usual. The young assistant said: The first time I washed a dead person's hands, I tried hard to imagine the dead person holding someone else's hand. I saw a life in their hands. Sew her up quickly, but sew her up well. It's easy. When you're done, wash your hands, and go on your way.

Salim looked at the wound. It was white. He imagined a key. Turning a key in the wound. When you stick a needle in a cadaver it sinks in, endlessly, there's no resistance in the tender skin. You could have thrown a stone. A huge stone. It would have gone right through her.

*

YEAH YEAH YEAH YEAH YEAH YEAH

look at the old dying horses
their bones piercing their skin
it's rational and wrong

just like the difference between one minute
and the next

a drill
moves closer to each temple
you know
babies don't do just anything
with their faces when they're born they don't
frown randomly
they imitate people
from the past

god carries your mantles
your illnesses
he is closer to you than his own veins
don't be hard on god
be soft
because he might have died

in a tractor accident
a train accident
a fire accident
a walking accident
or maybe he drowned
maybe he had an accident with machines
a bus accident
suffocated
or wounded by a bullet
a hunting accident
god has died in every accident
yeah yeah yeah yeah yeah

pages 71–72: Merriam-Webster.com, s.v. “Blood.” Merriam-Webster, accessed June 11, 2024, https://www.merriam-web-ster.com/dictionary/blood.

page 76: William Harvey, “On the Motion of the Heart and Blood in Animals” (1628). *The Harvard Classics* v. 38: Scientific papers; Physiology, Medicine, Surgery, Geology, with Introductions, Notes and Illustrations. Trans. Robert Willis. New York: P. F. Collier & Son, 1910.

page 162: Takuboku Ishikawa, *The Illusions of Self*. Trans. Roger Pulvers. London: Balestier Press, 2020.

LAURA VAZQUEZ is a leading figure in contemporary French literature and winner of the 2023 Prix Goncourt for poetry. *The Endless Week*, her debut novel, won the Prix de la Page 111 and was a finalist for the Prix Wepler. Her debut collection of poetry, *The Hand of the Hand*, won the Prix de la Vocation. She published her first play, the lesbian tragedy *Zero*, in 2024. Vazquez regularly gives readings around the world in venues such as the Ming Contemporary Art Museum in Shanghai and the Centre Pompidou in Paris. She lives in Marseille, France.

ALEX NIEMI is a writer and award-winning literary translator. She is the recipient of an NEA fellowship, the Heldt Prize, and the AATSEEL Prize for best poetry translation from a Slavic language. Her translations include *For the Shrew* and *Hekate* by Anna Glazova, as well as *The John Cage Experiences* by Vincent Tholomé. She also is the author of the poetry chapbook *Elephant*.

Dorothy, a publishing project

1. Renee Gladman *Event Factory*
2. Barbara Comyns *Who Was Changed and Who Was Dead*
3. Renee Gladman *The Ravickians*
4. Manuela Draeger *In the Time of the Blue Ball* (tr. Brian Evenson)
5. Azareen Van der Vliet Oloomi *Fra Keeler*
6. Suzanne Scanlon *Promising Young Women*
7. Renee Gladman *Ana Patova Crosses a Bridge*
8. Amina Cain *Creature*
9. Joanna Ruocco *Dan*
10. Nell Zink *The Wallcreeper*
11. Marianne Fritz *The Weight of Things* (tr. Adrian Nathan West)
12. Joanna Walsh *Vertigo*
13. Nathalie Léger *Suite for Barbara Loden* (tr. Natasha Lehrer & Cécile Menon)
14. Jen George *The Babysitter at Rest*
15. Leonora Carrington *The Complete Stories*
16. Renee Gladman *Houses of Ravicka*
17. Cristina Rivera Garza *The Taiga Syndrome* (tr. Aviva Kana & Suzanne Jill Levine)
18. Sabrina Orah Mark *Wild Milk*
19. Rosmarie Waldrop *The Hanky of Pippin's Daughter*
20. Marguerite Duras *Me & Other Writing* (tr. Olivia Baes & Emma Ramadan)
21. Nathalie Léger *Exposition* (tr. Amanda DeMarco)
22. Nathalie Léger *The White Dress* (tr. Natasha Lehrer)
23. Cristina Rivera Garza *New and Selected Stories* (tr. Sarah Booker, et al)
24. Caren Beilin *Revenge of the Scapegoat*
25. Amina Cain *A Horse at Night: On Writing*
26. Giada Scodellaro *Some of Them Will Carry Me*
27. Pip Adam *The New Animals*
28. Kate Briggs *The Long Form*
29. Ariane Koch *Overstaying* (tr. Damion Searls)
30. Renee Gladman *My Lesbian Novel*
31. Renee Gladman *To After That (TOAF)*
32. Lana Lin *The Autobiography of H. Lan Thao Lam*
33. Laura Vazquez *The Endless Week* (tr. Alex Niemi)

DOROTHYPROJECT.COM